THE SHIELD THAT FELL
FROM HEAVEN

THE SHIELD THAT FELL FROM HEAVEN

William S. Kerr

Groton Jemez Publishing

Santa Fe

With apologies and homage to
Alexis de Tocqueville and Poul Anderson

Pulaski County, Kentucky, U. S. A., 24 July 1861

Fornication, whiskey and fiddle music. These are, if Mr. Graham is to be believed, the three pillars of true American society.

Of course, by "American" he means his own people—those families whose serial evictions have moved them from Scotland to Ulster to the American east to places like this. If the three pillars define this nation, they also explain the expulsions and migrations.

Mr. Graham knows that his folk are not the majority—that they have never been more than one in ten. But he has his arguments and will deliver them at the barest breath of invitation.

This comes, though, I think, more from loneliness than from the usual motivations old men have for freezing the world in words. He does not, after all, give advice. At least, unasked. Whether he will give it on request is something I may soon learn.

I came to Somerset in a green, cool May. (The rains were on, but, even now, two months later, in the warmest month, it is not hot. The South is not all one place, apparently.) After a night in the Zachary House, one of the town's three sufferable hotels—I could have stayed in a tavern for twenty-five cents—I made it my first concern to be up and out early the next morning, looking for more permanent lodging.

There is a newspaper locally, and there were postings here and there around the town, so I had no difficulty in finding boarding houses and buildings for rent, but at noon I had not yet found quite the place. I was hungry, however, and walked back to the center of town—a longer walk than you would think, since Somerset, though not populous itself, is the capital of the county and surprisingly developed. It is also spread out.

As I neared the main square, which had been at peace not many hours before, and even before I turned my final corner, I began to be pierced by a loud, strident voice that faded and then jabbed, faded and jabbed. Once in the square itself, where I could hear better, it was clear that the voice never actually stopped for an instant at all, but simply rose and fell and rose again as if rearing back to gain strength for its thrusts.

That which, in manner and tone, shows soundness of character in a man, varies so much from society to society that it is not easy to deny it to any stranger. Still, it would be hard to grant it to this individual. He was the type who, on first meeting, strikes one as deficient at some deep level, as lacking substance all the way down. It is not simply weakness, either, since it can come with agitation and an hysterical energy, as in the present case. Perhaps these people lack souls? They are not unitary, in any event. Really, they lack what the ancients would have called virtue, but no one in these latter days will understand what that means.

Does it seem false that I could arrive at such a judgment so quickly and on so little acquaintance? Perhaps it is—I have had two months more familiarity now, and I may be projecting that back into my first responses. Yet, I am sure I remember thinking

4

something on those lines at the time.

I want to give you each person with whom I deal as much in his own words as possible. I would give transcriptions if it were civilly permissible to take them down, since that would be the most objective, most scientific method. What I can do is remain faithful to the content of what each says and convey something of the speaker's mode of speech.

This last cannot carry over easily into French. I had thought to do what the translators of Greek comedies do, substituting corresponding modern accents for Dorians or barbarians. It would be too much work. Instead, I shall simply say something about people's language as needed. Eventually, I should say something about local diction in general.

The speaker was dressed in faded formality of a kind common in the newly settled regions of America. He stood atop a wooden crate with a small group gathered about him, some on the few benches, some squatting, a few standing.

"One man in five lives in slavery in this state. One in five!"

I could barely understand him at first. My English is not perfect, but I can usually make out what is being said once I know where the speaker is from and can make a sort of shift in hearing to account for that. It took me some time in this instance, for the speaker proved, in the end, to have the thickest of what I have come to call a coastal Southern inflection. (I really do need to take time to discuss these things, and I shall.) His vowels differed even from most of the Kentuckians, and they were drawn out and drawled.

"We have kept our neutrality in the present conflict, but we shall not keep it long, and we must decide where we will take our stand. We must stand on the side of freedom or be counted in the ranks of the slave owners and their vassals. Those are our choices—our Lord, our

God, the beneficent author of our species, holds out to us no others."

I knew, before arriving, how divided the state was on this issue, and I looked around to see how this was received. The small crowd gave little away, however, beyond a mild attentiveness.

"Our President has called for our aid in his battle for liberty, and we have refused him. We may reap the fruits of that—to our pain, I fear. But it is not too late. Yet, even should we recover our humanity in time and rise against the despotism that threatens our union with dissolution, it will mean little if we continue to abide this institution which holds so many of our fellow creatures in chains.

"It will not be enough to take up arms against the usurpers, the armed contemners of divine justice. That would merely be to preserve ourselves as a sanctuary of iniquity in a land otherwise cleansed. We must immediately, of our own accord, repudiate the covenant we have made with wickedness in tolerating this system of bondage in our state. Slavery must go, and it must go soon, before we are dragged down with it into the conflagration prepared for sinners from the foundation of the world."

One man clapped, and some of the others turned to look at him, but, still, I saw little in their faces to betray how they were taking this.

The orator paused, then reached down for a jug on the box by his feet. This action, finally, elicited a more general response: a few cheered, at which most laughed or grinned.

One, whose face was almost entirely obscured by a bountiful beard and long, black, greasy-looking hair, shouted out, "A few swigs of that will put out that conflagration."

From his problems with this last word, I judged that he had already had a few swigs himself. The rest laughed again.

The hairy gentleman pivoted about unsteadily, assured himself that the audience was with him, then pulled a flat, glass bottle of dark yellow liquid from somewhere beneath his layers of dirty clothes. "Here, Elder Bell, I'll join you. You can always count on old Johnny Elliot," he said, making as though to drink, but really looking around again to gauge the group's response.

The putative Elder Bell, however, was not laughing. His face hardened and he rose with the jug in his hand. "This is no strong drink, you chimpanzee," he hissed.

He poured some of the contents on the ground. "This is pure spring water! All that I ever drink! The vintage God has given us in nature, and symbol of the only spirit you have need of! Sodden, senseless ape!"

Johnny Elliot was diminished under the glare from the crate. The Elder Bell drank deeply and set the jug down again. "But there is a lesson in this," he began again in a lower, calmer voice. "Too long have we viewed government as a convenience. Too long has this country seen the sword as a tool to be wielded only in defense of its pleasures. The authorities that exist have been established by God. The ruler is God's servant to do God's will. He does not bear the sword for nothing. He does not bear it as a hireling to barkeepers and fleshmongers!"

He was heating up again, perhaps too quickly for subtle transitions. "The ruler is God's servant, an agent of wrath to bring punishment to the wrongdoer! Why have we dwelt so long under this vicious despotism, the accomplices of thieves and robbers, of men-stealers and women-whippers? It is for our own ease, that we may continue to wallow in the filth of our own dissolution! The ruler is God's servant to do God's will! Not to smooth the path to our damnation!"

His voice cracked a bit on this last, and he was silent

7

for a moment, his hands on his hips, as he leant forward and scanned the listeners, peering at each of us with eyes that were, I think, meant to penetrate but seemed a little too bulbous, like a carrion beetle's. It was uncomfortable, nonetheless, and I dropped my own eyes when he came to me.

"The slave system is merely the most telling consequence of our neglect of divine polity!" he continued after a moment. "If every bondservant were released from his shackles today, we would be but little the better for it! It would be but the beginning!

"We would still have drunkards! Slaves to the bottle!" He looked significantly at old Johnny Elliot.

"We would still have adulterers and libertines! Slaves to their own lusts!" He looked at others who, for all I knew, were particularly appropriate targets.

"We would still have slaves to tobacco and medicine! To dancing and the theater!" He looked at me and, while this seemed fair to a degree, I resented the implied familiarity, though I still did not meet his eye.

"We would still have Sabbath-breakers, slaves to their own sloth and to the devil himself!" This was peculiarly vehement and was directed at a very old man seated on one of the few benches. This ancient, however, returned his glare with something like the same intensity.

"Only when the government returns to the role assigned it by the Lord's providence and becomes once again the scourge of sin will this land ever be truly free! Only then will the kingship of God be planted in our tormented land!"

It would have been a nice rhetorical coda, but he did not relax as he should have to signal an end. His attention was locked on the old fellow on the bench, and he stood bent in that direction as if awaiting an apology.

I would not have expected one. The elderly man still met his gaze, measure for measure, and I was in no doubt who was the more formidable. Who, on stricter observation, was the more dangerous.

I would have taken the old man for seventy or so (he is, in reality, somewhere over eighty—these people keep strangely casual track of their birth years), but a robust seventy (and a more robust octogenarian). His hair, yellowish-white, was longer even than the custom in these parts, but uncustomarily clean and tended. His clothes were worn but presentable and relatively *à la mode* except for his hat, the wide brim of which drooped in the front and which was obviously an old favorite. He wore a coat, although most in the crowd did not in concession to the warm weather. Boots, well made, reached almost to his knees and had a coating of dried mud. His right hand rested on his knee, holding a cigar with a thumb's width of ash.

A close-cropped beard of the same aged ivory as his hair covered a box-like, muscular jaw that seemed to hold a full set of teeth. The muscles were tightened now in vertical bands as he looked up at his challenger. I could not see how tall he was—I would say, now, about six English feet—but his shoulders were still wide and his coat sleeves were snug around his upper arms. His wrinkles were all deeply cut, not the spider-work one usually sees, and his anger had none of the elderly's soft petulance to it. It was ferric and fierce and held in a restraint that was therefore all the more threatening. Or, it would have threatened anyone more perceptive than the Elder Bell.

He finally moved, taking a long draw on his cigar, then resting his hand again. "The government, then, is going to tell me how to spend my Sundays?" His voice was inappropriately steady and strong, too, though hoarse and rough. The accent I will discuss more fully in time—it was striking.

"The government will tell you nothing that conscience does not," the other answered.

"My conscience is remarkably silent on the topics of

play-acting and dancing. It appears to me that you might be putting words in its mouth."

The Elder Bell drew himself up and shrilled, "Does it need my voice to make you see the sin in slavery as well? Does it need my voice to show you the wrong in using men as beasts?"

The sinews in the old man's face tautened until they stood out like ropes. "No," he said, very low. "And if you put words in *my* mouth again, you will regret it."

He patted his left breast lightly, but the man on the crate missed that.

"Slavery is its own peculiar concern. I address myself only to the other subjects you raise and your grander schemes of government. I have never owned slaves nor wanted to. Neither, I believe, has more than one man in a hundred in Pulaski County. The institution may go to blazes for all that I or most of us care. As may the slaveholders. I address myself to your more general view, and I suggest you take what I say with the meaning intended."

"Then, please explain to me, Hugh Graham, and to the rest of the gentlemen here, why the sword of worldly power should not be used for heavenly purposes. The ordinances of earthly law are established for our good, scripture tells us. How is it not good to refrain from that which harms the body and soul? And why, then, should the nation not put curbs upon our lecheries and winebibbing?"

Hugh Graham suddenly smiled, but it was not a pleasant smile. "The nation? You mean the government in Washington? It was bad enough when I thought you meant the county court!"

"Why not the highest power in the land? Righteousness is the same for all—for every state and every town and every man." The Elder smiled now. "But, then, you are not known to be a friend of righteousness. I suppose you, of all men, could be

10

expected to take your stand against decency and religion!"

Both had heated up, and I feared lest Mr. Graham would reach for his breast pocket again, but he sat there, visibly collecting himself and his thoughts. In a quieter voice, he said, "It's true that I haven't much use for churches. Not the way they've become. Not the way they've become thanks to people like you. But I am older than anyone here by a parcel of years and I remember what it used to be like. And my people—and yours, if your name is Bell—wouldn't have stood for outsiders coming in and telling them how to live. That wasn't the way of the old churches. My people came to this land to begin with because they were tired of killing people who were trying to tell them how to live."

The Elder Bell's smile became a smirk. "I suspect the old Scots Presbyterians may have had higher expectations than you remember. I have never heard that they embraced unchristian ways. To the contrary..."

He stopped and turned to take in the whole assembly again. "To the contrary. They had sterner criteria than we have now. Nothing I have censured would have escaped condemnation. God's statutes have not changed so much. I tell you only what our fathers would have told you."

Mr. Graham stood, more quickly and limberly than I could have predicted. "It's the telling that's the problem! They didn't stand for being told! It's not *how* they thought they should live that made a difference—it was being *told* how that got the tellers shot! And if you can't make that distinction, your head is as empty as your sacks!"

Elder Bell's face glowed a crimson red, and he made choking sounds as though food had gone down his trachea. Mr. Graham glowered at him, then turned and began walking away.

Abruptly, he stopped and swiveled his head. "And at

least we used to be able to drink in church! Made it tolerable."

Then he left. I stayed for a minute or two before it occurred to me that the old man was precisely the source I needed if I was to have insight into these people's ways of life and thought. Someone from the last century. Someone who had ideas about the course of things and their changing channels. News of the war was infrequent and tardy. There was not much action to digest. I had time to research the backdrop.

I knew which direction he had gone. Walking that way quickly, I could hear the Elder's voice begin to function again, angry now and brittle. I caught up with Mr. Graham around a turn.

"Pardon me," I said and was ignored. "Pardon me! Mr. Graham!"

I think he detected my accent in this second attempt, because he turned with a curious expression and not the hostility I half feared.

"Yes?"

"I wonder if I might converse with you for a while. I was interested in what you had to say about the older times and the changes that have happened."

"Who are you? French by the sound of it. *N'est-ce pas*?"

"Yes." I was startled. "Yes, I am."

"I passed through there in my youth. Paris. Probably shouldn't say why. But who are you?"

"Pardon me, again. My name is Edouard de Grimouville and I am originally from Normandy, although lately of Paris. I have been commissioned by Mr. Horace Greeley of the *New York Tribune* to be a reporter on the war between the states."

"Why Kentucky? We're one place where the war isn't happening."

"But that is exactly what makes it interesting. A state torn by loyalties. A place where all of the questions are thrown into relief."

"But why here? What do you expect to learn in the beyond's beyond?"

"I am relying on another *Tribune* journalist, a man I met in London, a Dr. Marx. He helped me obtain my position. He has analyzed the situation in Tennessee, and he thinks the war will pass through here."

He was doubtful—or I felt guilty and read that onto him. I could not allow suspicions of my candor, even in little things. "As well, the paper has more seasoned men in the western part of the state where everyone thinks the major proceedings will progress. I am new at this and have no status."

"I have no time at present and I don't live here in town. I'm just in for supplies and I have to get back."

"Might I visit you where you live? I really do need to become conversant with the customs I am studying."

He was amused for some reason. "Then, yes, you may visit me. It's not an easy trip, but, if you have the leisure, you can stay as long as you need. I have empty cabins— you can put up at one of them. You'll have to bring any necessaries and a bedroll. But I formally consent to be interviewed."

He gave me directions. His stead was about nine miles east, beside a Salt Lick Creek outside the town of Stirling. I was to take the road from Somerset to London. He joked about the latter town's name and I felt I had found a *sympathique* side.

"Not a bad road," he added. "A lot of the stumps are out."

Pulaski County, Kentucky, U. S. A., 25 July 1861

The war is now and truly on. Finally, a battle of some aim and scope has been fought. In Virginia, not far from the Union capital in Washington—the worst possible place, from a Northern perspective—the Confederates have confounded their foe with utter and humiliating dispatch. This was some days ago. We do not have telegraph lines out to here, but there is river traffic to Waitsboro, not far away. Intelligence finds its way slowly, but it arrives at last.

The North is near panic and Kentucky has risen still further in the scale of things. The Union must do everything it can to hold the loyal slave states. Kentucky's own Mr. Crittenden has gotten the Congress to pass a resolution to the effect that the war is not about slavery but about preservation of the Union.

I do not know what I believe about that. This may injure the North's moral position, perhaps fatally. But I do not know what to think. If the unity of France were at stake, that would be justification enough, but different principles may be legitimate in the case of a constructed nation like the United States. In general, I fear both centralized power and anarchy about equally. Secession by states may be such a violation of the country's founding principles as to signal lawlessness. Still, it is not my affair and I have no urgent reason ever to reach a verdict.

I know what Dr. Marx would say about the substance of the resolution. I have a draft of an article he is working up for the European press. He contends, against the English press, that this cannot be a struggle between free trade and protectionism. There were no serious tariffs until this very year, after the war had already begun. (He is, perhaps, too free in his chronology.) The South has always been the aggressor. The attack on Ft. Sumter was meant to forestall a constitutional convention that might have prevented war. (I do not pretend, yet, to be able to judge these declarations.)

It is true, as Dr. Marx says, that "Slavery!" is almost the battle slogan of the leaders of the rebellion. Is it true that their allies among the commoners have the same aim? That is the vital question. He himself points outs that there are only 300,000 slaveholders in the South's population of millions. But the others *want* slaves, he says, and therefore support slavery's expansion into new territories where they will have their chance. Is this true?

Dr. Marx thinks in systems. His entire world is a completed whole—I know this from many conversations on many topics, from the most universal and theoretical to the most detailed and practical (decisions about breakfast, for example). How much is he imposing on the American situation to make it fit a picture he has already?

Mr. Graham has a different view, though conceivably just as *a priori*. He is not as well read—perhaps not as intelligent—as my German scholar, but he is far older and more organically involved.

Pulaski County, Kentucky, U. S. A., 27 July 1861

I came across the Armstrongs' place not long after I arrived here, when my roving in the woods led me to the road running by it. The trees suddenly opened out into a clearing large enough for small fields of crops and a substantial homestead. A dog barked, and I began to quicken my step, not wanting to intrude on anyone's privacy, when I heard girls' voices from the near side of the house. By a creek, three young women were washing clothing, themselves variously *déshabillées*.

All were noticeably adolescent, one very young but the others nubile enough. They saw me and one waved, calling out something I could not hear. I stopped and cupped my ear theatrically. She shouted, then beckoned with her hands, in which invitation the other larger girl joined. I left the road and crossed the grassy yard to them. The dog, a big mongrel, came around the house but only pranced in timid welcome.

The one who had waved first had long, auburn hair, as did the youngest. The other was a brunette, though all three had much the same pretty face in different stages of development. I judged the leader to be the eldest, and this was disturbing. The two younger were covered by knee-length linen shifts and, however immodest the effect, we make allowances for youth and innocence. My redhead, on the other hand, had tucked the top of hers in about her waist, leaving her naked above. Yet, none seemed conscious of anything amiss.

I have not been among the Anglo-Saxons long enough to absorb their new prudery, but I have come to expect it. No detail in a picture is jarring in itself, if it is consistent with the setting. It is the perception of something out of place that scandalizes.

I regretted my impulsive acceptance of the summons, fearful that, any minute, an angry father would fly through the door of the house with an axe or rifle. It did not happen. There were only the three smiling faces.

"I was asking what you are doing out and about today," the redhead said.

"I am out for a walk." I riveted my eyes on her face.

"You talk funny," said the littlest. "Where are you from?"

"I am from France. I work for a newspaper and I am staying in Somerset for awhile."

"From France!" the middle one said. Her eyes grew almost comically wide. She raised her hand toward me, then caught herself. I think she was about to test me to see what I was made of.

Before I could say anything more, the eldest said, "Old man Graham's been to France. He's told us about it. Have you been to Paris?"

"I have lived in Paris a long time, although I am not from there. My name is Edouard, by the way."

"I'm Susannah," she replied. "These are my sisters, Toodie," she nodded at the brunette, "and Ella."

I turned to bow to Toodie and Ella, wanting to escape the temptation to look down at Susannah's breasts. Peripherally, I had seen that they were slightly conical, milk pale but freckled, with small but well formed nipples.

"I am staying in one of Mr. Graham's houses, as it turns out."

"I thought you were staying in Somerset," Susannah said.

"I spend more and more of my time here. I thought I would be spending it talking with Mr. Graham, but he is not being very sociable. Now, I stay because I prefer it to Somerset."

This loosed a stream of questions that I satisfied or parried as best I could, some about my personal ambitions, which I did not handle consistently well, not having worked out the answers acceptably for myself.

"Which house of Mr. Graham's?" asked Susannah,

finally.

"You can almost see it from here." I pointed. "On a hill over that rise."

That was a more freighted question than I saw at the time. When, at last, I could escape and continue on, I believed that was the end of the matter—of a pleasant, strange, but casual encounter.

Pulaski County, Kentucky, U. S. A., 28 July 1861

Sunday, and Susannah is spending the day in church. There are two in the neighborhood of Stirling. Even Somerset has only three or four for its few hundreds, so one would think two excessive for a town that is little more than a post office serving a tiny and scattered population. I am told it is not, but I am used to a doctrinal consensus for which one church per village (at most) suffices. Both churches in Stirling are Baptist— there are apparently no Presbyterians, the significance of which I believe I have learned.

Our friend the Elder Daniel Bell has some function in the establishment Susannah does not attend. I do not pretend to appreciate the details of the ecclesiastical polity.

I am bemused by Susannah's devoutness, considering all else. It is certainly not hypocrisy. I would dismiss it as inconsistency, a partition of her life into disconnected spheres, but I have known her now too long and too well. I sense a unity and harmony in her depths that would explain the matter if I understood.

These Ulster women are free, it seems, in their attentions. This is one reason the old New England Puritans encouraged the whole lot to slide on west. Are they all as liberal with their favors?

Mr. Graham suggests so. He thinks things are changing (and, on this topic, I find his thought genuinely worthwhile), but he maintains that weddings are still judged overdue only if the bride is actually showing. He says this last may even be the usual case.

At any rate, it would never have occurred to me to distinguish attention and offers. For those of my station, the distinction is rarely a practical one. Never, in my own experience. And now I am in difficulties. Susannah is pregnant. She does not wish to end the pregnancy.

In France, I might put this down to fear of the law. It

says much about the first Bonaparte that, however admirably grand he may have been on the whole, he was petty enough to legislate about something like this. There is a strict correlation between authoritarianism and pettiness. One needs to find more and more to control and necessarily turns to smaller and smaller objects.

Here, there would be no problem. The old English common law has always ruled the matter in this country. Quickening is the breakpoint. There is independent life only after the mother claims to have felt movement. That can happen at any time, of course, from the fourth month to never. I assume the rule was borrowed from the Church centuries ago—or, maybe it predates them both.

Regardless, Susannah wants to keep it, though she need not. It is clear she thinks she has trapped me. Perhaps "trapped" is the wrong word; the sort of embarrassment in which we find ourselves may amount to a prenuptial ritual. Dalliance, then, is acceptable, but only as part of a track that ends in marriage.

Mr. Graham tells of shotgun weddings. I do not know how much he knows of my affairs, and whether he speaks of these weddings as a warning. The community here is small, but he is not social. "Shotgun" is the Kentucky word for a fowling piece. It is the supposed incentive of choice for parents seeking to save their daughters' honor.

Obviously, this is no real threat to me. At worst, I would be safe in Normandy, but I doubt I would have to flee so far. Still, I want to stay here. I have my obligations to Messrs. Greeley and Marx—the one who has given me employment and the one who talked him into it. Beyond that, I have a duty to myself.

If Dr. Marx is right, Somerset is the place to be. The President sees Kentucky as a key to the war. For appearances' sake, he cannot lose his own birth state to the South, but, more substantively, he cannot let the South have the Ohio River. Kentucky is also one of the slave states still, mostly, loyal to the Union and likely to stay. If it goes, Maryland and Missouri might be less prone to stick it out.

When one side or the other invades, the western part of the state will be the arena for the grandest actions and, of my own accord, that is where I would be. The *Tribune* has sufficient presence there, however—sufficient and sufficiently experienced, Mr. Greeley stresses. That leaves the major city in the east, which Dr. Marx promises will be propelled to prominence soon enough.

I have no recourse but to trust his judgment. I have no credentials as a pressman but no other pretext for visiting this land at length. (To be candid, I am not indifferent, at this point, to the trifle of a retainer.) This country is still, scores of years after its founding, the weathervane of history. What I can learn of these people will hold, with a suitable lag, for all others. My time and place are therefore now and here. Should I have a hope of any life with any tinge of greatness to it, any glory or grandeur, it will be in letters, and only such as occupy themselves with grand themes.

Journalism is a start and an opportunity for the relevant studies. God knows I could not have tolerated the law for long, with its constrictions of the spirit. Politics held out something more, but the events have closed that life to me. There can be no public career with honor in France today. All the alternatives are base and distasteful.

No, this is where and when I need to be, and here I will abide, let all the Susannahs and shotguns in Pulaski County do their damnedest.

Pulaski County, Kentucky, U. S. A., 29 July 1861

I would have been better equipped to meet the Armstrong sisters if I had been able to speak with Mr. Graham beforehand. When I turned up at his door, however, to redeem his promise of lodging, he was annoyed and did little to hide it. After he conducted me to the cabin, I did not hear from him again until early June. I could have taken the initiative myself, but, to be frank, I was too leery of him. I would as gladly have put my hand into the burrow of an unknown animal. It resulted that I chanced upon the Armstrongs first.

Nevertheless, once I had the invitation and was seated at his table, we swiftly regained our old footing.

"So you used to drink during church? Was that common?"

"I never got more than a couple of nips every once and awhile. I was too little to have my own to bring." Mr. Graham punctuated this with a pull on his jug. We each had one. He distills his own whiskey in a still in the trees behind his cabin and stores it in oak casks. When he had invited me over, he had asked if I wished to meet a ewe with a crooked horn, which turned out to be this apparatus. I had said yes, out of mild curiosity and boredom.

"Why is it hidden?" I had asked.

"It isn't, really. But I could hide this plot pretty quickly. Taxes come and go in the different states, in my experience. The county court has already taken to licensing taverns. I can't trust how far it'll go."

As I have indicated, I am not trying to reproduce his manner of speech. It is anomalous. I can distinguish two or three types of Southern speech. There is the upper-class speech of the coastal regions which sounds almost British to me. A commoner variant is spoken by the more plebian or peasant inhabitants in the same districts. It has a similar drawl to it but overdoes it and, in general, lacks the smoothness and elegance of the aristocratic style.

One comes across this with decreasing frequency as one journeys west, but it seems to be expanding its scope. The Elder Bell has this accent, for example, and no one thinks him strange for it. It appears to be merging with the third kind of speech, which is that of Mr. Graham's Scots-Irish. In its unmixed form, this is very rough and abrupt, and it dwells on its r's.

Mr. Graham himself, however, has a lilt to his voice I have not heard in the others. His r's roll slightly. I suspect one would find the same traits in his contemporaries, if there were any—it is undoubtedly the vestige of the accent first brought from Ulster.

His vocabulary is peculiar at times, and he must stop and explain and apologize. Otherwise, I find that he can be exceptionally articulate and cultured if he needs to be in order to express a particular thought. It does not happen often, but it breaks out almost despite him.

He set his jug down overcarefully. "By the time I was old enough to join in fully, I had figured out that I could just drink at home and save the travel time. I left home about then, anyway, so I was free to do that."

"But it never caused disruptions during the service?"

"No more than any other enthusiasms—it was an aid to those, in fact. If it got out of hand, we dealt with it, the same as drunkenness outside church. This idea that tippling is bad is pretty recent, just in the past few decades. It's another sign of how wrong things are going. We expected propriety but we couldn't expect abstemption, and our standards of propriety were pretty relaxed. Same with fucking—as long as both wanted it and it wasn't adultery and the woman wasn't left in trouble, we let it be."

"As long as they did not do it in the public square?"

"Well, there was that. But some places they still roll around together in the fields when planting time comes.

Supposed to help the crops. That was always pretty public."

"And to what do you attribute the change in attitudes?"

He took another pull on his jug and I joined him. I had not and have not acquired a fondness for the taste, but the other effects were all that could be wished.

"More than one reason, I imagine," he said, clearing his throat. "The more immediate would be that the churches aren't persecuted any more. We've been hounded so long in so many places that our religion came to center on that. They even burned our churches in the east in this country. Finally, we made a religion of not giving in on our beliefs."

He cleared his throat some more. "The beliefs weren't the main thing, maybe. It was more important not to give them up."

"So, your religion was defined by opposition, after a time?"

"Yes. And then, with the revolution, there suddenly wasn't any enemy. We had to turn on ourselves if we wanted a fight. Then, the beliefs became the thing, and people needed to conquer themselves and bring themselves into line. And, more and more, they want to bring other people into line.

"Also, there aren't many more Indians to kill unless you move west. That was always the big outlet for our worst inclinations."

I pondered that for a bit. "You said there were other reasons."

"Well, at least one other. A people always values most the quality that it has the least, I think. So, once the Anglicans and Catholics couldn't bother us anymore, we started to value self-control. Liberty had always been our byword before. Actually, it still is, but only as a word."

As a rule—and a strategy—I try just to listen and remember, but my jug was a long way toward empty.

"Are those not compatible?" I asked. "One thing I've admired about the old New England puritans was their notion of liberty. They distinguished natural and civil liberty. Natural liberty they thought of as license, as the power to do whatever one wanted. They believed it turned men into beasts in the end, and that it was the one great enemy of truth and peace, against which the covenants between God and man and between men themselves are bent."

I realized, too late, that he might take this as a criticism and challenge—perhaps even an affront. I recalled his reaction to the Elder Bell in Somerset. I tried to marshal my words to better consequence, even as they followed my thoughts themselves off in an alcoholic reel. "At any rate, that's what *those* fellows believed."

He looked at me unblinking, and I could not interpret his expression. "And what did those fellows believe the other kind of liberty was?" he asked.

"*Eh bien.* Well." I tried to predict pitfalls in what I wanted to say, but finally just marched on. "Civil or moral liberty. The liberty to do what is good and just and honest. The kind that cannot exist without some authority to sustain it."

"That's nice if you have some simple definition of good."

"Well, your people had some notion of propriety, at least."

"My people did. The notion gets fuzzier to me as I get older. Even the old ideas are starting to seem whimsical now."

Everything was getting fuzzy for me. "You would agree that there are things men should not do openly if society is to survive. I do not care about private behavior —I am not of the middle class. Little can offend me. I would be difficult to scandalize. But, for the common person—must some deeds not be kept from his sight?"

"Why?"

"So that the doers do not become exemplars."

He rose, and I readied myself for what might come, despite the fact that, even in my state, my last remark did not seem especially provocative. He was ancient but agile. Then, he walked to a cupboard and carried back two new jugs.

"So, you're one of those who believes in different standards for different classes," he said. "At most, I can see the government controlling theft and violence, and maybe enforcing contracts. After that, I don't see that anything anyone does is going to bring things crashing down."

"You don't think weakened morals can destabilize the whole? Even lead to theft and violence?"

"Is there evidence for that?"

"Well, Rome is the usual illustration."

"Rome fell after it turned Christian and reformed its morals. That's the Empire. The Republic fell because it decided it needed a standing army and because the Senatorial class didn't restrain its own members. Once political crime started, other morals changed—not the other way around. Corruption has always been from the top down. It's the government we need to keep an eye on. We don't need the government keeping an eye on us.

"Besides," he added, "in our case, it's the moralizers who are changing things. I'm the conservative here. If the old ways worked, maybe we shouldn't fiddle with them. And the old ways were looser."

I was not concentrating well and knew that I would soon be too sleepy to continue. "We'll have to discuss this when I'm in better condition to put up a fight," I said. "Tangentially—in connection with something that happened lately—is it usual for young ladies to display themselves naked around here?"

He grinned. "Where was this?"

"I had rather not say, to avoid possible damage to reputations."

"It was pretty usual in the old days. Probably not around here, anymore. Must have found yourself some conservatives. Used to be, you couldn't be too particular. More often than not, there weren't any separate rooms, so modesty wasn't much use. Particularly if you were traveling—then everyone, family and strangers, man, woman and child, had to share rooms. Same big bed a lot of the time. It would have seemed odd to worry about what you were wearing. Who's parading around naked, by the way?"

"Women did not mind it?"

"A woman would have to be very unsure of her own virtue who was afraid to sleep in a room with a strange man. There wasn't any call for delicacy. No man would take liberty with a woman unless he saw a disposition in her to encourage him. Not that women's clothes covered as much as they do now, anyway. I miss the short skirts. Who was it you ran into?"

"The Armstrong girls. And now that I have told you that, I should start getting back. I am feeling sleepy."

I was putting on my coat when he said, "Ask the girls to do the cockle bread dance for you. I'll bet they still know that."

"Cockle bread?"

"Or cockledy bread, as I recall. Girls sing, 'My granny is sick and now is dead, and we'll go knead some cockledy bread. Up with your heels and down with your head. And that's the way to make cockledy bread.' They get up on a table and lift their skirts above their heads. Then they move their buttocks around or grind them as if they're kneading bread. Saw something like it in Paris, once."

"So have I. But what in the world? What is the point of it?"

"I don't know that it has a point. It's just playing. Cockle bread, though, is real. A woman moulds the dough with her nether parts, just as in the game, or she kneads it and then presses it against her quim. She bakes it and gives it to a man she's in love with, and it's supposed to make him fall in love with her."

"They believe in that?"

"I don't know about these girls. I expect it still goes on in this vicinity. There's always been a strong tradition of magic among our folk. Goes back to the Celts and farther."

"We should talk about that some other time. I cannot see it as anything but superstition, but I want a full picture of your tribe."

He laughed at this. "Arrange a meeting with Nick Bromfield. He'd be able to show you something that might change your mind."

"About my researches?"

"About superstition. He's the resident witchmaster."

If I had asked what that was, my departure would have been delayed yet again. I was at the door, so I opened it and said my goodbyes.

He came to the door when I had staggered about twenty feet toward the road. "If any Armstrong offers you bread, don't eat it."

Pulaski County, Kentucky, U. S. A., 30 July 1861

I sent a dispatch to New York today, the first with usable content. Things are stirring to the south, and I have a chance to justify my stipend. Not that I have been guilty of idleness—no more than my situation imposes—but the paper could not make use of most of my labors.

I have, until now, had little to report that did not consist of general Kentucky politics, and they have this already from correspondents closer to the scenes and whose responsibility those are. Much is happening in the west, but affairs in the east are rightly mine.

The greater part of my efforts has been more anthropology than journalism. While I regard this as necessary to preparation if I am to comprehend the things on which I report, my motives are not pure. The topic is worthy in its own right and deserves a treatise. I had been planning a broad study of American society all along, but I appreciate, now, after my weeks here, how facile my categories were. My framework determined my observations.

So, recently, I have tried to compensate and perhaps gone too far off the mark to the other side. I have volumes of notes, chiefly from transcription of interviews. These are all necessarily from memory. I get less—or nothing—when I ask questions with a pen in my hand. Simple conversation is the key. Too, more comes from conversations around a bottle, and these are easiest to start, while most difficult to write down on the spot.

I shall have to devote some space to Kentucky whiskey before this account proceeds too far. It has more consequence than one might imagine.

But to return to my records. I have taken in much but allowed little time for digestion. That is the main object of this journal, however widely it seems to range.

On the war front, what I have is this: The Unionist faction in Kentucky is stronger than the Secessionist, but the state has struggled to maintain its neutrality. Its leaders are in constant negotiation with the Union army and the governor of Tennessee to forestall any intrusion. This may not succeed much longer.

There are Confederate troop movements in eastern Tennessee, near its juncture with Kentucky and Virginia. A General Zollicoffer has been ordered in with 7,000 men. Unionist sympathy is strong there—there has even been talk of a counter-secession—and the rail connection between Virginia and Tennessee runs through that area. On the surface, the South is simply being cautious, and no one, Kentuckian or Northern, has expressed any worries. Yet, there is little credible threat to the railroad. The region does, however, offer convenient natural entry into Kentucky. A moderately sized force might successfully seize the east and, conceivably, march unopposed all the way to the port of Cincinnati on the Ohio River. This would be disastrous for the North.

Closer yet to home, animosities are coming to a rolling boil. The American constitution makes explicit mention of citizen militias, and how they are to be armed and organized, but this appears little heeded in practice. The militias' official status can be cloudy. They are a singular example of the Americans' habit of substituting private voluntary associations for state action in addressing perceived social needs. There is also a long-standing prejudice against a standing army.

Militia units are raised at the local level (though normally instigated at some higher level) and may or may not be affiliated with other units, and may or may not receive government support. In Kentucky, this has led to some competition.

In Pulaski County, we have, first, the Somerset Artillery, mostly Mexican War veterans but open to anyone willing to contribute three dollars. This may be, in truth, principally a drinking club—they own no actual artillery. Still, they are liable for war service.

Then, there is the State Guard, organized by the Inspector General. This has somehow come to be dominated by Secessionist partisans.

Lately, we have the Pulaski Sentinels, associated with the newly formed Home Guard. This Home Guard was created by the legislature as a pro-Union counter to the State Guard. The two Guards are being given simultaneous legal recognition.

The county court, exercising vague authority, has ordered that forty muskets of unclear provenance be taken from the State Guard and given to the Sentinels. The decision has more symbolic than practical importance, since, I am told, the arms are too old to fire safely. Be that as it may, it is neighborhood news and something I can report as a reflection of native sentiments.

To be honest, I spend more and more time reading, alone or to Susannah. Mr. Graham has a surprising library, gathered as he has been able and therefore eclectic. The greater part is historical or reference material, in accordance with his tastes, but he has Milton, much of Shakespeare, Bunyan, and many of the Waverly novels. He says his collection is not untypical of his people. He acquired *Tristram Shandy* and *The Vicar of Wakefield* "to see what Andy Jackson was on about," these being the only two things the late president ever read besides the Bible. (Mr. Graham has a Bible, in pristine condition—none of the pages have been cut apart.) His philosophy is all Scotsmen except for Montaigne (in French!).

Susannah has been listening to me read *Kenilworth*, an old favorite of mine. She enjoys the plot, but demands much explanation. Rather, she did at first. Remarkably quickly, she has built a context for herself and a sense for the idiom. Her grasp of Elizabethan English will soon be better than mine. We should, perhaps, apply ourselves to

31

the Shakespeare next, although I am curious what she would make of *Rob Roy*.

Pulaski County, Kentucky, U. S. A., 31 July 1861

My own reading, apart from the recitations to Susannah—who, by the way, can read perfectly well but would rather listen to me—has been a translation of Plutarch's *Lives*, borrowed from Mr. Graham's history section. He has, or once had, some Greek and Latin, imparted by what he calls a "classical school." As I understand it, classical schools are institutes the Scottish Irish used to set up to educate the one son per family relegated to a clerical vocation. The consignment was not honored in Mr. Graham's instance. He claims to have lost the languages over the years.

I was reading the account of Numa Pompilius today when Susannah came rapping on the door. She listens to the Plutarch engagedly when I read it to her, but her questions do not have the intensity of interest that other works invoke. I set the book aside when she entered.

"They say you went to the fiddle contest without me," she said, without preliminary greetings. This way of hers is not rudeness—it is meant as evidence of intimacy, and she knows that I find it charming.

"Was that a contest? I just came across it, walking into town to ask for my letters. If I had known about it, I would have asked you along."

"Was it good?"

"I enjoyed it, if that is what you mean. If it was a contest, the criterion seems to be tempo. Many of the tunes I have heard before, from Mr. Graham, and some are quite interesting, but, at speed, they all sound very much the same."

"Well, sometimes they play for the melody and sometimes they play to show what they can do. Do you like the rhythm, at least?"

"There is something to be maintained for it."

"He says with his usual enthusiasm for everything."

"No, I do like it. I am just not habituated to it the way

you are."

"We need to dance sometime. Next time there's a dance. We can dress up and go."

"Can you do that in your condition?"

She laughed her delicate, lovely laugh—possibly her most engaging mannerism. "That won't work. I'm not even showing."

"I do not have anything to wear."

"How can you not have anything to wear? Aren't you an earl or something? Dudley in the book has all sorts of ornaments and straps. You could go in full regalia—blow the chawbacons back into the woods. " As with Mr. Graham, her vocabulary keeps catching me off guard, both in its extent and its diversity.

"You think I packed along a collar with double fusilles interchanged with knobs, supposed to present flint-stones sparkling with fire?"

"Or something along those lines. In your case, something less cheery. Maybe something darker, supposed to present coal."

"I do have ornaments, but I did not bring them with me. I have told you that I do not like to call attention to my title."

But I must, here, I suppose. Our association has included much consumption of Mr. Graham's liquor, with which he supplies me at a trifling price. It was inevitable, ultimately, that some allusion to my nobility should slip out. Susannah, of course, is taken with the idea, especially given our reading. On the frontispiece of our edition of *Kenilworth* is a picture of the Earl of Leicester that Susannah claims resembles me. It does not, except, perhaps, in coloring (hazarding immodesty, I do think that I am somewhat better looking). She is well aware of the fact—and is, I suspect, disappointed—that I am not the earl in my family. My eldest brother has that title—or the title of *Comte*, at any rate, the French equivalent. My other older brother is *Vicomte*, and I am left to be *Baron*.

"But you must have brought something to wear in the city."

"I have traveling clothes and formal attire, but neither is proper for a dance."

"No one will recognize that. They'll think it's the fashion. They'll just notice that they're expensive."

"*Were* expensive. I have not had the means to buy anything new for some while."

I stress my poverty constantly, trying to discourage her plan to marry. Destitute as we are, except for land and some negligible rents, I cannot even contemplate what my family's reaction would be if I returned home with Susannah on my arm and a Pulaski marriage license in my pocket. I cannot and do not take the prospect seriously, yet I would like for Susannah to be the one to reject the idea. The possibility of hurting her is almost as unpalatable as thought of marrying her.

"Good thing you've found employment, then. Meanwhile, you can borrow one of my father's old suits. My mother has kept everything he owned. You may end up with all of it, anyway."

As has come to be my practice, I changed the subject. "Does *everyone* play the fiddle?" I had the answer already from Mr. Graham.

"Everyone I know plays an instrument, usually a guitar or dulcimer if it's not a fiddle. Or sings, as I do. Toodie plays the piano, but we don't have one, so she only gets to do it at Mrs. Crozier's, when she takes lessons."

"I didn't realize you sang," I said blandly.

She grimaced, since I had heard her sing many times. Her voice is astonishing for someone without training, high and light and pure, with a decent range and, always, a wistful quality. She will sing as readily as Mr. Graham will opine, seizing the slimmest pretext.

"Let me hear you do it," I said.

A shy but pleased look came over her, and I knew my ploy would succeed. I pushed a bit farther, "You've never told me which song is your favorite."

"I've never sung it for you. I'm afraid if I do it too much, it'll ruin it for me."

"I am intrigued, now. And, if it is your favorite, it really should go into my collection. Sing it and then help me write it down. It might be lost forever, otherwise."

"So, your interest is scientific. Just the thing to put me in the mood."

However, she could not resist for long. This is what I came away with in the end (the melody I have noted down on the loose sheet between these pages):

> *"Cold blows the wind on my true love.*
> *Softly falls the rain.*
> *I never had a love but one,*
> *And in greenwood she lies slain.*
>
> *"I'd do as much for my true love*
> *As any young man may.*
> *I'll sit and I'll mourn all on your grave*
> *For twelve months and a day."*
>
> *When twelve months and a day had passed,*
> *The dead began to speak,*
> *"Who is this that sits all on my grave*
> *And will not let me sleep?"*
>
> *"'Tis I, 'tis I, your own true love*
> *That sits all on your grave.*
> *Just one kiss from your sweet lips,*
> *That is all I crave."*

"My lips, they are as clay, my love.
My breath is earthy strong.
And if you should kiss my clay-cold lips,
Your time would not be long.

"O think upon the garden, love,
Where you and I did walk.
The fairest flower that blossomed there
Has withered on the stalk.

"The stalk will bear no leaves, sweetheart,
The flower will never return.
And your true love is dead, is dead,
And you do naught but mourn.

"The stalk has withered dry, my love.
So will our hearts decay.
So make yourself content, my love,
'Til death calls you away."

Pulaski County, Kentucky, U. S. A., 1 August 1861

I visited Kenilworth nine years ago, when I was in my early thirties. I was staying in Warwick and had toured the castle, which left me exhilarated. Nothing is left in France so redolent of feudal times and their long story of freedom and servitude, criminality and virtue, and relentless energy. No one with a trace of poetry in him could remain unresponsive.

Modern Warwick held nothing for me—at least once I had eaten. In my mood, the contrast with the castle was unendurable. It was late, but I managed to hire a good, spirited horse, not without reactions of incredulity, but with the tolerance the English grant to those who can afford their follies. (The family had not yet then reached the end of its funds.)

I flew through a windless, cloudless night under a full moon, young and intoxicated with chivalry. Kenilworth was a few miles from Warwick and worse, if anything—it had a railroad station. When I came to the outskirts, however, I could find no one awake. I pounded on the door of an outlying house until a lovely, tousle-haired young woman opened a window. I asked the way to the ruins. Again, I was met with astonishment, but I was given friendly direction, mostly, I suspect, as the easiest way to get rid of me.

Leicester's castle was a mile from there, over ditches and through closed gates. Thirty minutes later, I found it standing in somberness, silence and desolation. Nothing remained whole above the ground level. The moon shone through the gothic windows in the ivied walls, and its funereal rays warned that I had entered a house of the dead.

My footsteps may have been the first in untold years. When I had explored my fill, I sat on a rock in the center, feeling myself carried into the far past. But it was not the historical past, the past of Elizabeth and Raleigh and

Cecil. It was the past of Amy Robsart, the past of Scott's novel. That delightful, unhappy heroine, object of Susannah's anguished solicitude, haunted the place for me. I almost seemed to hear her final cry as she fell into the chasm prepared for her. (I had forgotten that she died at Cumnor.)

Enrapt, I might have sat the night there, but my horse, impatient, began kicking the gate. I fell from poetry into prose. Nonetheless, I had been in a place more real than reality. Is the dead superior to that which never was? Both exist by the will of him in whose mind they act their parts. Neither has being outside that mind. On the points of interest and vitality and value, the fictional may have the advantage. Why, then, the privilege accorded history?

Pulaski County, Kentucky, U. S. A., 2 August 1861

Susannah came to my door two days after I first met her and her sisters in their yard. By coincidence, it was the day after Mr. Graham first relented and granted me an audience. I was still recovering from that conversation and trying to write down some of what my impaired memory had been able to keep. There came the rapid knocking at my door that has become so familiar since.

I was both curious and dismayed. No one came to the cabin—no one aware of its existence had reason to think it inhabited besides my landlord, who went beyond his own fence only under pressing need. On the other hand, I was not fit to receive visitors, nor had I yet summoned the will to repair the disorder in which I awoke.

She smiled as she took stock of things, then said, "Good afternoon. I am here as a representative of the Temperance Union, and your name has been given to us as an ardent supporter of our cause."

She was respectably clad. Only slowly did I recognize her and, even more slowly, that she was joking. "You should be asked in, I suppose, although I would not recommend that you accept the invitation."

She accepted immediately, however. In my stupor, I only just moved out of her way in time.

"Why, this is horrible!" she said, surveying the scene.

"Yes. Ruffians were here not thirty minutes ago. They had heard there was gold hidden in my effects and they left things in this sorry disarray. You can see in what sad state they left my person."

"And was there gold?"

"Scarcely copper."

"You're lucky, then, I was free to come by," she said, and forthwith began to tidy.

I believe I felt, mistily, the oddity of the presumption, but, mostly, I simply felt ill, so I sat and watched without protest.

"What are you writing?" Her labors had reached my desk.

"A complaint to the county court. How do you spell 'Susannah,' by the way—with an aitch?"

"It's sunny for once. You should be outside."

"I imagine I would die were sunlight to touch me."

"We could walk along the creek, under the trees."

"We could, but what would your parents think about that?"

"Well, my father died three years ago, and my mother is at her shop on the road to Somerset, so I don't guess that either of them will find out anything about it."

"And you yourself find nothing improper in the suggestion?"

"Improper in what way? We're just going for a walk along Tickle Cunt Creek."

"*Mon dieu*! What? Of which creek are you thinking?"

For the first time, then, I heard her laugh. "The original settlers on Salt Lick Creek were from Virginia, and they named it after a creek back home. There was a Fucking Creek, too, and it almost got named that. It got changed to Salt Lick later on—Mr. Graham was one of the campaigners for the change."

"That does not sound like him. But I would feel safer walking along Salt Lick Creek."

"Let's go, then," she said, in a tone that ruled out opposition. She opened the door and made insistent gestures with her hand. I collected my coat and hat and obeyed.

We climbed down off of my hill and continued downward to the innocent little stream with the deplorable past. My nausea came and went, as did the pulsation in my head, but both gradually abated with the exercise. It was cool under the trees by the water, and the ground sloped hardly at all once we reached the path along the bank. I came near to enjoying myself.

"Your mother has a shop?"

"Just the other side of Stirling, on the London road."

"That one. The general store." I went there often and had dealt with the proprietor when the boy who usually waited on customers was not around. She was a handsome woman for her age and pleasant enough. Still, I wondered how she would respond to a report that her daughter was roaming around with a forty-year-old Frenchman.

The bank was slick with mud at places where the footpath veered near the water's edge, and we stepped cautiously and wordlessly for long stretches.

"How old are you?" it occurred to me to ask.

"Nineteen. Toodie is seventeen and Ella is fifteen."

"It is good to be systematic about these matters. No brothers?"

"No. They wanted one but they gave up." She stopped to pick up an old walnut and probed its seam idly with her thumbnail, then threw it in the water.

"Who is the boy who works in the store?"

"That's John Foster. His family lives in Stirling. He's not very bright."

"Oho. Sounds like a romance gone wrong, to me."

She rolled her eyes. "You've seen him, haven't you?"

"Even so, there cannot be that many likely beaux available."

"There are *none* if 'likely' means conceivable. Toodie's young man lives in Somerset. He's an engineer."

"So, if in Somerset, not the train variety."

"No, he builds things. He's what's called a civil engineer, but there isn't enough work in that around here, so he does everything. Toodie met him when he came through looking at ways to improve the London road. They're going to start working on that, any time now. But now he just takes whatever job people need done."

The path was increasingly narrow and shallow with more branches across the way. We were getting scratched.

"Where was he educated?"

"At West Point."

"But he is not in the army, now?"

"No. He says he just went for the engineering and scientific training, and it was free."

"How old is he, if Toodie is only seventeen?"

"Twenty-five. He was very young when he went into the Academy. But it's all very chaste—he cannot visit very often, and my mother chaperones. Or I do."

"That last reassures me considerably."

She ignored me. "They're going to be married when she's eighteen. He's trying to put away some money. He's very nice."

Finally, there was scant passage remaining, though a trail continued visibly on. "We should turn around," Susannah said.

"Where does it lead from here?"

"It keeps going a mile or two, until you're at the end of the settled spots. But I don't like to go any farther than this. It's too hard."

"Let us try regardless. I have never explored this far. I shall keep the trees from getting you."

She was quiet for a moment, as if deliberating a confession. "That's not the reason. I just don't like going too far in this direction."

"What is ahead that you do not like?"

"A man has a house in a ravine where the stream splits. We try to avoid him. He's dangerous."

"How so?"

"People have disappeared who've gone to his place."

"Have the authorities looked into the matter?"

"The only local authority is Josh Moffat, whom we made constable part of the time because we're so far out. He came out with some men and asked questions, but nothing came of it. He's pretty useless except that he's big and can threaten people. I think he's probably scared of this man, too."

"Then, there is no evidence against the man in the ravine. Has he done anything else?"

"I don't want to talk about him. Let's go back—I have to get some chores done before my mother comes home."

I yielded, and we retraced our route. Susannah slipped once in some mud and grasped my wrist, almost precipitating us both into the water. After that, she clasped my hand until we were out of the small gorge.

"I'll come back next time you're sick," she told me when we reached my porch. "Tomorrow, I assume."

"I am not seeing Mr. Graham this evening."

"I'll stop by to make sure." Before I could retort, she kissed me on the cheek and walked swiftly away.

Pulaski County, Kentucky, U. S. A., 3 August 1861

A bad day. I spent it alone, which, for one of my temperament, is not healthy. Rather, it feeds a sickness already there. I cannot cure it. It is a debility in my very constitution. I have from my father an inherited need for frequent and sharp stimulation. It is a great source of vigor at times—this is its sole benefit—but typically it agitates for no reason and to no purpose.

This has been the chief impediment to the life of action I have always felt my due and duty. I lack perspective—I see things larger or smaller than they are. At my best, I am among the most clear-sighted and judicious of men, but I am rarely at my best. The serenity that would allow it can always be shaken by the smallest irritations. In the presence of grandeur— grandeur of conception or affairs or even physical perception—I grow calm and steady, but the continual abrasion of day to day life robs me of that. People are the worst annoyances, and yet I am drawn to them for stimulus and escape.

The ancients were right to counsel moderation and tranquility, whatever Mr. Graham may say about a nation always valuing most the quality that it has the least. I need to limit my desires, especially since no good thing can satisfy me. I despise everything, yet seek it all to rouse myself from the torpor that comes whenever I fall back into myself. Worst of all, I know that the most glorious objects, once achieved, would leave me as discontented as the pettiest.

Life has long ceased to hold any merit in itself. It is the ultimate pettiness. I only endure it by the thought that value can be instilled into it through doing one's duty and serving one's fellow man, taking one's proper station among them. One is then free to see life neither as treasure nor trial. One neither hopes nor fears overmuch. Life becomes a simple given, neither a joy nor a burden, but carrying an obligation to acquit ourselves as well as we are able.

I find this gets me through the night. It has also released me from the decade-long paralysis I fell into after the *coup* and my resignation. I had expected too much of men. Now I only expect myself to do my proper work, and I leave outcomes to Providence.

As a consequence, I have less tolerance for Mr. Graham's views on politics with each discussion. Paradoxically, in the same measure as my distaste for his attitudes grows, my fascination with him as a person intensifies. This is a puzzle well worth examining.

Pulaski County, Kentucky, U. S. A., 9 August 1861

I am returned from a week in Somerset. Much too much time had passed while I worked here on my own projects and read day-old newspapers. I tried to atone by shipping off chunks of dispatches, though, initially, I had nothing to report exclusively eastern in its compass. My bank drafts from New York had persisted in arriving, but I feared that might soon come to an end. Only an incursion by one side or the other, soon and into my share of the world, could save me.

I took the opportunity to pay Mrs. Irvine, my landlady, more rent in advance. She seemed startled by my reappearance, but my rooms and belongings were as I had left them. One noontime, I dined with Mr. Robert Selby, Toodie's suitor, to whom I had been charged to deliver a letter. He is an intelligent, likable young man, current on all the latest scientific advances—or, at least with those on which I, myself, have kept up—and we passed a very pleasant hour. I shall have my approval relayed to Toodie.

Otherwise, I accomplished little else by the end of my week that would justify the trip. Unionists have triumphed in elections for the two houses of the state legislature and are now proof against the governor's veto power, but that was anticipated. Only as I was set to return to Stirling was my salvation granted: I learned that in Garrard County—to my near north and well within my portion of the state—the Unionists have established a military training center, Camp Dick Robinson. A retired naval officer commands it, and the troops are mainly Home Guard units, but these are being equipped with legitimate weapons and drilled in a professional fashion.

The governor is outraged but toothless. He is appealing to President Lincoln to close the facility down but has no grounds for optimism. According to rumor, the former naval officer is a confidential agent for Lincoln.

The governor is friendly to the South, but genuine neutrals, like Congressman Crittenden, are anxious as well. A competent military force this close to the Cumberland Gap into eastern Tennessee could well provoke a preemptive attack by the Confederacy.

While confirming the particulars for this story in a tavern, I was given to understand that another Home Guard camp, at Barbourville in Knox County, has begun to receive and organize Unionists fleeing Zollicoffer in Tennessee. This camp has been around for some time, but was an amateur business that aroused no apprehension in the Southerners. Now it must: Barbourville is thirty miles from the Cumberland Gap (and, incidentally, in my territory).

I communicated all of this to New York. The previous dispatches had all been posted directly, since they had no urgent content. These items I sent to Louisville to be telegraphed to the Associated Press. Then I returned to the tavern, where I heard more news, though this was nothing I could exploit: the United States has adopted a three-percent tax on all incomes above $800 a year.

I shall have a Roman holiday confronting Mr. Graham with this. At present, however, I am tired and must sleep.

Pulaski County, Kentucky, U. S. A., 11 August 1861

I should continue to copy out my talks with Mr. Graham in the order in which they took place—I have a tremendous reserve of notes. Then, again, they are all of a piece and can build on each other in whatever arrangement they are given. This should speak well for him, pointing to an overall coherence to his positions. I find it wearying after so many weeks, the more so as it clarifies my disagreements. Also, he repeats himself, and I have concluded that is more self-satisfaction than forgetfulness.

In any case, I shall violate the sequence and describe our exchange yesterday, rather than record it twice.

I rang the bell beside his door and a chair scraped within. I heard his deliberate, unhurried steps as he came to admit me and I saw, on entering, that he had been reading at his desk.

"What is this?" I asked, pointed to the volumes.

"I thought I would look at Livy again. Your borrowing the Plutarch put me in the mood."

"Thank you again. It is finer reading than I remembered. I began somewhat distractedly but now I find a wonderful appeal to it. What a devil of a world was antiquity!"

"Or, perhaps, a hell." He went to the cupboard for jugs.

"But with more latitude for greatness! You see that better in Plutarch than anyone else. He animates characters one usually sees merely as statues. They become human, or only slightly larger than ordinary human scale. The effect is arresting and inspiring."

"And dangerous, maybe."

"Maybe. I become so caught up in it that I fear at times I may go mad after the fashion of Don Quixote. I get overfilled with urges toward a heroism that does not suit our times. Then the present world intrudes, and I am deflated."

"I have to admit that it happens to me, too, if I don't watch myself. I used to have a Macaulay sickness a few years back—and I was old then. 'Hail to the great Asylum! / Hail to the hill-tops seven! / Hail to the fire that burns for aye, / And the shield that fell from heaven!' The trick is to remember where most of it led."

It seemed early to begin drinking, but, after a few swallows, I decided I could reconcile myself to it. "I have only read Macaulay's history of England. But that is the shield from Plutarch's *Numa*, is it not? I just read that recently."

"Yes. In Livy, too, indirectly. A shield sent by the gods to safeguard the health of the state. If the gods really wanted to help us, they would send a shield to *protect* us from the health of the state."

He knew how I felt about his more *outré* opinions and he was goading me. "Rome," I said, "was all that drew us from barbarism."

"Mostly by exterminating barbarians. My people have done that too, I'm ashamed to say, but we didn't mechanize the process. Julius Caesar probably killed a quarter of the population of Gaul, and that set a pattern for how the Romans treated Celts. *Auferre, trucidare rapere falsis nominibus imperium, atque ubi solitudinem faciunt, pacem appellant.* 'To steal, to massacre, to usurp under false titles, they call legitimate authority, and, where they make a wasteland, they call it peace.'"

"I thought you had forgotten your Latin. But for every Caesar, there was a Brutus or a Cato. The Plutarch reminds that it has always been a mixture. You know the repugnance I have for the politicians of our day when they treat principles like merchandise. I come near to believing that any claims to ideals and standards are simply dissimulated self-interest, and always the most paltry, transitory interests."

The alcohol was doing its work. I took some more and tried to remember where I was going with this. "But Plutarch is letting me see the same tendencies in the most beautiful eras of the ancient world. We are not all contrast, and that gives me hope."

"I'm afraid I need to make a short visit to the shack out back," was his response, and he arose and left the house.

I have begun to talk too much. Partly, it is because I have tired of listening to Mr. Graham lecture and I wish to forestall him. Our acquaintanceship may be near its end. I have had from him what he has to provide and I am sated.

When he returned, I said, "Did you hear that the federal government is now to tax all incomes?"

This did not affect him in any of the ways for which I could have hoped. What those were, I am not certain. Apoplexy, perhaps.

"That's been a long time coming. Is it *all* incomes?"

"Those above $800."

"I'm safe, at least. I don't have any income at all unless I sell some land. I'll just need to keep it below that amount. I lose enough on the watch tax."

The county taxes gold watches at $100 a watch. Mr. Graham has one, and I am sure he would feel no guilt about keeping it hidden, but everyone knows that he has it. He brought it out for me, once. It is inscribed: "For fond memories, Lydia." His wife's name was Margaret, so I do not know who this was, and he did not offer to enlighten me.

"There will be conscription soon enough," he continued. "That should put an end to Lincoln's posturing about involuntary servitude. Should, I say. It won't."

"And yet," I said, "the Union cause is gaining in popularity. Why would conscription be necessary?"

"It's easy to be hot for a cause when you don't expect to risk your own skin."

"What about the latest elections in Kentucky? The Unionists were overwhelmingly victorious and no one around here who has taken sides appears averse to military service."

"No one around here *would*. I've told you—the Scotch Irish are a warrior nation. It's our fatal flaw. We'll join in any war going as long as someone tosses the word 'freedom' around. The government would never be able to make slaves of us if they went about it honestly. It'll be our own faults, our religion and our martial nature, that do us in."

He invariably found a way to turn any question into an opening for his pet maxims. This had turned down a road all too terribly familiar. I picked up my jug and settled back to wait him out. When I get around to writing out my notes on the earlier (and fresher) interviews, the same terrain will be charted.

I examined the room in which I have spent so much time and which I shall seldom see again if I follow my inclination. The building itself is, like mine, a relic from the age of first settlement. It is about forty English feet long and fifteen high. The walls and roof are formed of the untrimmed trunks of trees, the gaps filled with moss and red clay (which may be original). The interior has been subdivided more recently—finished boards have been used, and they look relatively new—but the greater part of the house is still one large chamber.

This room has one window in the right-hand wall with a muslin curtain; the opposite wall is devoted to an immense fireplace of compacted clay, filled with ashes. Over the mantel hang a prehistoric musket, a large animal hide and bouquets of eagle feathers (I think). On the left side of the chimney is a gun rack holding more up-to-date weaponry. On the right side is a map of the world. Next to this begin the shelves for his books, which

extend around the corner and onto the next wall. Next to
the books is Mr. Graham's desk, and next to that is a
large *armoire* containing I know not what.

Then comes the door into the other room or rooms—
this is precisely opposite the door to the outside. I have
never been through that, but there must be a bed and a
kitchen somewhere. The remaining empty space is
covered with overclothes on hooks or pictures of ships. In
the center of everything is a slab-like table, its legs still
covered with bark and looking as if they are growing out
of the earth. Empty jugs and old issues of the *Somerset
Democratic Gazette* occupy a great deal of the table's
surface. This is where we sit on two of the mismatched
chairs and talk.

I do not recall how this homily ended. Pertinently or
not, I suggested that the outcome of the election proved
that local support for the Union was sincere. "Either
position can be portrayed as a crusade for freedom, after
all. Why such a hostility to the South?"

"The enemy will be whoever invades first. It's as
simple as that. If the North comes in first, you'll see a
sudden shift in allegiance to the South. Camp Dick
Robinson only survives because it's all local boys. But,
we'd rather not support either side."

"Still, why did the Unionists sweep the races?"

"Because no one voted. Only Unionists voted. The
Confederate faction and the neutrals kept out of it. And
what does that tell you? It tells *me* that everyone thinks
the South will launch an offensive first. The state will
throw in with the North. There's no point in working to
elect people who'll be tossed out in a month or two.

"By the way, you should be interested in this—I hear
that some seseshes, at least, are planning to set up their
own government and wait for the rebel army to arrive
and hand things over to them."

"'Seseshes?'"

"Secessionists. Another load of them are running to

Tennessee to join the Confederate army. This is all beside the point, though. The important fact is that most people are neutral and most people don't vote even in normal times. Most people just want to be left alone to live their lives. And why would a rational person vote? We've got trained animals to do that for us."

He was tweaking me again, so I retorted, "If you despise American politics so much, I am surprised you are not more sympathetic to the rebels. They are taking arms against the government, whatever their motives may be."

"I sympathize with some of the soldiers, the ones who are only fighting to get out from under the thumb of outsiders. Those are my people, and we have never benefited from slavery—it makes it hard to get work if you can't make a go of farming. On the other hand, they've wound up fighting for slave owners, and I can't countenance that.

"And the war will not end government. The Confederacy will have taxes and conscription of its own, soon enough. Probably before the end of the war. It's in the nature of things."

"So, on balance, you would oppose the South if it intruded into your domain."

"I would have harsh things to say about it. Whether I fought or not would take a lot of considering. It's not my job to set things right, and I don't think things ever stay right for long, anyway."

He looked drained, of a sudden. He has reserves of youthful vigor upon which to draw, but they are not bottomless. His voice had hoarsened with so much talk, and he gargled some of the whiskey before swallowing it.

"That is a shame," I said, when he did not continue. "You have the instincts of an anarchist, but not the drive. You will never discharge your proper function."

"I'm not against government. There's such a thing as legitimate government. It's that collection of vermin you don't kill right away because you think they'll be useful for keeping someone worse out of power."

But he was flagging. We needed to leave this theme.

"Mr. Graham, I am going to have to spend more time in Somerset from now on. I shall not be able to converse with you very often. The one area I have not researched well enough is folklore. We touched on it a few weeks back, but only superficially."

He looked distinctly grey. "We can do this another time," I said.

"No, no." He fluttered his hand. "I'm just having these moments, lately. I lose all energy. It passes quickly. Do you mean superstitions, again? I've told you about the Baptists."

"Superstition is part of it. Stories are the biggest part."

"All the stories I know come from Scotland and Ireland. Or England. We used to have a lot of songs about Robin Hood, but I don't remember them. There are better people to go to for that sort of thing. I do remember there were stories about the fairies—the details are all gone."

"So, there is an American species of little people. That is interesting. I had not heard of such a thing."

"No, they're not local. Come to think of that, it's evidence that they really exist."

"How is that?"

He smiled. "If they were superstition, we would have kept it up, and there *would* be tales of a native species. Since no one claims to have seen any, it's evidence that the old stories had a tangible basis. There are fairies, but only in Europe—none of them made the trip."

"Engaging, but hardly proof."

"Not proof, just evidence."

He did not believe this. It would violate his essence to believe in anything.

"Did you meet with Nick Bromfield?" he asked.

"Who?"

"The witchmaster I told you about."

"No. Everyone denies knowing who he is."

"They would, I suppose. Must hurt the witchmastering business something awful."

"But what is a witchmaster?"

"He cures diseases caused by witches. And he can catch witches."

"And is there a great need for that?"

"You've put your finger on the problem. It got to where there was no one around anyone felt like suspecting. Except Nick. He looks odd, he keeps to himself, and he has some strange experiments going. Alchemy, I would guess."

"That ended in France with Lavoisier." A man of my class, a *vicomte* and a lawyer, though his title was purchased.

"Well, not in Pulaski County, Kentucky. If that's what he's doing. Something outlandish, anyway. When people had witch problems, he was the obvious one to blame. Finally, a group of boys went out after him at night—about six of them, armed—and never came back."

"Wait, please. Is this a man who lives down on the creek near the edge of the settled area? A hunchback with long, white hair and beard, and spectacles?"

"That's your man."

"Susannah—Susannah Armstrong—believes that he is hundreds of years old and comes from pre-Christian Britain. It took me forever to coax her to say that much."

"He is about eighty and comes from New Jersey. We have strong connections with that place—Somerset was founded by two gentlemen from New Jersey. They came from Somerset County. But Nick is from Camden. His family moved to Virginia about the same time mine moved there from Pennsylvania, so we were close. I used to protect him from the other boys.

"We stayed close until we had some...disagreements...

over a business venture. I left the country about then. He did too, for awhile, though I don't know where all he went. I've only seen him a couple of times since he moved here. He came here when he was older, following his family, who came with mine—our tribe's families tend to form partnerships and migrate together. Now, everyone has drifted off to Illinois and Texas except for him and me.

"Anyhow, he's someone you might want to interview. He was always attracted to that sort of thing."

He was not looking any better, and his breath seemed to be fading. "I'm sorry, but I'm going to have to call it a night," he said.

"Are you going to be all right?"

"Yes, yes." He waved my concern away again. "Come by before you take off for good."

"I propose to be around frequently."

"Well, that cabin is yours any time you need it. You can leave anything you need there. It's not going to be used, otherwise."

"Thank you. I appreciate that. Also..." I was hesitant but drove myself on. "Also, there is another matter about which I wished to get some advice. Nothing with which we need to deal now. A personal matter, but one regarding which I truly need your expert judgment."

He was too weak for curiosity. "Any time. Right at present, I'd better sleep."

I left him still slumped at his table.

Pulaski County, Kentucky, U. S. A., 12 August 1861

The house Mr. Graham has lent me is about ten English feet square and, like his, made of logs. It cannot have been used much since the earliest days. Mr. Graham owns many of these, as I have said, with the plots they stand on. He bought them up as his family and friends drifted west and north. I have made repairs and caulked the chinks in the structure with the ubiquitous red clay.

It could not have been a farmhouse, I suspect. Those are in the low places, chiefly around water. Mine presides over one of the hills that undulate throughout this country.

The road is not visible from my spot, so all I see are billows of oak and maple and pine. These are not Normandy's gentle ripples. The surface dips and swells, mounts and sinks, quick and sharp. Little valleys make a maze with thousands of bends. One can imagine anything might be found down there, just around the next turning. I can see what drew people on and on, deeper into this land. Always, there was one more curve ahead that might reveal...who knows what?

When it rains, the mist can hide it all. But, sometimes it merely obscures and one sees only hilltops, like islands rising from a sea. The valleys and hollows are especially mysterious then, concealed and concealing. I wander in them then, sometimes, never finding and always, still, expectant.

These hills are old. Somewhere down in those corridors must be something worth the seeking. They cannot be empty, unless emptiness itself is the secret.

Pulaski County, Kentucky, U. S. A., 13 August 1861

I went on an outing today with Susannah and Toodie. Toodie brought along her admirer, Mr. Robert Selby—in for the day—and a friend, Miss Percina Johnstone. Miss Johnstone invited a Mr. Willis Gilchrist, so, all together, we made a sizable party.

It was meant to be a *piquenique* in a broad, level, grassy field by the creek, but, when we gathered at the post office, we found an assembly collected around a crude platform. Nearby, a flagpole had been erected and was flying the Confederate flag.

"What is this?" Miss Johnstone asked a woman standing near us.

"It's supposed to be a talk by an officer from the Home Guard. That's him over there in the uniform. He was going to speak for the Union states, but representatives for the other side appear to have gotten here first." She nodded at a hard-featured group.

"Is the officer going to take it down?"

"He doesn't have much right to. It's a free state."

I was as happy about that as not. The assembly as a whole was substantial and no doubt contained abundant enthusiasts for both sides, however neutral the greater part may have been. My impulse was to get the girls away from the place as speedily as possible. I was about to recommend that to Mr. Selby when I was jostled by Miss Johnstone.

"Excuse me," she said and immediately turned to her escort. "We *cannot* allow that sickish rag to float upon Pulaski breezes. Do something about it."

Mr. Gilchrist, a very young man, looked inquiringly at Mr. Selby and me.

"I must not be involved," I told him. "I am a foreign national, and it would not be fitting."

Mr. Selby asked him, "Do you have friends here?" (I

presume that his officer training was revealing its stamp.)

The boy looked around. "Jimmy!" he cried, spying someone.

Jimmy came over and, between the two of them, they soon rallied a score of acquaintances. One left and returned with an axe while the others were plotting their strategy.

"We should take the girls as far from this as we can," I advised Mr. Selby.

He nodded, but then pointed to Miss Johnstone and Toodie, who were in the thick of the planning debate. "I don't know that we can. You might see if Susannah is willing to go."

"Susannah, it will not be safe here long," I said.

"I can't leave Toodie here. Toodie! Get out of there! We're going on to the field. Bring Percina."

They ignored her, however. The little troop moved toward the flagpole, the boy with the axe bearing it before them like a banner.

Then about six of the seseshes climbed upon a fence and declared that the man who cut down the flag would do so at peril of his life.

Our side wavered for a moment until Miss Johnstone took the axe and advanced again upon the flag, telling the others to stand guard.

She and Toodie took turns hacking at the pole until it began to fall. Unfortunately, it lodged in a tree instead of dropping. Mr. Gilchrist completed its descent with a couple of strokes and dragged it flat against the ground.

The men on the fence kept a flow of abuse running the while, but asserted themselves no further.

"Cravens!" shrieked a voice I knew. I made out the Elder Bell in the crowd. "If this is the mettle of the forces of rebellion, the party of righteousness will celebrate its victory soon enough. Weaklings and cowards!"

I perceived that he had positioned himself so that the

mass of the Unionists was between him and the gentlemen on the fence.

He wore the derisive half-smile I have grown to despise so in the past weeks. I interviewed him in my first days here but could evoke nothing to my purpose. He was all oratory and spite, all delivered in a reproving tone as though I were an ally of whoever his foil of the moment happened to be.

When I have encountered him in town—if I have not seen him in time—I have been gracious and reserved. Yet, he has always felt obliged to slip some little acridity into our exchanges. They have been insinuated slights, never enough to call him on. It has not been subtlety— that is not for one of his breeding. That is a thing with which I have vast experience and can contend. It is his lack of manliness. If one must be common, one should at least put on an honest peasant candor.

I took no notice of whatever else he had to say to the seseshes. Mr. Selby snatched Toodie and her friends from their followers, and Susannah and I picked up all of our neglected baskets. We snaked our way to the edge of the throng.

As we emerged to wait for the others to make their way to us, I almost walked into the Elder, who, I assume, was working to maximize his distance from the forces of rebellion.

"In this country, we are not expected to yield the way simply because of another's birth," he said.

"You have my sincerest apologies," I replied. "We were in haste to escape to a more pastoral setting."

He looked at Susannah with that disdainful, mirthless smile. "Ah. So your wanton is along for the show."

I cannot say why he thought I would abide this. I conjecture that he had finally decided my long forbearance was weakness. One interprets others in conformity with one's own character.

"I am sorry. I am afraid that I misheard you just now.

What did you say?"

"I remarked that this woman has apparently accompanied you to watch these proceedings."

"I do not believe that was precisely your wording. Might I advise that you apologize to the lady for your ill-chosen language."

As with Mr. Graham in Somerset that day, he was not sensitive to threat. It can only be that he had dismissed me so thoroughly that he could not imagine any danger. He thought that I was, as they say here, "bluffing."

He squeezed his lips together, then said, defiantly, "I will not. It is not for me to apologize. It is for this slattern to apologize for her shameless conduct."

With three straw baskets in my hands, I was carrying my walking stick under my arm, almost vertically so as not to stab people as I walked through them. Clumsily, I set my load on the ground and then grasped the stick under the silver pear at its top—I could not strike him with that end without injuring him more severely than his transgression warranted. Then I began to thrash him.

I have only had to do this once before, in Normandy, when a drunken rustic insisted on annoying a young lady. That man had bellowed deeply, like an ox; the Elder screamed like a child. It did not last long—he curled up like a prawn and his coat absorbed the force of the blows. Once his face started bleeding, I avoided striking there.

By this time, the others had reached us, and I motioned them toward their baskets. The rest of our little holiday was very pleasant, once everyone began talking again.

Pulaski County, Kentucky, U. S. A., 14 August 1861

Miss Johnstone's performance yesterday restores some of my optimism about the American prospect. Granted, the better part of those present may only have been on hand for the spectacle, but the young woman's zeal was unprompted and heartfelt, and must have its roots in some native nobility. I mistrust the patriotic fervor the Lincolnites have drummed up—it is too brittle and desperate—and I am near to ill when I reflect on the cloaked, twisted malevolence that must drive an Elder Bell.

As best as I have been able to discover, Mr. Graham's portrait of his fellow westerners is accurate in the main. At their best, they can be spurred to splendid deeds by appeal to their love of liberty or, second best, to their warrior spirit. More typically, they are prone to sever themselves from any concerns that go beyond themselves or their families or their friends.

When the westerner has thus formed a miniature society of his own, he willingly leaves the larger world to itself. The virtues of public life, unnourished, wither and weaken. From Mr. Graham's perspective, this is all to the good—he has no use for the public-spirited, admitting no distinction between interest in the common weal and officiousness. He holds that the most important public virtue is a willingness to "leave other people the hell alone."

There is something to be said for this. If we call it self-interest, it is not so on a narrow construction. The westerner looks to the interest of his limited circle. Further, it is an interest rightly understood, which Americans as a whole have always espoused as the surest foundation for morality. They value morality for its usefulness, not as an end in itself.

This frees them from the tyranny of abstractions and

preserves them from baneful enthusiasms. At least, it has in the past. Mr. Graham maintains that too much has changed in his lifetime. He thinks this war will be the killing blow for the old America, and I am inclined to agree. The apocalyptic language of the Lincolnites, and the crusading spirit it is meant to engender, may be the sign. This country will go the way of France, abandoning its freedom and its local loyalties for a centralized state and the glamour of power. We took that route with the devaluation of the aristocracy under the Old Regime, and all our revolutions and transformations have only confirmed the change.

Then again, Mr. Graham's people go too far to the other extreme. Their traditions do not encourage even those civic ideals requisite for a free community. The townships of New England hit the proper mean. There, men have learned how properly to identify their personal freedom with the interests of the political whole. These Scots Irish never made the historical step from family to city. They are a "ruined fragment" of a people, as Dr. Marx's friend Mr. Engels would say—they have as little chance for survival as their old Highland neighbors.

And this is why I am finally tired of Mr. Graham. He refuses to understand this and he looks with equal indifference on all the ideas that can stir society, be they right or wrong, honest or ignoble. He is virile enough in himself, and passably healthy, but his political agnosticism is not. He does not see how well his attitude accords with the bourgeois complacency he despises and which has led to this new world he laments.

I am prey to the same temptations as he. I have lived among these people—these neutrals—long enough for that. The experience is very like that I have when I observe Susannah's religious devotion: an acute yearning to think and feel the same way, even while I know it is impossible. The situations in France and America seduce one to apathy.

Yet, I cannot cease struggling. What I shall be in the end, I do not know. But it would be easier for me to enlist in the Union army, or run off to Tennessee to join the rebels—or run off to sea or to China, for that matter— than to lead the life of a potato, like these decent people here.

Pulaski County, Kentucky, U. S. A., 16 August 1861

Another lively day yesterday and a very long one. Susannah came by in the morning to ask if I wanted to go "sang-picking."

"Is it a musical occasion?" I inquired.

"No—ginseng hunting. It's hard to find, so it's mostly an excuse for exploring, but, if we find some, we can get a lot of money for it. But there *is* a dance tonight, and I thought we could go after. Wear anything you want.

"And give me one of those cigars."

I happened to be smoking one of those I have from Mr. Graham, who, like most in the region, grows and cures his own tobacco. He could probably preserve meat in the atmosphere of his front room. I shall miss the free cigars and free liquor in Somerset.

Taking one from the box on my desk, I handed it to her. I almost encourage the practice among the young people here. The alternative is worse: I have never known Susannah or Toodie to chew tobacco, but their sister Ella does. Mrs. Armstrong requires only that she and her little friends not spit in the house, I am told.

"Will the whole town be there?"

"Just church members—and Toodie and Bob and Percina and Willis," she said, biting the end from the cigar.

I held my coal to it while she puffed it alight. "Do you know, Susannah, I feel out of place in your circle. I am so much older."

"Bob is older, too."

"Not as old as I. I like them all, however."

"Good, because they're coming sang-picking with us."

This was announced with such implied finality that I did not bother to pursue the subject.

"I would also, I think, feel uncomfortable at a church dance. I am not of your faith."

"We'll go late. Everyone will be liquored up by the time we get there and won't notice you. Except Pastor Taylor—he doesn't drink."

"A pastor who does not imbibe! I was given the impression that none of them dare stand up to deliver a homily unless they have prepared themselves with a few cups."

She smiled her saintly smile, and that sight exercised its customary influence on me. It tore at my heart this time. I had not informed her of my plans.

"The sermons are generally better when the preacher's prepared," she said. "The spirit comes through more powerfully."

"And Pastor Taylor is willing to sacrifice that for a moral scruple."

"A moral scruple? You think he's a temperance man? He wouldn't keep his position if he were. No, everybody knows he just has too much of a liking for morphine. It doesn't do to mix the two."

She turned the chair at my desk around and straddled it to be near the ashtray. "He's a very happy, easygoing man. You'll enjoy him."

For a minute or two, she said nothing more, smoking and looking off into the dark corners of the room. The smile disappeared by stages.

"What are we going to do?" she asked in a small voice.

"I do not know."

"Couldn't you really keep me hidden away on one of your properties? I would be satisfied with that."

We had played with this solution, in jest, while reading the Scott. At least, I had passed it off as a joke. "Amy was not. She was not content with that even in her native land. You would be removed by an ocean from everything and everyone you know."

"Then what are we going to do?"

It was the moment. "Susannah, I shall be spending more of my time in Somerset from now on. It is necessary with the state of affairs developing as they are. I cannot follow the war adequately from this place."

"Take me with you."

"That would not be feasible in Somerset. As what would we represent you? Queen Victoria's hold is much stronger there than here."

She had never wept in my presence before. I was at a loss—nothing truthful I could say would carry comfort.

"Come here," I managed.

I put my arms around her and held her. "We can devise something, in time." Or not, I reflected, and straight away despised the thought. But what am I to do?

"It's just a hard thing," she murmured against my breast, "when I like you so well, and you don't love me in return."

"We shall work something out," I repeated, and then, distracted by her unwonted tears, undid myself. "Even if it means installing you in a ruined castle."

The slender form stiffened. "Do you mean that?" she asked, still pressing her face against me.

"Yes," I answered, too slowly.

It was enough. Her distrust was evident, but she dried her face and smoothed her thin calico frock. "We had best hurry. The others are waiting."

We met them coming up the path to my cabin. Mr. Selby and the boy were wearing packs on their backs.

"We were tired of waiting," called Toodie in cheerful rebuke, but, when she came close and saw Susannah's face, she looked troubled. However, she merely said, "There is one spot left that might have 'sang. It's beyond that big patch of poplar across the road."

"Protected by difficulty of access, apparently," commented Mr. Selby.

"It wouldn't be an expedition if it were easy," rejoined Toodie.

Our destination was at some distance, and the girls felt it essential to quick-march us until we were among the poplars with no clear trail. At that point, we were allowed to halt and regain our breath.

"Did you bring cigars?" Susannah asked me.

I offered them all around. Susannah and Mr. Selby accepted, but Miss Johnstone's countenance crinkled up. "I do not smoke. I cannot endure the odor. Neither can Willis."

The boy himself was carefully expressionless.

"You will have to bear it this once," said Toodie.

I turned to her. "What about you, Toodie?"

"I have something better."

She drew out a leather pouch, ornamented with Indian beadwork, and opened it to reveal loose tobacco in tiny flakes. As we watched, she poured some of this into a fold of paper and rolled that into a tube with practiced movements.

"A cigarette!" I exclaimed. "The sin of Elizabeth Tait!"

"That was years ago," she said. "And we are hidden here."

"And she is a willful child, anyway," said Susannah.

There is a history underlying part of this banter, which I shall explain when I can give it due attention. It has interesting implications.

Our break concluded, Toodie herded us through underbrush until, on no observable basis, she declared we had arrived. The others she directed to search in assorted directions; I demurred on the ground that I could not tell a ginseng plant from a ground squirrel. Toodie and I stood on a rise, guarding the packs from, I assume, bears or some such.

"So you are to be married," I said.

"When I'm eighteen. Bob will be twenty-seven and almost make the culling list, but I'll be safe by a margin."

"The culling list?"

"People who are too old to marry. It's twenty for women and twenty-eight for men."

"Who keeps this list?"

"It's not really a list—it's an understanding."

"And it's taken seriously?"

"It's supposed to be a joke, but things really do work out that way. Or used to. I guess people can always move to a city these days and find someone who's desperate. I expect even you could still land somebody."

"Mr. Selby would appear to be a very good match. I have been much impressed by him in conversation."

"Well, I think so, naturally."

This exhausted our conversational invention, so we waited there in mute discomfort. Mr. Selby was the first to abandon the hunt, and his return finally rescued us.

He had removed his coat and was perspiring through his shirt. "I fear that the species is no longer to be found in these parts. We have mined the region out."

"Let's catch the others as they come by, and then we can eat," Toodie said.

No one, in the end, was successful, so we dined on cold cuts of pork in slices of a bread made from maize. The hike had sharpened my appetite, and I devoured my share and most of Susannah's.

Because of the dance, we were driven homeward twice as quickly as we had come. I took my leave of the others and went to the cabin to rest in preparation for the evening. Trusting in Susannah, I laid out a set of my ordinary day clothing, and washed and slept.

It was darkening when she came to fetch me and full dark by the time we made it down to the church. Had we not known the way, we could simply have followed the glow of the multitudinous torches and lanterns set up outside and in the great church hall. The blaze was visible even from the lowest places.

It was warm in the August night, and a considerable number of the attendant clustered or danced outside, where tables were stationed with tubs of water and ice and trays of cups. Others were loaded with jugs and jars and bottles—whether supplied or conveyed individually from home, I could not tell.

We were accosted by a dignified but amiable woman of stout middle years who had watched us approach. "Susannah," she greeted us, nodding. "And this is your famous Frenchman. I have seen you around, but never had the chance to say hello."

She clutched my hand with both of hers. "I'm Hettie Taylor, and I'm pleased to see you here."

"Mrs. Taylor's the pastor's wife. She arranges these occasions for the congregation," Susannah explained.

"I thank you very much, Mrs. Taylor, for your hospitality. I am Edouard de Grimouville." She still had possession of my hand, so I just bowed.

"The *Baron* de Grimouville," my companion supplied.

I scowled at her, but she returned my look with an elfin smirk.

"Then we're especially honored to have you present," said Mrs. Taylor. I am not sure that she took Susannah's claim seriously, and, in any event, counterfeit nobility are not uncommon on the American frontier.

"The musicians are inside, as I am certain you can tell." The music was hammering at us through the open doors of the hall, and I could see movement and leaping shadows. Our hostess nodded at the jug Susannah was carrying. "You can set your refreshments anywhere except the tables in the side yard. We're trying to keep the little shits corralled there."

We thanked her and continued toward the doors. Susannah took hold of my arm.

"Little shits?" I asked her.

"Children," she translated.

Inside, it took a few seconds to adjust to the commotion. I was acquainted with several of the tunes played by the massive band, though the tempo was, when we first entered, comparatively slow in order to oblige the dancers. It accelerated as the evening progressed.

The dance itself was a sort of quadrille, which meant

that I had an approximate notion of what to do when, at last, I consented to be drawn in. There was also a gentleman who chanted instructions, and this helped somewhat when I could understand what he was saying. More helpful were my trips to Susannah's "refreshments" outside, which relaxed my diffidence. (The other dancers' trips outside ultimately erased all pretense to decorum, and that was most helpful of all.)

At the outset, however, I wanted merely to watch and analyze the rules. My aspirant partner, thwarted for the moment, walked off, to reappear presently in the company of a tall, thin, greying man with a clerical collar and a beatific visage

"This is Pastor Taylor."

We shook hands. His grip was slightly too easy, albeit preferable to the competitive pumping one often gets from Americans. It corresponded to the steady but overly mellow voice that said, "Edouard, Edouard— welcome, welcome." Then he embraced me.

I disentangled myself as gently as I could. "Pastor, I am very pleased to meet you. Susannah is a fervent admirer of yours and has spoken much about you."

He was probably flattered. It was difficult to tell, since his face was already blissful. "Miss Armstrong is too kind. Everyone is always so kind."

"I am trying to work out the conventions for this type of dancing. Susannah expects me to take part in it."

"Just go to it, my boy. Love and do what thou wilt, as one of the churchmen said. No one but God is watching, and he has more important things to judge."

"It is Susannah's judgment before which I tremble."

"Not even God, perhaps, can help you there."

She punched him in the upper arm (too forcefully, I thought). "I've told him that I don't expect him to be good. But he does have to do it."

The pastor beamed at her. And kept beaming, saying nothing further, until it became strange.

"It has been a distinct pleasure to meet you, Pastor Taylor," I finally declared. He set his beam on me, and I nodded and tugged Susannah toward the dance. "No time like the present."

But we did not reach the dancers. Our way was blocked by a trio of men of markedly villainous aspect. One held out his hand to block our advance.

"You're that Frenchman, aren't you?" he growled.

"I'm one of them."

"But you're the one gave Elder Bell a whipping at the political meeting." (I believe the word he used was "whipping." Various forms of it were uttered in what followed, but the vowel never quite settled down.)

"Yes, I am," I said, and I set my feet.

"Then I want to shake your hand," he said. He proffered a huge, grimy appendage, and I obliged him.

"It *is* him!" he told his fellows, and they all wanted to shake. This attracted the attention of all around, who, after explanations, encircled me, waiting their own chance to shake my hand or slap my shoulders. Some even dropped out of the dance.

I should have recognized the man who initially approached me. He turned out to be none other than that Johnny Elliot whose contributions to Elder Bell's discourse in Somerset I have described earlier in these pages. Later in the evening, he was able to satisfy a bit of curiosity I have had for some time: He and his friends all wore large daggers, almost miniature swords, in scabbards on their belts. I suspected these were the famous Bowie knives, specimens of which I have never before actually seen. Dr. Marx has an eccentric prejudice against them, using them in his essays as a distinguishing concomitant of frontier thuggery. Having examined them, I must have one.

I am off the main thread of my narrative, however. At the time, Mr. Elliot and his friends, Mr. Daniel Shays Routledge and Mr. Henry "Toeless Harry" Carruthers, seemed to provide a pretext for outdoor socializing, but Susannah wrenched me back toward the dance.

I did escape from time to time to join my new friends by the tables, often for extensive periods. Always, I was tracked down and towed back into the fray. My proficiency increased rapidly, though, as it was reaching a peak, disorder began to infest the whole. More and more couples and individuals broke ranks and adopted freer techniques. In the end, Susannah herself discarded the formalities. She tried to get me to follow suit, but I could not, so I retired to the perimeter and observed.

As I noted earlier, the music sped up over the course of the evening. Now, it approximated the swiftness at a fiddle competition. Some of Susannah's steps seemed skillful, showing traces of traditional forms, but, for the most part, she danced as the music led her, twirling and skipping with spontaneous abandon.

They moved to give her space, and she became the focus of the room, all other dancers now mere satellites. Her reddish-brown hair spilled out of its fastenings and swung with the cadence of her movement. When her dress could no longer accommodate her motions, she took the hem on both sides in her hands and raised it to her thighs. Then she simply flowed, transported, her eyes almost closed in rhythmic ecstasy.

Her legs are slim but muscled, like a ballerina's. In fact, this night, despite the frenzy of her dance, she brought nothing so much to mind as the sylph in a ballet I saw in Copenhagen. She was ethereal, otherworldly, but still my Susannah—not transfigured, but revealing an aspect I had only otherwise sensed when she sang.

Then it all ended. For the rest—how we took our leave, the journey home, even going to bed—my memory is vague, and what I do recall I see as through a mist. It was not the alcohol, which rarely affects me in this way. Another power was at work.

Pulaski County, Kentucky, U. S. A., 19 August 1861

Life in Mrs. Irvine's boardinghouse imposes a regularity that sits badly after my weeks of independence in the forest. Meals are at appointed times, for one thing. I could eat on my own, but I pay for the board regardless and I cannot rationalize the added expense. In addition, our landlady insists on entering the rooms once a day to tidy. It is obvious to all of us that she is as much concerned to monitor our use of her accommodations as she is with cleaning them.

In return for the annoyance, I am acquiring little information that I could not have had just as well on Salt Lick Creek. The only significant news nationally is the issuance of Demand Notes by the United States government, and this solitary development is several days stale. The notes are to pass for currency but are effectively a way for the government to incur debt without paying interest. They are designed to resemble banknotes but have no backing apart from a promise to redeem them for real money on demand (at a limited number of government offices). Washington will use them to pay its soldiers and those of its contractors willing to accept them. By reports, prospects for the latter are dark. Then again, seventy women have been hired to sign the notes, so the scheme is not wholly without beneficiaries.

The consensus among patrons in the taverns is that it would be foolish to accept the notes as payment for anything of value. They fear that redemption will be suspended as war expenditures mount. There is also suspicion that the notes will ultimately be declared legal tender in order to compel their acceptance. The system would thus become a devious method of taxation, since the Union could print as many notes as it wanted, transferring purchasing power into its roomy administrative pockets.

This automatic assumption that the whole thing is a "confidence game" may, it occurs to me, make this newsworthy if it is indicative of broader local feelings. I would guess that it is—it would be in harmony with the traditions. I shall have to see what I can do with it.

In the meantime, because I have no more constructive way to fill my time, here are the notes from another early interview with Mr. Graham:

Edouard de Grimouville: I do not understand your conviction that America is fundamentally Ulster Scottish. My inference from my reading has been that the two prominent groups in British America have been the New England Puritans and the Southern cavaliers. Both are from the south of England. Your race has always been a small fraction of the population.

Hugh Graham: You're forgetting the Quakers.

EdG: I am not forgetting them, but they are another small clan of restricted and declining influence.

HG: I don't know that they were unimportant in the beginning. But, as to the Ulsterites, well, first, we're scarcely a race. We should leave that for a minute, though. We've been the majority in some states all along, and we still make up most of some counties all over. I'd say that one in two men I've ever met in the South has had a Scottish or North English name—the border had two sides, so we're not purely Scots. A thing to remember, besides, is that we're the ones that did all the settling. Most of the country was originally Ulster Scots. Geographically, we've usually outweighed everyone else —our territory is bigger than Napoleon's ever was.

EdG: All right, but you have not set the tone for

American society. The revolution itself was the work of Virginia aristocrats and northeasterners, as was the constitution.

HG: And we set the tone for that. Everybody knows about Jefferson's declaration of independence, but his wasn't the first. We came up one more than a year before he got around to it, in Mecklenburg County, North Carolina.

EdG: I have heard of the Resolves. I understand that it is not clear what they actually said.

HG: I had family who were there. Regardless, we were the ones behind the spirit of the thing—the ones who pushed most for independence. About half the signers on Jefferson's declaration were our people. If you check into that, I'm sure that's what you'll find. We were also about one in three of those who did the actual fighting. You can check on that, too. Your Southern aristocrats' major achievement was to surrender Charleston. We had to turn things around again at Kings Mountain.

EdG: The constitution itself, however, drew on more universal principles. Parenthetically, Washington was one of those aristocrats.

HG: The constitution would have been a betrayal of the revolution if we hadn't opposed it and made them change it. We *were* the anti-federalists. We made them tack on the Bill of Rights before we let the thing pass. And since we're the ones who gave the final nod to the document, there are only certain meanings it can be given. No interpretation that wouldn't suit the old Scotch Irish values can be valid. And no view of the country's purpose. Not today's degenerate Scotch Irish, but the ones at the time.

EdG: Of what are you thinking?

HG: I'm thinking, for instance, of when Patrick Henry—who was one of ours—said...I used to have things off pat after reading them once. Let's see. ..[He searches through his shelves and opens a book. Much muttering.] "And those nations who have gone in search of grandeur, power and splendor, have also fallen a sacrifice, and been the victims of their own folly: While they acquired those visionary blessings, they lost their freedom."

EdG: You see that as a real tendency?

HG: Those who want a strong central government have been using language about national greatness from the beginning. That's why he talks about it. If we'd wanted to be part of a great nation, we would have stayed with Britain. The point of having a government is to keep people from meddling in your life. If it didn't do that, we wouldn't need it to start with. And if it's the one doing the meddling, then it's no different from the criminals we set it up to curb. People like Daniel Bell, who want to tell us what we can eat and drink and smoke, are the people we have governments to protect us from.

EdG: There is one sphere in which centralization is advantageous, perhaps indispensable: war—even defensive war.

HG: Who's going to attack us? The Mexicans? The British?

EdG: I agree, I agree. You're in the fortunate position of having oceans on both sides. To the extent that you avoid foreign entanglements, it would be worth no one's while to mount an expedition against you. I am thinking in more general, theoretical terms. Not all countries are so happily situated. And in the case of France, we have a heritage of grandeur that must be preserved and continued. You do not carry that burden. Still, does nothing in this talk of greatness and power and nobility speak to you?

HG: I'm not a philosopher. I'm not interested in coming up with abstractions to guide other people's affairs. I'm not one of your European liberals. My tenets are based on what my folk have always held to—their customary attitudes and practices—and I'm only concerned about the practical circumstances we find ourselves in. But the Scottish borders were always under siege, and we never needed a permanent dictator to keep us free.

EdG: The borders were also a waking nightmare. We should talk about that some time. Now, however, what as to my question about greatness?

HG: Is that something you can give arguments for? You said it was an inheritance—the only difference between your legacy and ours is the particulars. Can you argue that there's more to it than that?

EdG: There are philosophies of the beautiful.

HG: I'm flattered that you think I know what you're talking about. But I do, a little. *De gustibus non est disputandum.* There's no accounting for taste. That's my philosophy of the beautiful.

EdG: There are those who would argue against that.

HG: Let them try. But, as I said, I'm not a philosophical liberal. I just hold to the traditions I was born into, and I would like to see them conserved. But, funny enough, maybe an American conservative has to be a European liberal.

EdG: You have not yet substantiated your identification of "American" with "Albano-Hibernian," or however we want to put it. When you point to the disproportionate role your race has played in American political life, you are conceding that there are other, larger, groups relative to which your role has been disproportionate. Let me try that again.

HG: No, I got it. We've only succeeded in doing what we wanted because so many in the larger groups agreed with us. That was also our doing. It means we've turned them into us. Your mistake is that you keep thinking of us as a race. We're not. We're a group of people who have—or had—certain beliefs and attitudes and things we regarded as worthy. Anyone can join, and almost everyone has. And now that we're corrupted, everyone else is too.

EdG: But you have an identifiable history and a limited set of surnames. I can probably recite most of them.

HG: The major fact of that history is assimilation. Do you want to hear it?

EdG: That is my objective here.

HG: How much do you know about the history of the Scottish border?

EdG: I have a good dilettante's acquaintance with it. It has never been a focus for me. I have read general histories of Britain. I recollect, especially, depictions of the Reiver period in Elizabeth's time. I have read the Roman authors on Britain and I have read much of Walter Scott. Otherwise, I remember something about

Edward I and William Wallace from a commentary on Dante.

HG: Then, you'll recall that the occupants at the time the Romans came in were Picts and Celts—if those were two different things. At the least, there was probably some mixing of peoples going on already. The Romans put up a wall on the border and never managed to hold any area beyond it for any length of time. They tried a second wall to the north, but had to abandon it. They did, however, manage a further combination of stocks. Their soldiers were from all over the Empire, so you had Africans and Asians and Italians added to the blend. Meanwhile, a different group of Celts started sailing over from Ireland and became the Gaels—the Highlanders—and they started to make their contribution. When the Romans left, you had all manner of Germans coming in. We may be more Saxon than Celt—the Highlanders always called us *Sassenachs*. Then Norwegian Vikings, and then their cousins the Normans, who were already part Frank and part French Celt. When we moved to Ulster, we probably picked up more Gaelic blood. We definitely mixed it up with Huguenot Frenchies, who were there for the same reason we were. That's the first big example of people being added in because of beliefs. When we came here, we married anyone who was willing, and that brought in every nationality available. Finally, there were a lot of Cherokees and other tribes. Families are so much the thing for us that the whole family of anyone who married in became kin. And, always, they seemed to take on our ways, and not the other way around. So, people with border names may have taken the lead in the political matters, but they had the support of a lot of Schmidts and Picons. And, between us, we set the tone for most of the country. Grahams and Armstrongs and what have you are just the kernel of the thing.

The delivery, as you would imagine, was not as continuous as my account suggests. This is all reconstruction and summary. It is true to the content and sense of what was said, however, and I am confident that much is verbatim.

Pulaski County, Kentucky, U. S. A., 21 August 1861

I have been reproached by friends—the closest, in fact —the ones who feel themselves on sure enough footing to say such things—for maintaining too reserved a manner, approaching iciness, in social settings. I am unwilling even to feign an interest (they say) in those who displease me in the slightest respect. I am often taciturn, purportedly, and overly careful to preserve my distance and dignity. I have never remarked this in myself, and, were it true before, it certainly cannot be so now.

I have been too successful in my anthropology, too powerful a magnet for confidences and imprudent opinions, to be indicted on the charge. Something I have that invites such intimacy. Whatever it is, it must be warm, not cold, close, not remote. Or, perhaps it is the accent.

I will not publish my takings, even here. Mr. Graham's are the exception. He would publish them himself if he could bring himself to care. Instead, I use the rest to give substance to the world I am trying to portray; they are the material that underlies my words and gives them unity. They need only exist for me, the artist—there is no reason the spectator should ever see the canvas under the paint.

This is imperative for the kind of work I am attempting, the journalism as much as the scholarship. I have not only to relate facts, but to revivify and represent sentiments and values and desires. I must straddle the divide between science and art. I cannot, consequently, stand aloof from my subject. My material is human, with all the sweltering vitality that entails.

This has a price, it appears. I miss things now, and that is new. I have lost my detachment, and now the world has laid claim to me. I miss my life on the creek, and I miss the people. Above all, to be honest, I miss

Susannah. But it is not only the near present that has hold of me. I miss my past, which never held me as I lived it. I want to go home—to my real home, to France—as much as I want to return to Stirling. I have fallen into life, I suppose, though I never thought myself out of it.

The very journey that brought me to this place has a nostalgic grip on me. We left in the early morning, in darkness but under fair weather. All was so tranquil that the ship seemed to slide over the ocean, not through it, as on a sheet of ice. When the light came, we saw that birds had followed us, great flocks, almost as many as the fish that frisked in the waters around us. There were always sails in sight. But, shortly, all that vanished. We were solitary, isolated, our own silent world to ourselves, with only an unchanging sea outside. Not until we neared the other shore was there any sign of other beings, and it was a curious sign: the sea began to shimmer with the light of millions of phosphorescent animalcules. A storm caught us then, and the foam we cast up in our passage was like a fire around us, our track a tail of fire like a comet's. We steered south and reached New York after a month's crossing.

Much different have been my steamboat travels, especially the last, which brought me to Nashville and, by a short leg, to Waitsboro. The great system of rivers in North America is such that the steamboats can bring you within easy reach of even the more remote locations. I used them in my tour of the east, as well, for shorter trips. The boats are colossal mechanisms, the size of hotels, and have all the amenities of these. The size of the suites, saloons and dining halls are such that one is hardly aware that he is in a watercraft. One embarks in one place and, unless one goes on deck, arrives at his destination with little sense of the miles covered between. I, however, always spent most of my time on deck, inspecting the changing landscapes and habitations.

I wrestle with a longing to jettison all my plans, throw everything overboard, and make the journey in reverse, back, homeward, to the place of familiar things. But, more than that, I want to take the crude road to the east about three leagues. I do not know how it will end, but, for now, at least, I cannot do without Susannah. If the child must be born, it must be born. We shall manage something. It would not be the first by-blow in my family's long record, and most have prospered. Blood shows through.

Pulaski County, Kentucky, U. S. A., 24 August 1861

I did not receive the reception for which I prepared in my mind. I anticipated gushing gratitude for my return to her arms. She is cold, aloof, unresponsive. She does not tell me to go, but she does not seek me out. She tolerates me. I understand that, if I try—I simply did not expect it and I am ill-equipped to meet it. Although I never told her I was not coming back, I did not leave her assured that I would. She has set her mind to live without me, and that will take a while to thaw.

If not, I am at loose ends. There is nothing else keeping me here. All my bright, warm associations with this place turn out to take their coloring from her. It is, without that tint, a stark, empty spot. Somerset is only marginally preferable—I picture myself vegetating there, waiting for something to happen and going to bed each night with the same disappointment. Someday, someone will move against Kentucky, but, by then, I shall be an atrophied husk on the floor of my rooms.

Have I enough to commence my great treatise? I do not believe I have seen enough, or ranged sufficiently, or talked with the variety of people the work requires. I am at the beginning of my researches. Mr. Graham has merely handed me a thread.

Home again, I would drop back into my decade's sleep. I know I cannot bear the law—I gave years to that as student and as apprentice judge, and that was a fair trial. My political activity, which climaxed with a seat in the National Assembly, ended with our second Emperor's ascension. I cannot go crawling back and say that I have recanted and am ready to be a good little drudge. With amnesty and liberalization, others have done it, but the people showed what they have become with the referendum that validated the coup. The deep problems are beyond solution: the universal dedication to material comfort and the willingness to abdicate control. Even a new republic would change nothing. There is nothing to be done.

Our Napoleon Minor is a symptom, not a cause. The rise of the central state and the growing uniformity and deadness to life are as inextricably established in France as they are inexorable in America. The man himself is a monomaniac, wedded to an imperial ideal, no matter what maneuvers he must make to disguise it. He will undertake no radical structural changes. History itself is in the seat, and any one man will only serve it as an instrument—or fall. Power will abide in the center from here on out.

I made my last stand almost ten years ago. We awoke one winter's morning to find the walls of Paris covered with announcements that the National Assembly was dissolved. Several of my colleagues, I learned, had been arrested. I went to the Assembly, where other representatives had gathered, but the doors were barred to us by a detachment of troops. We made to enter despite that. One of our number was struck, and the rest of us were driven back with bayonets. Some were injured.

We determined to retreat to the city hall in the 10th administrative district, where about three hundred of us were already assembled. Others continued to arrive after us, but a second detachment of soldiers prevented them from entering the chamber. There we passed a decree to the effect that the President, Louis-Napoleon Bonaparte, was guilty of high treason for dissolving the Assembly, and that all citizens were obligated to withhold obedience to him.

As soon as this had been signed by all present, soldiers appeared at the door, commanded by officers with drawn swords. They did not dare enter. One of the acting presidents of the Assembly read them the decree and ordered them to leave. They were confused and ashamed, and finally decided to go for further orders. The doors remained blocked, however. We opened the windows and read the decree to the citizens and troops in the street.

After a time, the soldiers returned with two police commissioners, who took custody of our acting presidents. We followed as a body, arm in arm, and were subsequently marched off to the barracks at the Quai d'Orsay. Though the people turned against us in the end, on this occasion they were moved by the sight by of so many great men—former Ministers and ambassadors, generals and admirals, celebrated orators and writers— being dragged *à pied* through the mud like criminals, encircled by bayonets. "*Vive l'Assemblée Nationale!*" they cried.

We spent the night on the barracks' boards and tiles, with no fire and little food. I slept in the arch of a window. I had awakened ill that morning, and this worsened over the next two days, when I was released. As soon as I was healthy again, I tendered a—purely formal—resignation from the Assembly and retired to our estates. The worst excesses of the new regime have passed, but nothing has occurred since to give me hope for the future.

Pulaski County, Kentucky, U. S. A.,
27 August 1861

The frost has softened for a season at least. There is too much gentleness in her to shut me out of doors in the cold for any long time. Whatever I deserve. We went to the old field by the creek—not a natural meadow, I think, but reverted farmland. It is grassy enough for an idyll. One can hear the water's sound, like the plink of silver coins, and little else. We lay there and talked of everything but my absence.

I pulled some grass and sprinkled it on her head. "Soft falls the rain on Susannah Armstrong's grave."

"Don't," she protested, though she laughed. "That's not how it starts, anyway." She patted if off and tried to throw pieces at me.

"How does it go, then?"

"I'll sing it for you again, some time, but I'm not in the mood now. It should be your turn to sing something."

"Where did you learn it?"

"There are a lot of old songs that everybody knows. They probably go back to before we even came over here."

I did not pursue the matter. I was not in the mood for some things, myself, and deliberate continuity was one of them. I sank back and was still, following my own disjointed musings.

"I had a simple idea of British America before I came here," I said aloud, after a space. "I thought there were two sorts—Puritans in the northeast and Cavaliers in the southeast. Everyone else was a degeneration of type. It was such a nice, tidy conceptual arrangement."

This was more to myself than her. She has an excellent, inquisitive mind, and will not let my ramblings pass without elucidation—when she is interested. When she asks nothing, it signifies understanding or apathy. I know I have worn down her patience on my pet themes, so I felt free to drivel on as I would, at present, confident that she did not care what I said. Our conversation was merely an accompaniment to our real purpose, which was to be idle together in the late-summer grass.

"When I first saw Kentucky—the northern part, along the Ohio—I was struck by the difference between the two banks of the river. The climate and the land on both sides are identical, but you rarely see anyone on the land to your left—perhaps a flock of slaves standing around among badly tended crops. It is principally still forest. From your right, however, there is actually a sound, if you listen for it. A humming sound, as from a busy hive. The land is cultivated, amply, and buildings are being erected, many quite elegant.

"I put the divergence down to the effect of slavery. I had settled on this even before, during my travels in the east, but the contrast along the river sharpened it for me. The Northerner must rely on the produce of his own labors, and he comes to reverence labor itself, probably to excess. The Southerner comes to scorn labor, with its associations of servitude. He cherishes leisure and independence. He despises even money. He wants it much less than he wants pleasure and stimulation. The vigor which his northern neighbor directs toward profit, he bends toward hunting and sports and martial activities. I set this all down to the account of slavery."

Susannah made an indistinct noise, now and again, to prove she was listening.

"But then, I realized that I had not tracked the difference to its source. Why slavery in one region and not another? Partly, yes, because agriculture differs in Massachusetts from Virginia. Still, I had been thinking of the two folk as deriving from a common stock, and they did not. The northern seed was Calvinist and carried a passion for gainful labor from its very beginnings on these shores. The south had its origins in the English aristocracy, if augmented by gold hunters and adventurers. I began to see the troubles in this land as the final act of the English civil war.

"Then I came among you people. I took you for Southerners, and you are not—not in the way I had construed them. You do not have slaves. If you do not care about money it is because you have never cared about money. It is a different civilization entirely. And Mr. Graham has convinced me of this, at least: that your ways are based on principles and not a falling away from them. Even your corruption is the embrace of new principles."

"We're Westerners, maybe," said Susannah, to my surprise. The vague murmurs were the most for which I had hoped. "We've moved west with every generation. What's called the West by other people is wherever we happen to have moved. I'm told you'll find the old ways strongest out on the real frontier, the far West. Half the people I've talked to think we should just let the South go. It has nothing to do with us—it's just another place we lived for a time."

This last is my experience as well. Mr. Graham is, as one would anticipate, one of those who agree—"and good riddance"—but it is a popular opinion generally. Dr. Marx does not agree, according to an article he has sent me. He is captivated by theories of sweeping scope, however, and sees the world in large and simple terms. I have grown cautious about that sort of thing. I look for trends, not causes. The latter are too complex. Even Salt Lick Creek may be too complex for the style of analysis Dr. Marx is doing. (I pray, in fact, that history has no order—that is all that might save us in the end.)

"I need to visit the far West. I have seen too little for the work I would like to do. It may exceed my capacity, anyway. Too much needs to be studied. Too many little items, even here."

"Like what?"

"In good conscience, for instance, I should be

collecting all the old songs you know. That anybody knows. I should talk to a slave from this area. I talked to some back in the east, but I was always suspicious of their honesty. They never voiced complaints about their lot. It was not plausible."

"Finding a slave will be hard. It's not just that we don't have many—abolitionist feelings have always been strong here, too. My own father was a big emancipationist. The Northerners who run the coal mines in Pulaski and in Laurel County are about the only ones who use slaves, and they keep them at work in the mines, out of sight. I doubt they'd let you talk to them."

"Well, then, I also need to interview people about your folklore. I'm supposed to introduce myself to Nick Bromfield. Whose identity, it turns out, you have known all along, despite your protestations of ignorance. He is your wizard of the creek. The most suitable penance, I judge, is that you accompany me on my visit."

She did not take this as the joke intended. It was spiteful of me, indeed, to present it. Faint freckles were visible through her tan, as had happened before when the blood left her face.

"*Eh*, well, we shall find another appropriate punishment. However, I myself must see him. Mr. Graham assures me he is harmless. They were friends when young."

This perplexed her. "That may be, though I've never heard anything about it. Discuss it with others, first. Talk to my mother. She's been wanting to have you over for supper, anyway—it would be a good chance. Maybe I'm wrong, but there've been so many stories, and those men *did* disappear. I've never heard anything good about Nick Bromfield, and plenty bad.

"And I can't see how Hugh Graham could have known him."

Her distress was intense and all for me. The tenor of the day was broken, and she was not easy in her mind when we parted, but we are no longer at odds, and she still cares for me, beyond question. Then, again, she has engineered a dinner where I must face her mother. If Providence has ever turned a charitable eye on man, there will be other guests.

Pulaski County, Kentucky, U. S. A., 28 August 1861

I have to say that I now see no convincing argument why the South should not be set loose. If the Union had the historical identity of a France, a recognized character, forged by the centuries and not by late convention, secession would be unthinkable. But it was created by voluntary contract of the states, and these, by uniting together, have not forfeited their nationhood, nor have they become a unitary, homogeneous people. If one of the states wants to withdraw from the contract, it is difficult to deny its right of doing so, and the federal government has no grounds to dispute its claims.

The rough draft of Dr. Marx's article asserts the nationality that I cannot perceive. (Ironically, this places me at variance with Mr. Graham as well.) Dr. Marx maintains that the South has neither natural geographic individuality nor any national distinctiveness. "The South," for him, is not a country at all—it is only a battle slogan.

He returns to his argument that the Confederacy has been waging an offensive war from the beginning, not defensive. It deems Kentucky and all the border states to be its territory, along with everything south of the Mason-Dixon line as far as the Pacific Ocean. It is engaged in a war of conquest and will not stop until it has subjugated three-quarters of American territory. The very intention of annexing Kentucky, against the will of most of its population, gives the lie to its pretense of defensive war.

Slavery is not popular in the South, he says. The slaveholding oligarchy has gained power through adroit political manipulations. Further, they have used their power to restructure the state constitutions with an eye to enslaving the white working class. Their intellectual advocates work, not to justify racial servitude, but to endorse the irrelevance of color: It is the working class as a whole that merits slavery. They are born to it.

Were the secessionists to succeed, they would control the Mississippi River and most of the American seaboard. They would dominate the North economically. The white working class in the North would become slaves in all but name. The war, he concludes, is a struggle between two economic systems, not soluble but through victory by one side or the other.

Mr. Graham read the article when I first received it. He saw at once how deterministic an intelligence is Dr. Marx's. "He thinks everything comes down to money, doesn't he?"

"That is typically his inclination."

"Can he explain why the Southern workingman is willing to fight?"

"I am sure that he can."

"My sense of him is that he can always explain everything. But his world is too simple. It has too few particulars. The South may not be a country, but Tennessee is, at least in its people's minds. I can tell you why the rebels are willing to fight, and it has nothing to do with money."

It is a tiny and unavoidable step for Mr. Graham from being able to tell and the actual telling. "Please deign to enlighten me," I said.

He chose to heed the encouragement and not the tone. "First, bear in mind that I have nothing to say against secession. If the southern states go, we'll rid Kentucky of slavery soon enough. The Union will finally be free of a poison that's been working on it from its birth. We'll also strengthen the status of the individual states against the center by recognizing the right to secede."

He slouched back and thought for a moment. "I don't know if you know that Kentucky, not long after it became a state, passed some resolutions to the effect that acts of the federal government could be nullified by a state if the state decided they were unconstitutional. Thomas Jefferson wrote the resolutions, secretly. Virginia passed a similar one, secretly written by James Madison. This was after the Federalists came up with laws limiting freedom of speech. That was one of the first big moves by the centralizers. I'll tell you about some others, sometime.

"Anyway, everyone—for them or against them—took the resolutions to mean that states could withdraw from the Union if they thought the terms of the constitutional contract were violated. So, that notion's been around right from the beginning, and it's always been especially popular in the states I've lived in. Kentuckians just don't like the particular cause these seseshes are fighting for. But, if other states want to go, I think it's a mistake to help stop them. It just helps the centralizers."

"And this addresses the question of why the rebels are willing to fight?" I asked, disingenuously.

He made an impatient gesture and drew his chair closer to the table. "It's just background. And to show I'm not for secession or against it. I'm looking at the matter impartially. But it does show why a lot of the Southerners fight—the Scots Irish ones. They don't want outsiders telling them what to do, even if they agree it's the right thing to do. And they distrust the motives of the tellers. And they're right to do so. You think Lincoln's really against slavery?"

"Can we deal with Mr. Lincoln some other time?"

"All right. Anyway, they're fighting for their rights against people who would just as soon do away with rights altogether. But, that's just part of the South. There's another big part that's fighting just because the authorities told them to. The coastal Southerners, the ones with the slow, drawly accents. The ones who came from southern England."

"I would have thought they were the ones acting from self-interest. Or, at best, a chivalrous ideal. The slaveholders are from aristocratic stock, are they not?"

"I'm not talking about the slave owners. How many people do you think own slaves? And you think they're mostly from the nobility? Wouldn't that be a contradiction? An aristocratic society is aristocratic because most people are at the bottom. Most southeasterners are from peasant stock—they followed their masters over as indentured servants. Their ancestors were serfs for centuries, and they've inherited a taste for servility. And now, they fight because they were told to. And if the North wins, they'll be the biggest little lackeys for the United States that you can imagine. Anything to have a master. Natural slaves themselves, practically. And they're like that no matter whether they're poor or not—money doesn't have anything to do with it."

"And your people were not peasants?"

"They were not serfs. Serfdom never took hold very close to the border. They tried it in the lowlands to the north of us, but it never got its legs. And when *we* started to get something like it, we all headed west. If you went much south of the wall, though, it was serfs all the way down.

He smiled tightly. "And in the rest of Europe."

"My conception of Scottish society was very hierarchical. Clan chiefs and such."

"We weren't Highlanders. We chose our leaders for their ability and kept them only so long as they showed that ability."

"And I was given to understand that you people converted everyone with whom you came into contact. I cannot remember who said that, at the moment."

"And it was true, whoever said it. But that's in the past. As we've weakened, we've become the ones converted. Mostly, we've done that to ourselves, but the southeasterners have had their influence. It comes from standing still. Those of us who've kept moving west are still free. Those who've stood still have lost their traditions and their spines. They've been absorbed. Easterners and eastern ways have followed us all the way out here, even, and they'll follow us farther."

"*You* have stopped moving."

"I'm dying."

My surprise and distress must have shown, for he added, "Not soon, I hope. I just mean that I'm too old and too close to death for it to matter whether I move or not. And I'm ossified—there's no danger of my being converted into anything. Except bone meal fertilizer, maybe."

The fact that I cannot evaluate all of this is more evidence that I am not prepared for the task I wish to undertake. I do not have the experience I need, nor could I obtain it in a lifetime shorter than Mr. Graham's. Certainly, too, I cannot rely on one man's testimony. I console myself with the belief that all science is partial and all history is simplification. If I have learned one good thing from Dr. Marx, it is not to let that interfere with one's endeavors. I, however, will try to retain my self-awareness in the process.

Pulaski County, Kentucky, U. S. A., 30 August 1861

The Armstrongs' home is, I judge, older than any of the Graham properties. There have been additions, but the original core is evident from the aging of the wood. It must have been two separate dwellings, each about fifteen by twenty English feet, connected by one large roof. The open area between has become an internal hallway in the expanded building.

The two old houses are a parlor and a dining-room, both decorously appointed and worthy of a middle-class family in any city. I had expected something *à la* Mr. Graham, but it is a house of women, not a slovenly old man. The furniture is modest but professionally made, and the utensils and most of the furnishings were purchased. The effect overall is a bit lacy for my tastes, but neat and homey.

Besides the mother and the three sisters, there were present—thank God—Mr. Selby; John Foster, the boy from the store; Mrs. Taylor, the pastor's wife; and a robust gentleman with a large, brown mustache. Susannah and I were the last to arrive, and the others were already seated in the parlor. Mrs. Armstrong set down her clay pipe and rose to greet me, as did the large individual, who, however, kept the most enormous cigar I have ever seen fastened in his teeth.

"Mr. de Grimouville," said our hostess, beaming, "I believe you know everyone here except Joshua Moffat. Mr. Moffat, Mr. de Grimouville."

We shook hands more energetically than was quite comfortable. He stood a head taller than me, and it was a massive head, though in proportion to his frame. His height and form—a muscular, inverted triangle—would have graced the royal guard in any European country were it not for his round, red face. This glowed with broken capillaries, like a lump of smelted iron, new from the furnace. On his leather vest was a metal star, and I recollected that this was the constable of whom Susannah had told me.

"Josh," he corrected. "Call me Josh." He spoke in a deep, relaxed drawl which I decided was a personal mannerism and not an accent, since he otherwise used the clipped syllables of the Westerner.

"Please feel free to call me Edouard." I have been extending this invitation to everyone, recently, but only young women seem prepared to accept the offer.

When we had acknowledged the others, we sat while Mrs. Armstrong exited to bring back tumblers and a bottle of whiskey with no label.

"Ella," she said, "just wait and I will get the sugar for yours."

"I want sugar in mine, too," said Toodie.

"You're too old for that," Susannah told her.

"I don't care. It's how I like it."

Susannah turned to me. "I told you she's a willful child."

"You keep saying that," her sister cried in mock indignation. "And it isn't true. *You're* the one who always wants things just so. All I want is a bit of sugar in my drink."

"That sounds like willful talk to me," I contributed in a stern tone. Toodie stuck out her tongue. "You are right," I said to Susannah. "She is now irredeemably willful. It is too late to save her. But there is still time for Mr. Selby to save himself."

"If only he will," Susannah said in a sorrowful voice. "If only he will." She paused. "But, if not, at least we'll be quit of her."

Toodie sneered and held her glass out for the sugar to be spooned in. Then, she sat back and began to roll one of her cigarettes.

I addressed Mrs. Armstrong, "The girls have told me a story about an Elizabeth Tait, who was driven out of town for smoking cigarettes. They did not know many of the details."

"Apparently. She ended up here. She was driven out of a place east of here. This was years before the girls were born. The Taits have moved on since." She finished serving Mr. Moffat and, placing her tray on a small, three-legged table, took her own seat without filling a glass for herself.

"Is that the authentic story? I cannot picture anyone around here troubling themselves about such a thing. It would violate the Ulster Scottish ethos."

"Around here, they wouldn't. This, however, was back in the woods where people had been settled for a long time. An old community. We tend to go bad if we stop moving. Especially if there are a lot of English around— and there were in that place."

"What was wrong with cigarettes?"

"Just that they were unfamiliar. They were unusual. It could have been anything. A group of northeasterners came traveling through the same area not long ago, camping along the way. The women were riding cross-saddle. The people there rode into their camp one day with guns and rousted them out. They didn't have anything in particular against riding cross-saddle—they'd just never seen women do it before. It comes from staying in one place too long and associating with the wrong sort."

"Mr. Graham theorizes that you are all becoming like that because you are no longer persecuted. He says you have turned on yourselves in order to have something to fight and subdue."

She took a minute to work at the bowl of her pipe. "That has something to it. Some may keep moving because they can't suit the new ways and some may just *get* moved. That's a sort of persecution and it may be what saves a part from degeneration."

Succeeding in rekindling the pipe, she rose. "It may

be what saves the degenerate part from getting their arses whipped—it would be a sore miscalculation for Southerners to push Westerners too far. They'll find that out should they be the ones to invade first. Come, Ella, we must finish preparing the food. The bottle is on the table—please help yourselves. There is more."

"Hear, hear!" exclaimed Mr. Moffat, followed by the boy John Foster. I could not ascertain whether they were cheering the prophecy of Southern humiliation or the availability of liquor. Perhaps those were more nearly linked in their imaginations than I could see.

"Ella," called Mr. Selby to the girl before she could reach the hallway door. "Are you excited about going back to school?"

As she turned at the door, I saw a subtle squirming in her facial muscles before they resolved into a variety of smile. "Oh, yes. Very much so." She spun and escaped before he could press for more.

Mr. Selby laughed and told me, "Mrs. Taylor is the children's teacher. Poor Ella could scarcely have answered otherwise."

"Oh, I believe I encourage more honesty than that," the pastor's wife said. "And it is not as if they don't complain to my face. Besides, Ella does very well—she is much more diligent than her sisters were. And tractable. That Toodie was a hellcat when her vinegar was up."

"I will leave if everyone insists on teasing,' said Toodie.

Mr. Selby patted her hand. "I don't think she's teasing. Just reporting. Mr. de Grimouville is trying to obtain an accurate picture of our community. He may as well know the worst. She revealed that Susannah is very wicked too, so you're not the only one."

Toodie arose and left, saying, "I will see you all in the dining room when supper is ready."

There was general laughter when the door closed.

"How many years of schooling do children receive?" I

asked.

"As much as they can tolerate," answered Mrs. Taylor. "And as much as their parents can spare. Susannah stopped a couple of years ago, but I do hope that Toodie continues until I can place her in a Normal School. If she were a boy, I would encourage her to attend a university. She has a mind for great things."

"Would she want to go away for so long?"

"There are some fine colleges in Kentucky, Mr. de Grimouville, like Transylvania University in Lexington. It's a shame that our own folk no longer found them."

"But they did in the past?"

"Oh, yes. We founded the College of New Jersey in Princeton, New Jersey, among others. It was considered an obligation. Where did you study?"

"I was privately tutored by a priest until I was sixteen. Then I attended the *lycée* in Metz where I studied rhetoric and philosophy. Afterward, I studied law in Paris."

"And did you become a lawyer?" asked Mr. Moffat with surprising interest. I had, I suppose, anticipated scorn.

I gave them a *précis* of my life and elicited many sympathetic noises from all. The one misstruck note sounded when Mr. Moffat inquired about my military service, of which there has been none.

He was gracious about it. "I expect not everyone has the time if they're doing important things. I was in Mexico, myself, but I've never minded a man not being a soldier as long as he doesn't call for other men to do his fighting for him. That is what I despise—a man, if you can call him that, who talks about national greatness and glory and honor, who wants everyone to march off and fight in some grand crusade, but won't risk his own skin."

I hastened to redirect the current of the talk. "There cannot be many of your people who meet that description. Mr. Graham says that military duty is bred into you."

He mulled that over. "It's true. Even Hugh Graham, who doesn't regularly give a damn about what anybody does or thinks, was in the militia. It's an instinct. But some don't do it, and as long as they're not trying to stir up other people to fight for them, like a girl, I don't think any the less of them."

"Like President Lincoln."

Mr. Selby came in quickly. "No! Lincoln was in the Illinois militia. He was captain of a company in the Black Hawk War. He didn't fight, but that wasn't his fault. Lucky, too, because we might end up having to join his war, and it would be hard fighting for a complete mountebank. He may be one, anyway, but not that style. A lot of the Unionists are that type, though—they've always been a glut on the market in the North—and I can conceive of nothing more contemptible."

"So say we all," toasted Mr. Moffat, echoed by the others, including the women and John Foster, who, in my experience, has never actually uttered a word except in business or exclamation.

The door to the hall opened, and Toodie emerged to curtsy and announce, "*Mesdames, Monsieurs, Mademoiselles*, Susannah—dinner is served."

We filed through the facing doors into the dining room, Mr. Selby snatching the bottle as he passed the little stand. I had observed that, glass for glass, he had the heaviest investment in the enterprise.

"We have only one such in the entire region, do you know?" he said to me as I completed my passage. "That little piece of filth Bell. You did better service than you know, the other day."

"What is the theme?" asked Mrs. Armstrong, who had come through another door with a beautiful, flowered tureen.

"Disesteemed people," I said.

"To wit, the good Daniel Bell," added Susannah.

Ella was adjusting the place settings. "Elder Bell wants a law against morphine," she informed no one in particular, her eyes on her task.

"What a helpful observation, Ella," her mother remarked.

"I am not offended, Cora," Mrs. Taylor said. "Ella and I are used to one another. And it is no secret that my husband is exceedingly fond of his medicine. It does no harm and improves his nature. As vices go, it is economical as well—it costs next to nothing."

Mr. Moffat flourished his tumbler, losing some of its contents in the gesture. "Here's to Elder Bell being the biggest jackass in the state. Any American who'd want such a law is a traitor to his country."

Those who had their glasses returned the toast. Happily, I had left mine in the other room—I could not quite accede to the sentiment. Its sponsor aside, such legislation does not seem without merit, outlandishly novel as it may be in conception and impracticable in implementation.

We seated the ladies and girls and took our own places. Mr. Selby might have spared himself the capture of the bottle—Ella was filling or replenishing glasses from a new one, and others made a sort of centerpiece. There was also a pitcher of lemonade, which served Mrs. Armstrong when she had time to sit and eat with us.

"Are you not fond of whiskey, Mrs. Armstrong?" I asked.

"No, I'm not. It's horrid of me, I know, but I have simply never enjoyed the giddy feeling I get."

"Just as well," said Mr. Moffat. "Your abstinence has spared your looks. You could counterfeit one of your own daughters."

Our hostess flushed a blazing scarlet, as profoundly colored as the constable himself. She tried to respond but could not.

He turned to me. "She is truly a fine-looking woman,

isn't she, Mr. de Grimouville?"

"Oh, certainly," I answered, trying for a balance between undue enthusiasm and ceremonial assent. Either could be taken badly in several ways. I saw two things—Susannah's mother had, indeed, resembled her daughters in some former era, and she had preserved enough of her charms that a man might still be drawn to her. Did Mr. Moffat perceive me as a rival? If so, his question was more arch than I think he has it in him to be. I had been admiring his bluntness and frankness of character, which is always refreshing in its proper bounds.

"Fairest of her daughters Eve," interjected Mr. Selby, to our general puzzlement.

As an appetizer, we had oysters that had been tinned and suffered from it. They were meant to be a special treat, so I did my duty by them until the soup arrived. This was turtle with vegetables and herbs, all fresh, and it more than made amends for the oysters. The courses were not many but ample: roast pork, then a salad of greens, then a large pastry full of apples. Potatoes and beans were at hand throughout, along with butter and large slabs of bread, both maize and wheaten. I avoided the latter until I was sure that others were eating it.

It was plain, satisfying fare and went far toward freeing me from my suspicions about the purpose of the dinner. Mrs. Armstrong interrogated me no more than she did any other guest, and this in an apparent spirit of warm interest. If anything, I have begun to worry, not that she may object to my association with her daughter, but that she may like the idea too much and presume too much upon it. I still have no clear plans.

Mrs. Taylor knocked over the salt in the later proceedings and threw some over her shoulder. She felt it necessary to apologize: "It's not good practice for the pastor's wife to encourage superstition by example."

There was an odd pause in the table chatter.

Susannah broke it by saying, in a controlled voice, "Well, throwing salt seems harmless enough. And not all seeming superstitions are baseless."

I know her well enough that this gave the game away. The dinner was a contrivance, as I had originally suspected, but I had misapprehended its author and object. Susannah had devised this, not her mother.

Another pause until Toodie looked at Mr. Selby and asked, "You were going to say something?"

Her partner, who had been holding a bottle up to gauge its contents, looked back in confusion, then cleared his throat and said, "Yes, I was just going to point out...that is, I feel it necessary to suggest...that we keep an open mind about some...things. I mean to say that, while I don't personally put much stock in witch tales—I view myself as a scientific man—I don't believe we should prejudge the case."

"Why witch tales in particular, Mr. Selby?" I queried.

He opened and closed his mouth, then said, "Well, just as an example. Of superstition, you see. I thought that's what we were talking about."

Susannah came in with, "Yes. That's a very good example, there. Witches. I find it difficult to believe that there is so much witch lore with no reason behind it at all."

"I should hear some of this lore," I said. "It is in the area where my studies have been most lacking. I need some preparation if I am to have a fruitful meeting with Mr. Bromfield."

That set them back a bit, as I intended it should—I thought it fitting repayment. "In what, precisely, does witch lore consist?"

"Well," Toodie responded to a glance from Susannah, "things like how one becomes a witch, or how to know a witch is after you, or how to break a spell. Useful knowledge, mostly."

"How does one become a witch?"

"Different ways. You usually have to go to a mountain top at dawn, but, after that, you have alternatives. Mostly they involve guns. You can shoot through a handkerchief at the sun and curse God three times, or, if the moon's out, you can shoot at that nine times with silver balls and curse God each time."

"What did people do before there were guns?"

"You can just take a spinning-wheel with you, I think, but I'm not sure how that one works. And it would be harder."

Mr. Selby snorted. "As in all aspects of our modern life, technology has provided greater ease and efficiency."

Toodie elbowed him and he brought his features into a simulation of sobriety.

"If you have tangles in your hair, it shows that witches have been riding you," volunteered Ella. "Same with horses."

"But you can tie corn shucks in a horse's mane, and that will keep them off him," said Toodie.

"Why do witches do all this riding?"

No one knew.

"Mostly, they're interested in spelling people or stealing milk and butter," Toodie continued. "They have all sorts of ways of doing that—or just drying cows up or making churns stop working."

The schoolteacher had a sad expression but said nothing.

"But they do like to ride!" Ella burst out. "And if a jack-o'-lantern gets on your back, it will ride you till morning! You have to wear your coat inside-out to keep that from happening."

"But that's not witches!" Toodie said indignantly.

"But it happens." From her grin, it appeared that the little girl relished the idea.

Mrs. Armstrong took over. "Of course, there's really no reason to take any of this seriously. No one does, really, anymore. There are a variety of ways of protecting yourself. And there are professional witchmasters who can handle the difficult cases."

"As Mr. Bromfield is supposed to be," I noted, trying to force the game to its conclusion. "Do any of you truly believe any of this?"

"Well, Mr. de Grimouville," said the constable, "that's a tangled mess of rope. I don't expect that most folk concern themselves much about any of it these days. But you bring up Nick Bromfield, and there's a more troublesome matter. He's doing strange things out there, and he has powers. Think what you will about everything else but trust me on that. Whatever he's doing—or can do—isn't natural."

He was so much in earnest that I did not know what to say. I looked to Susannah, who nodded, her brown eyes solemn. Behind her, Mr. Selby merely shrugged, disclaiming any judgment.

"He's speaking honest fact," Mrs. Taylor said.

"Don't get me wrong," Mr. Moffat went on. "I'm not saying he's up to the mischief some people claim against him. He's a tolerable fellow when you meet him, in spite of how he looks. There's something wrong, though, about all those books and jars and tools he's got. I've never smelled anything like his house. He's doing something a few degrees off true.

"And, then, people who bother him disappear."

"That has happened more than once?" I asked.

"A few times."

The others at the table expressed surprise. "I know more than you do," he told them.

"He is, however, a 'tolerable fellow,' you say, to those who bear him no ill-will."

"That's just my own experience. I don't know what it takes to get on his bad side. Might not be much. Better not to chance it. You'll learn nothing to your purpose that you can't get somewhere else."

"Mr. Graham believes him safe enough."

"I can only advise you according to my lights. My advice is, stay away from him."

To Susannah he then said, "There. I've done my duty. Whether he profits from it is his own lookout."

The evening's cordiality was broken, and, though we tried to mend it, we could not succeed. Soon after, by unspoken consensus, the guests began to murmur about taking our leave. At the door, Mrs. Armstrong squeezed my hand, too warmly, and I determined yet once again to find some resolution to the Susannah problem.

Outside, I stood for a minute with Mr. Selby, who was waiting to escort Mrs. Taylor home. "If you're going to go see Bromfield, I'll go with you," he whispered. "I'm supposed to help talk you out of it, but now I'm just curious."

Pulaski County, Kentucky, U. S. A.,
1 September 1861

The first of September, nearing autumn but not near enough that I should feel a change. Yet, I do. The light should not yet have the slant that signals the sun's spiral to the south, yet I sense a difference, and it is enough to put me in mind of the coming season. It seems cooler already, though that cannot really be.

I am beset by the nostalgia and melancholy the setting of the year always brings upon me. Nostalgia for what, I could not say. For autumns past, certainly, but not for any particular time or any remembered occasions. It is not my chronic homesickness—I experience the same aimless longing every year even at home.

The hills are still as green as in July, and they will be for weeks to come. Still, I see the trees differently. Their transience shows in the changed light. Soon enough, the leaves will trade their green for October colors. Then, they will fall, and that picture is already before me, their reds and golds and purples, and their fading, and their drop, all here in this present moment.

The world presents itself to me more and more in these comprehensive, complete moments, and their end is always a perishing. It is not conducive to the work I have set for myself, which rests on hope for perpetuation and growth. One needs to live in a perpetual spring and not the everlasting autumn in which I find myself increasingly. Perhaps it is just age. But age is supposed to bring insight—this eternal dusk of the year may simply be the truth of things.

The hills themselves are solid, I suppose, but they retreat into hiddenness if examined too long. This happens especially in the mists that accompany the rain. There is much rain this week, though August was comparatively dry. It is not expected to last, but, while it does, the hills flow in and out of being and have no clear outlines. They are as fleeting as the trees they bear, as evanescent as the leaves.

I wonder now if there is anything to be found in the winding valleys. Were I to go down into them now, I half suspect I would vanish into the formlessness. I am as transitory as all else—there is no reason my identity should hold. My general melancholy gives force to the notion, but the melancholy itself is bittersweet and imparts that savor to all it touches. I am not altogether averse to dissolution.

I shall go for a walk, I think.

Pulaski County, Kentucky, U. S. A.,
2 September 1861

I did go for a walk yesterday, which led me, by chance turns, to Mr. Graham's door. I had wanted to speak with him, anyway, about the proposed call on Nick Bromfield. As set as Mr. Selby and I were upon the visit, and as little acknowledged credence as we gave to our friends' concerns, I was apprehensive. Suggestion is subtle but insidious.

To my surprise, he volunteered to go with us. "We're both nearing our ends. There is little rancor left between us, if little love. We've talked since he moved here, but not for a long while. Perhaps it's time again. Something may have changed, and I would welcome that. I wasn't without fault when we fell out.

"It's also true that he's dangerous, whether you're willing to believe that or not. It wouldn't hurt to take someone he knows."

I thanked him politely, concealing, for dignity's sake, the intensity of my relief.

After some pleasantries, I made to go, but he stopped me. "You said once that you wanted my advice about something. Some personal matter. You still want it?"

"I am not sure that it is anything with which you can help, now. I have ruled out the courses of action on which you might have advised me. Not that my direction is clear, but it is all a matter now of having a positive plan."

He chewed the end of his cigar idly, then asked, "Is this about Susannah Armstrong?"

"Yes, it is."

"Well, with a family without men, there's no question of feud law. That used to be the big risk you ran in seducing and abandoning. That doesn't seem in your line, though, if I read you right."

"No, that is one of the courses I have rejected."

"Then, there's the pregnancy." I could not tell if he grinned—his face tightened, however. "Any notion on what to do about that?"

"It will apparently go to term. Susannah does not wish to end it, and I respect her desire. For my own part, I would as soon it were not born."

"I thought you Frenchies were against that sort of thing."

"Only our two Napoleons. They have authored our laws on the subject. But I take my moral bearings from the Catholic Church, not the Bonaparte family."

"You know that there's a move to outlaw it here. Not in Kentucky—the old ways still hold sway too much. But people in other states say that too many Catholics are moving over from Europe, and we need to increase the number of Protestants to meet the competition."

"I think the Emperor's argument has a similar, if opposed, aim."

"Funny sort of war." He chewed some more. "But on your particular problem: you're right—I have no recommendations. All I can say is *bon courage*. You'll need it with that girl."

Today, then, we made the journey down the creek, slowed by Mr. Graham's stiff gait. He is not what he was even the few weeks ago when we first met. We stopped often to let him lean against a tree or shoulder, his skin the ashen color that had worried me so that night at his table. He talked not at all a few minutes into the hike.

"Is this a good idea?" asked Mr. Selby. "We appreciate the favor, but there's no use injuring yourself."

"No, I can go on. I'm doing this as much for my purposes as yours."

When we reached the point where Susannah had turned us back, we were all impeded by the condition of the path. We two younger men fought with the vegetation, and Mr. Graham regained some of his vigor.

"Not much farther from here," he informed us. "It's

just hard going. Nick doesn't get out much, and no one goes in."

At last, we came to an opening where the main stream was joined by another that ran from a narrow valley to our left. In a glade at the mouth of the valley was a cabin much like mine, the timber blackened by humidity. I had been expecting dogs, but none came.

We all halted. It was early afternoon, yet the surrounding rises blocked the sun and threw the scene into a twilight that, I imagine, never lifts but only darkens with the waning of the day. I may have heard an owl—I do not know the regional bird life well enough to be confident it was not something else. There was no indication that the place was inhabited.

"He has another building behind this one, that you can't see from here," Mr. Graham told us. "A laboratory of sorts. He may be in there. But let's check the house, first."

We let him lead the way. The one large window was covered on the inside by a curtain of yellow cloth drawn so tightly that the corners must have been fastened to the sill. No glow of any light showed through. Mr. Graham knocked and, after a wait, knocked again with no better response.

"Then, we shall try the laboratory." He took us around to the back, where the other structure stood, also weathered but longer and constructed of unpainted boards. Knocking there met with no better luck and our guide then tried the handle. The door opened readily, despite creaking protests, and we entered.

This building had no window at all. By the light from the door, we saw an array of oil lamps along the walls, stretching from the very front into the darkness beyond. An atmosphere both mephitic and sour was thick enough to make us cough. Mr. Selby found a box of lucifers on a table by the door and struck one. This revealed several benches crowded with indistinct equipment.

"Shall we explore?" he asked us.

"Probably not a good idea," answered Mr. Graham, "but let's. Light some of the lamps, if that's possible. We can say we were concerned not to find him. That's partly true, for my part."

The lamps lit easily, and Mr. Selby continued down the rows, emboldened by the illumination, meeting the rear wall forty feet back. We were indeed in a laboratory, but such a one as seldom seen in this century.

Much of the apparatus would have been at home in any modern chemist's work quarters, though the retorts and alembics and crucibles all were cloudy and blackened with much use, and cobwebs covered the whole. The charcoal ovens and reverberatory furnaces were antique, but I have seen their equivalents elsewhere.

It was the large slate boards set everywhere around the enormous room, and the ornate symbols and diagrams chalked onto them, that distinguished this place from any establishment I have visited. Some markings looked vaguely astrological, others like freeform artistic design.

One table held an armillary sphere with the earth at the center.

Nothing had been placed with care for rectangularity. Tables met cabinets at random angles, none, except by chance, parallel to the walls. I examined shelves and found jars of every manufacture, labeled in a spiked, unsteady hand and stored by no discernable rule. I remember "Flowers of Tin Stone" standing next to "Purple Vitriol," "Liver Ore" next to "Needle of Bismuth," "Philosopher's Wool" neighboring "Saltpeter Rot," "Butter of Arsenic" with "Plumbago" and "Perspired Antimony."

"Alchemy, indeed," I said.

"Alchemy for a certainty," said a croaking voice. I turned to the front of the chamber, where a small, stooped figure stood beside the door, holding a revolving pistol. There could be no doubt that this was Nick Bromfield, hunched, squinting through spectacles like telescope lenses, his white hair and beard reaching almost to his waist.

"If you would care to introduce yourselves, I might delay metamorphosing you."

"Nick, I think we've already been introduced," said Mr. Graham.

"Hughie," the man acknowledged in a flat voice. "You've been a rare sight. And who are your friends?" He indicated us with a sweep of the gun.

"These are Mr. de Grimouville, a writer from France, and Bob Selby, an engineer."

"An interesting combination to bring me."

"Mr. de Grimouville is interested in local folkways, and I told him that was your profession. Bob...well, I don't quite know why Bob's along, but he wanted to come."

Mr. Selby finished lowering a notebook to the bench in front of him. He had been doing this by slow decrements, trying to avoid alarming Mr. Bromfield.

"I'm marrying into the neighborhood," he said. "I thought I should get to know it."

He started toward Mr. Bromfield with his hand out, but the gun rose.

"Nick, there's really no call for that," said Mr. Graham. "If you want us to leave, we'll do that obligingly enough."

The gun came down. "No, no. You've made the trip—you might as well stay for a bit. I'll see what refreshment I can spare. But let's go into the house."

As he left the laboratory with a beckoning motion, it was clear he could barely walk. "I heard your knock," he informed us outside. "It's taken me this long to get out of bed and make it this far. I'm not doing well."

"What are your symptoms?" Mr. Selby inquired.

Mr. Bromfield ignored him, but addressed his old

acquaintance: "I'm tired all the time. And sick. I can't keep food down. And there's a pain in my gut that never goes away."

"Sounds like old age to me. But you should go by a doctor."

"I'd never make it out. And little point to it. It'll either kill me or it won't, and I'm getting to where I'd welcome the former. I've been long enough for this world and never took much joy in any of it."

"Reasonable enough, then."

When we were settled with glasses and a tray of inedible biscuits, our host took a seat opposite me. "You know something about alchemy, do you?"

"Not in substance. I cannot say I have met any practitioners. My countrymen flatter themselves that they have superseded the old chemical researches with a more systematical, analytical approach."

"But we old alchemists are the ones who invented distilling. That alone has established our superiority for the ages." He pointed to the jug. "I make that in the laboratory."

Mr. Selby set his glass down and did not touch it again for the time we were there.

The other continued. "You need to realize that the new and old sciences aren't trying to do the same thing. For us, it's never been about the substances. It's the process of transformation itself that's the subject of study. If we can understand that, chemical transformation becomes just an instance."

Looking at him sitting there, twisted and hurting and half blind, I thought I understood what motivated him. But I asked, "What does understanding transformation achieve?"

"If we can understand it in its general patterns, we have the key to its application. To anything."

He took a sip from his glass and winced, then sipped again. "To the spirit, especially. It would give us the key to transcendence, a way to refine the human soul by a change as radical as a transmutation of lead to gold."

"Transcendence to what?"

He leaned forward and examined me through his magnifying lenses. "I don't know that anything I could say would be intelligible to you." Then he dropped back. "Or entirely to me, for that matter. I've never succeeded, for all the years I've put into it.

"But it's in my capacity as witchmaster that you want to talk to me, isn't it? If you're interested in the reality of it, the reality is that it's all superstitious shit. If you're just interested in collecting the old beliefs, though, I could recite you a list. I used to cure a bewitched cow by taking some hair from her back and putting it into some of her milk, then boiling the whole thing over a fire.

"But you could just make up this kind of thing on your own, for all the significance it has. The details aren't meaningful. The only thing they tell you about the folk who believe in them is that they believe in witches. Or used to."

This last was forced out. His features warped with pain, and he sat staring at his glass until, finally, he extended his hand and caressed it. Then he drank and winced and drank again and seemed recovered.

"I've lost that trade. And my researches have come to nothing. I've lost track of my family. So, a doctor will do me no good, whatever he figures out. I've never had anything real to begin with, so I'm not going to lose much."

We all bent forward as though to speak, but none of us did, and all for the same reason, I think. There was nothing that could be honestly said that would bring any comfort. We could only look at each other emptily.

But, then, a hint of deviltry began to glimmer in Mr. Graham's eyes. He is, natively (or, at least, in his distracted moments), a kind man, but not on principle. Caprice or, perhaps, a pinch of the old enmity, led him to say, "Well, you do have a pile of bodies hidden somewhere around."

The other old man lifted his head, his pupils wide. Mr. Graham's hand slid beneath his coat.

"Not a pile," Mr. Bromfield said, gently but breathily. "I'm a competent enough chemist to do better than that."

"My point is, you have curious skills."

"Not a skill. Though, yes, I do have one real thing. Something I picked up in my travels and studies which, I suppose, means they were not altogether barren. It has merely preserved me as I am, however—it has been no route to metamorphosis."

"So, what is it? I was never impressed by mystification—not yours, anyway. How did you do it? You have half a county in terror."

"Oh, the killings? That just took a Navy revolver. No trick to that. Getting the bulge on them and having time to shoot is the hard thing."

"And..."

"I'm not trying to be mysterious, just cautious. I'm coming up on my end, however it happens, and I'm not leaving a will. To tell what I've got is to bequeath it, unless I can hide it well enough. I don't know that I want any of you gentlemen for my heir. I don't know that I want an heir.

"Tell you what. If I decide to pass it on, it'll be to you, Hughie. We've had our differences, but so long ago it was almost another world. I've been thinking on the times before that more and more, lately, and I do feel gratitude. And affection. You're the only one I could contemplate leaving it to. If I leave it to anyone. You're least likely to misuse it, of anyone I've known. At any rate, you won't use it worse than anyone else."

"Do I want it?"

"Maybe not, but you're the kind of cuss who's suited to it. I can't get out, so come by once a week and see how I'm holding up. If I don't hold up, I'll set the thing up for you to find."

"It's hard for me to get around, too."

"It's the best arrangement I can make. Get one of these young fellows to help you, if you want. But if they come by themselves, and I'm still here, they won't be going back."

When we left, which could not be soon enough from Mr. Selby's and my perspectives, Mr. Graham paused in the doorway and looked back at the shriveled shape in its chair. "You know, Nick, I think more and more on the old days, too." He paused, then: "I'm sorry things didn't turn out better for you."

He made as if to say something more, but changed his mind and simply came out and closed the door softly behind him.

"Does he really have something?" I asked him when we were in the less demanding stage of the journey back.

"I expect so. I don't reckon that what you saw there could put up much of a defense without help. Even a few years back."

"What do you think it is?" Mr. Selby asked.

"I guess we'll have to wait and find out. Shouldn't be long."

"An unfortunate life," I commented.

There was no response.

"Did he never have a wife?"

The corners of Mr. Graham's mouth twitched. "Did he seem like someone who would have a wife? Anyway, he's one of those men who prefer...whose proclivities run toward... Well, let us say that he's Hellenistic in his tastes. Was when he was younger, anyhow. Never understood that sort of thing, myself, but it happens."

"How did your people respond to that?"

"I can't really say. I don't know how many knew. He was so tormented for his looks and general strangeness that it would be hard to tell, anyway. It only happened when I wasn't around, so I never got the specifics. I would just go out afterwards and knock some heads together."

"But what was your people's stand on the phenomenon as a whole?"

"Couldn't tell you that either. Never came up much."

He was still laboring, although the going was easier the farther we went.

He stopped. "All I can say is that it didn't seem to matter much on the borders, from what I've read. The Reivers had leaders with names like 'Buggerback' Elliot and 'Davy the Lady' Armstrong. They didn't let it interfere with business. That's the best I can do for you on the subject."

We left him at his place in little better apparent condition than we had left Mr. Bromfield. I do not know that he is up to the proposed weekly visits. The great secret may never come to light.

Pulaski County, Kentucky, U. S. A., 4 September 1861

The long deferral continues. Outside of Kentucky, the war proceeds in its dragging pace. Two things of note have occurred. One is not an event in the narrow sense: the blockade of Southern ports—a policy announced in a proclamation last April—has now reached maturity with a slow increase in the Union navy's effectiveness. There are, at last, enough ships and suitable to make a genuine effort.

This should have real consequences for the South's ability to carry on its enterprises, both military and civil. Of greater interest to me, a proclamation of blockade apparently bears with it official acknowledgment of the enemy's rank as a sovereign power. It implies that the Confederacy is not a mere collection of provinces in revolt—it is a nation. The way is opened for foreign states to recognize the South and, conceivably, ally themselves with it.

Does this have a practical significance? It has a legal one. England and France may treat with the rebels in whatever ways they find most advantageous, with less danger of formal guilt. I suppose there is some value in preserving the accords—it does not undermine the appearance, at least, of international law. A pretense of order is better than unconcealed chaos.

This is what Mr. Graham does not see with his insistence on stripping things to their bare fundamentals. He would have me grant that governments are armed gangs—I may believe that in my most dismal moods, but I will not grant it. Man is such a creature of appearance that even the flimsiest illusion can have substance enough for him.

I am personally concerned in this. I know that the Emperor has designs on this hemisphere. On Mexico, specifically. The rebellion promises, at a minimum, to keep the United States too occupied to do more than protest at anything France does. An outright conquest of Mexico is not unthinkable. At best, Bonaparte (or his puppet) could have an actual ally on his northern border —one who might afford him tangible support if this war concludes in a Southern victory.

I, however, may awaken on any morning to find myself an enemy alien through no intention and with no choice. It would mean the end of many hopes.

The other occurrence has the opposite tendency. The state of Missouri's neutrality has not met with the same respect as Kentucky's. Missouri, to its misfortune, has long been host to a United States Army arsenal, and this has drawn the state (by a progression too detailed to describe here) into open conflict with the Union. In effect, the North has been first to invade and has thus assumed for itself the role of enemy.

General John C. Frémont, commander of the Union army west of the Mississippi, has placed the state under martial law. He has also issued a proclamation emancipating the slaves of anyone who has taken up arms against the United States.

The Union cause now has, in concrete fact, the moral grounding that was heretofore the stuff of misty rhetoric. I would not have thought it possible. The President's policies toward slavery have taken the health of the Union as their guiding principle. In an attempt to keep the South from leaving, he gave his support to an amendment guaranteeing constitutional protection for slavery. This was passed by both houses and was to be sent to the states for ratification when the onset of the war rendered it pointless.

Mr. Greeley—a personal acquaintance of his since their days in the Congress some years back—has assured me of Mr. Lincoln's personal dislike for the institution, but this has only whetted the edge of the editor's contempt. It was he who told me that the President's *credo* is that "the preservation of a strong, centralized state is inestimably more important than human freedom or human lives."

All due adjustment having been made for hyperbole and bitterness, I suppose I have been taking my bearings from this. Now, however, I wonder if I was misled. I may have done injustice to a great man. I was once open to the possibility of great men, but that was long ago. I have prided myself on my experience and detached maturity, but those may simply be age and myopia.

If this really is to be a battle for freedom, it will change how the world perceives it. No ruler, monarch or democrat, is wholly immune to popular opinion, and France could very well weigh in on the Northern side. How active the support might be, I cannot say. It need not be much, for my purposes, which are only to work and live here unhindered by diplomatic complications. It would be enough if Louis sent Abraham a card expressing his best wishes.

Above all—above deliberation on my personal interests, especially—I am elated by this slimmest, most blurred glimpse of a political world not bounded by vulgar calculation. Whether there is, indeed, a way out of the muck, I am still afraid to affirm, but, if it is a mirage, it is a pleasing one, and I must take my pleasures as they come.

Pulaski County, Kentucky, U. S. A., 6 September 1861

The war has come to us, at last. The news has reached us with only a couple days' delay—almost instantly, by our standards. The South has lost the game of patience and occupied Columbus at the farthest western end of the state. If one wished to invest Kentucky, it is a likely spot, giving control of the Mississippi River and a major railroad depot. One side or the other would have moved on it eventually. We are now a Northern ally, lacking only an official declaration, which should not be long in coming.

Rumor has General Ulysses S. Grant of the Union Army preparing to move on Paducah, a similar town on the Tennessee River and another key railroad connection. His troops have only to cross the Ohio from Illinois. He, too, is uninvited but will retain our blessings by the grace of a day or so.

The Confederate commander, a Leonidas Polk, has committed the additional offense of being an Episcopal bishop—an Anglican—and thus carries in his person the weight of bitter centuries. He is not present, however, having dispatched a General Pillow to command the *soi-disant* "Army of Liberation."

Why did the South leap first? The line I am vending (and, coincidentally, believe) is that Camp Dick Robinson has become too much an irritant. The garrison there has grown too large for comfort. It has also become, quite openly, a way station for Northern arms on their way to the Unionists in Tennessee. Time was on the Union's side. The Confederacy has been out-maneuvered rather adroitly and has now lost the state. The governor will presumably call for a resolution condemning both sides for violating Kentucky's neutrality, once the expected deluge of troops commences, but it is clear where our allegiance has been lodged.

There has been no actual fighting, to my knowledge, nor do I think the west will see action until all of the pieces have been placed. This is a most dilatory war. To the Americans' credit, I think a true horror of shedding fellow countrymen's blood has made them slow to act, as though they think something might happen to make it all unnecessary if only they delay as long as possible. What battles there have been have appalled everyone. They have not grown the European callous. When they do, it will be a different nation.

I believe the fighting will start here in the east. Zollicoffer has been pent up by the Cumberlands, frustrated in his desire to take the offensive. He cannot control his district of Tennessee as long as Union sympathizers have the scope to act freely in eastern Kentucky. Now, he will be loosed on us. He has only one avenue of ingress, the Gap, which will bring him up the old Wilderness Road. This is, ironically, the route that brought the Scots-Irish into Kentucky, and the region is filled with them still. His way will not be smooth.

Not long ago, I would have welcomed what I think is going to happen. I cannot, anymore. The conflict is too close, and I dread the thought that it will spill over into this place. That must happen of necessity—London is on the road and will be a target, and we shall be in the line of march between London and Somerset, whichever direction that takes.

Perhaps I can convince people to leave before it is too late. Everyone I know has always refused to consider that course, but those were hypothetical discussions. The looming reality may change their minds.

Susannah, so far, is unyielding in her intention to stay. I spent the morning in town, sifting through all reports I could gather for the outlines of a coherent image of affairs. I spent the afternoon writing up my assessment, which I shall take to Somerset tomorrow, then went to the Armstrongs'. All was calm there—they had heard nothing. All remained calm after I told them the news.

"Isn't this what we expected would happen, one of these days?" Susannah asked me. "I'm sorry that you're actually going to have to do some work, but we've been living with this hanging over our heads for months. It was going to happen, and we've already set our minds for it. What do you think has changed, that we should get upset?"

I explained my forebodings. "I think you and your family should make preparations to leave the area. Go to Somerset, at least, if not somewhere farther north."

"Where, and do what? What would we live on? Here, we're pretty much self-sufficient even if the store comes a cropper. We don't live near the road, so there's no reason anyone should come out here. But, mostly, we can't just pack up and go."

"You don't know war. It doesn't follow rational lines."

"And you do?"

"I admit I am not always perfectly consistent..."

"I mean, what claim do you have to know war?"

This was an unfair thrust and uncharacteristically cruel. She knew that this has become a sore point with me since the dinner with Mr. Moffat.

"I know much *of* war," I said. "I know that it is unpredictable and that safety is only assured as far from it as possible."

"Well, we cannot leave. If it's unpredictable, it may very well pass us by altogether. Let's not speak of it—if you're going into Somerset, let's find something more agreeable to do. I won't see you much from now on if you're going to be traveling around reporting on things."

She stiffened as with a sudden pain. "But you're the one who's going to be in danger, poking around into things. Oh, Edouard, do be careful. I hadn't thought that you would have to be around the fighting. But, you will, won't you?"

"I can only promise that all wounds will be in the front."

"Don't joke about it! I don't know how I would live if anything happened!"

"You will sit on my grave for twelve months and a day and then find solace in John Foster's arms."

"Now I'm getting angry. It's not something to joke about."

I tried to kiss her, and she pulled away, so I seized her shoulders and had a clumsy success. "I am going to make every effort not to put myself at gratuitous risk. And I am doing that expressly for you. Without you, I would have no reason to value my life."

This is perfectly true, and she saw that. It put things right, though she could not allow herself to relent immediately. "If you do get shot, it'll probably be in the arse, and that will serve you aptly."

It was a wet day, not precisely a rainy one. Enough drizzle came down, at intervals, to give us the mist that frees this valley land of all clear lines and all set contour. The house was too filled with sisters sheltering from the dampness and unseasonable chill, and I was tired of my cabin. The creek seemed the right setting for a walk, down in the thick of the murk, at the very bottom of everything.

"But not in the direction of your friend's place," Susannah insisted as she bundled herself into her rain gear. "The other way. Downstream." She will never be brought to trust the man.

Our shoes were heavy with mud and dead leaves even before we reached the water itself, so we walked along freely, unmindful where we set our feet. The sense of premature autumn has stayed with us, and the smell of wet decay was heavy.

"I was serious about taking care," she said. "Not just for me. You do have it in you to do something great, something splendid, whatever you may feel about yourself. If it's this scientific study you want to do, it will be a production of consequence, but you'll go on and do more than that. It shines out of you—people see it. I wish you could see it."

There is no clever response to such a remark, so I gave a skeptical grunt and walked on until enough minutes had passed to start us on a different thread.

"How will the people respond to the invasion?" I asked. "Among themselves, I mean—as a community. Will it change things?"

"It will turn some against others," she answered. "I know there are factions in the church, already, and the seseshes will probably secede. If only for consistency's sake."

"I am surprised that secular politics would have that power. Can you not agree that there are bonds more vital than party loyalty?"

"It won't be many. Most of us would still prefer to stay neutral as much as we can. But there's never been a sense that unity is the most important thing. Churches split at the sweep of a hat. It's always been our way. You know that the two churches in Stirling used to be one, don't you?"

"And I know that they used to be Presbyterian. And I have gathered that the change had to do with local autonomy and not with anything substantive. I do not see that church discipline amounts to much or that what you regard as doctrinal differences can really be of great interest to anyone."

She spied something on the ground and stooped to take it in her hand before I could see what it was.

"It's just part of our way. Authority in the Presbyterians was too much, more and more, in hands of a few people far away, and they spent too much time telling us what we should be saying and doing."

I did not like the way she was standing, suspiciously tensed, her fist still closed.

"Could it have been that onerous? Was there anything that mattered? And how could they police you, anyway?"

"I don't think they told us any particular thing that we disagreed with. They wanted more regular attendance—fewer people skipping out on Sundays to gamble or fish or go to shows. We felt guilty about that, anyway. The gambling and fishing, that is—there's no place to go to shows around here, though I guess that's a problem in the bigger towns. We do get together for music, but that's usually in the church and decided on by the congregation the week before."

"So, did it matter?"

"It was the telling that counted. It meant the church was turning into what we joined it to get away from. And what they were worried about gave the game away—they want it that man is made for the Sabbath, and not the Sabbath for man. That's not scripture. So, yes, doctrinal differences let you know what kind of men you're dealing with. People work hard around here, and they don't need religion adding to their chores. Religion is supposed to brighten your life, not make it harder. Religion should have cheerfulness and hilarity. I don't even want to be around the kind of people who would deny that."

"And, so, you distance yourself from them by seceding. Makes me wonder about your other sympathies."

She looked at me with the face of a sly angel. "Oh, we like secession well enough. We just don't like being told to secede. When you finally understand that, down in your bones, you'll understand all there is to know about us and you can write your great book on Americans."

Then, she dropped something moist and cold under my collar and ran off laughing.

It was a worm. "Hilarious," I said, letting it fall into the mud. "Reeking with the fragrance of sanctity."

"Was that awful of me? I'm trying to be better, but I couldn't resist."

"If your moral resources were any richer, our association would be the poorer for it."

"I recall that you were the one whose power of resistance was put to the test."

"And fell short, and I am much the better for it."

But, I have let my pen run on. I should be preparing for my journey to Somerset. I grudge the time I must spend away from here, and my absence must only increase with the new developments. Developments I have awaited for months with almost carnal longing. They have arrived and they are almost distractions.

I am in turmoil. I wish to go about my business and I wish to stay. I flit from one object to another with infantile fickleness. The future opens out into a thousand paths and I cannot settle on any one. I cannot think—I am sinking into numbness worse than grief. Susannah herself would not want me to sacrifice my hopes, especially now that she is convinced, at last, of the constancy of my love. I see that in her every little manner. All is informed by a subtle happiness and ease. This calms me in return—just seeing the serenity my presence can cause.

I had feared that my duties and the approaching separations would rob her of this new-found security. I am sure now it will not. At least, I have stronger misgivings about my own state. I am disordered. At moments, I feel my reason is going. I realize that, until this pass, I have had no inkling of the violence of passions.

This woman has undone me. Or altered me into something so much better that I cannot yet compass it. I recognize that she has made me accepting of men and of actions I would have denounced without a thought a year ago. I wish, I pray, I might be given an occasion to carry out good and glorious things, whatever dangers they might entail, by the use of this inner fire now within me, fed by I know not what.

You see, whoever may read this, how far from lucidity I have been driven. This is not strange with me. It has been chronic my life long. The acuteness of the attack is, however, unprecedented. I should learn from Susannah, who thinks and feels with passion and intensity, with fierce and anguished sensitivity to any evil that happens or impends, but who comprehends how to take pleasure in what good may come. She is not distressed by trifles. She understands how to let peaceful or joyful circumstances manifest themselves in their own full, unprompted, unhurried fashions. To learn that, though —to absorb it—I would need to stay, and that is the very problem. I am picking up the knack, I think, but I lose it if I am away from her for any duration. I begin to tremble and grind like a cogwheel out of gear.

I must, somehow, put this journal to rest for the day. I am finding that exceptionally difficult. It gives me a chance to linger on that which most engages me. At my age, I am only now become aware that there is nothing truly firm and truly sweet in this life but friendship with a woman willing to make the attempt to decipher you and sympathize. Only with my father did I ever share such closeness. All other intimacies are incomplete and ineffectual. All other sympathies, even the most genuine, are maladroit and obtrusive.

I have found Susannah by sheerest good fortune. I could never have had this at home, in my station. Among my order, this most central concern in life, the choice of a mate, is conducted with the care given to the choice and purchase of a pair of gloves.

I need to stop writing.

Pulaski County, Kentucky, U. S. A., 9 September 1861

I went to Somerset to find little changed there except for a stir. My reconstruction of events turned out accurate in all regards. Grant has Paducah. The governor is calling for a condemnation of both sides and a demand that all troops withdraw, but the legislature is likely only to denounce the Southerners.

I came back to Stirling to find little changed here. It will be a week since our adventure at Mr. Bromfield's, and Mr. Selby can scarcely curb his eagerness to be off again and see what the great unknown is. Mr. Graham is game enough. We will go tomorrow. I, myself, anticipate nothing. The old wizard strikes me as a fraud all round, trading in false mysteries. He will announce he has decided to take his legacy with him to the grave, and he will never be required to pull the handkerchief off the empty hat. I am impressed that he managed to ambush his enemies, but there need be no more to it than that. Mine will be simply a mission of mercy, carrying provisions to see him through the brief time left him.

Susannah continues cheerful, with stout complacency about the future. She has even given up her scolding about the visits to the house on the creek, only smiling benignly while Mr. Selby and I make our plans, as if we were proposing to hunt rabbits. She is more worried by my intention to scout out the Cumberland Gap for signs of activity, but affects to be comforted by my vow to leave when the first wisp of danger blows my way. If anything is happening, I assume I shall know before ever coming in sight of a grey uniform.

Miss Johnstone's Willis is going for a soldier, as they say. John Foster wants to join, too, and would certainly be accepted in some capacity, but there is a general conspiracy to dissuade him. None of the women think he can survive outside their supervision. Mr. Moffat is torn between zeal and age.

Mr. Selby will probably go, in the end, but admits his reluctance. "It's not the prospect of war that I mind. It's being back in the military." For the present, he is too avid for Mr. Bromfield's contrivance to think of volunteering. He speculates about its military applications, ranging as widely as his complete lack of particulars will allow. He is in for sore disappointment.

I encountered Mr. Johnny Elliot in town, who did not know that anything has occurred. When I explained the situation, he slapped the knife on his hip and threatening to disembowel and skin the first sesesh to enter the county. There was no talk of formal military service.

We start early for Mr. Bromfield's. Afterwards, I must consider how best to make my way east to Knox County and as far south to the Gap as is prudent to go.

Pulaski County, Kentucky, U. S. A., 10 September 1861

It is the most remarkable thing. No, that is far too restrained. It is the most stupendous thing, the most marvelous and terrible in all my knowledge. The great mystery was not a deceit at all. It is no hoax and no conjuration. No illusionist has the art for what we have seen.

I was near enough to losing my wits from all that has come upon me. But this is far, far worse than the strange passion that has unsettled my soul or the deeds that threaten the little world I have made for myself here. The order of nature has been shaken, and there is nothing solid anywhere.

Only once before has doubt done such violence to my view of things, and that attacked my certitudes, not my entire universe. I remember that I lived most of my youth without reflection, until, at a distinct point, or in a distinct period, I seemed suddenly to acquire consciousness, and, with it, a need to question. It was obvious to me, at first, that the world was full of demonstrated truths, and questioning was only a way of examining things in order to see those truths most clearly. When I set myself to do this, however, I discovered nothing but inescapable doubts.

I cannot do justice to the awful condition into which my mind and feelings were thrown. It was the most miserable I have been until this moment. I was like a man overcome by dizziness, who thinks that the floor has begun to move and the walls to shake. The memory still horrifies me. I did desperate battle against my doubt, desperate in the strictest sense of that word.

I do not know if the end was victory or truce, but I concluded that the chase after absolute, demonstrable truth was as futile as the hunt for perfect felicity. There may be such truths—if so, they are few. For the rest, we have probabilities, plausibilities, and that is enough foundation for action. To ask for more—to despair because one has no more—is to wish to be more than a man.

Yet, the pain of my lost faith in certitudes has never wholly left me. It is an unhappiness to which we are born as humans, next worst after only disease and death. The metaphysical speculations that have such a hold on so many, I cannot see but as self-torment, as though one directed one's every second thought to death. It is useless, at best, for the purposes of life.

Now, probability has deserted me. The ground begins to tremble anew, and the walls to move around me.

Mr. Selby, on the contrary, rides it like a jaunty sailor on a rolling deck. He is almost in raptures. He anticipates a new era of discovery and a new set of natural principles. It is a gift to be unwrapped. Mr. Graham is intrigued and dismissive almost in the same breath. He will not be seen to be moved by anything. (However, occasional, elusive comments show that some deeper thought is going on.) Neither perceives the horror that I do. Neither appreciates that this is the destruction of centuries of intellectual progress. Our systems are laid waste, and, Mr. Selby's reflexive optimism aside, there can be no assurance that we shall find something to take their place. The world may be such as to escape systems altogether, to escape reason and understanding. There may, at its core, be nothing comprehensible. It may be all madness underneath.

Still, narratives impose an order, whatever else may be truer, and I should apply myself to this one. It may concentrate and calm me.

So: We reached Mr. Bromfield's residence at about the same time of day as on our first visit. We knocked and listened and knocked again. There was no response, so Mr. Graham tried the door and found it unbarred. He cracked it open a few inches and called, "Hello the house!"

"Open it," we heard in a moment, in a voice almost inaudible.

We entered—not without hesitation—Mr. Graham first, by unspoken consensus. Unilluminated, with windows draped, at the bottom of its shadowed hollow, the interior was black as a cavern. It smelled like an animal pen. "Nick," said our leader, "where are you? I can't see a damned thing."

"To your left, on a table, are a candle and friction matches."

With fumbling and profanity, the candle was lit, and we could make out Mr. Bromfield swaddled in blankets on his bed.

"You've come. Good. And good that it's you. I'm beyond protecting myself. You can see the lamps on the wall. Light them if you want."

These were the same type of oil lamp as he had in the laboratory. While my companions lit them, I eased my pack to the floor and said, "We have brought you provisions."

"Thank you for the thought, but I've no need for such." He did not look at me. "I've decided it's time to go."

"For where?" asked Mr. Graham. "Or are you making plans to die?"

"I will be leaving. I have made out a bequest, proper and signed, giving everything to you, Hughie. If your attendants are willing, we'll have it witnessed."

"Certainly," said Mr. Selby, "but surely we can be of more assistance than that."

"Does this pup never stop barking?" the man said with frail vehemence, then began to cough. Droplets of pink spittle dotted his blankets.

"They will witness, if you want," said Mr. Graham.

"The document is in the drawer of that desk. You'll see where it needs to be signed."

We carried out the ceremony and I tried to hand it to him, but he nodded at Mr. Graham. "To him. It's his."

His beneficiary folded the paper and put it in the breast of his coat. "And now that that's out of the way, can we have a more civil reception? Can you point the gun in another direction, anyway? I can see the bulge under the covers."

The Navy revolver emerged and was laid on a stand next to the bed. "You should take it when you go. It's going to be yours, anyhow. Balls and caps are scattered around. Take care of it; it's been a trusty servant."

"Always wanted one. I didn't really need more land on my hands, though. I'll have to pass it on, myself, before too long, and none of my kin are here to manage it."

"It's your problem, now."

I took a chair and sat. Manners did not seem warranted in this situation, and I was weary. The others followed my example.

"I don't have the strength or the time for socializing," said our host. "Or a liking for it. Help me up, and I'll show you the item I was telling you about."

We got up again and helped him to his feet. I kept hold of him to support him until he hissed, "I can stand, you muggins. Leave me be."

This suited me exactly. His odor was intolerable and his clothing had a greasy feel that stayed with the hands. I wiped mine, unproductively, on my trousers.

From some unclean recess in his clothing, he produced a flat, oval object. It was slightly larger than a pocket watch and greyish. From its color and smoothness and sheen, I took it, at first, for a polished stone.

"Do not come near me," he commanded us. "Come outside with me, but stay at least five feet from me until I indicate otherwise."

He moved slowly through the door and did not stop

until he was some distance from the building. We went out and stood, watching. He turned and pointed to me, then beckoned with his hand. I moved forward and stopped short of him by the requisite interval. He frowned and repeated the gesture. Two or three feet from him, I encountered an invisible obstacle.

I ran my hands over it and seemed to be feeling an unseen, curved wall. Pressing on it gave no result. At the top was a plane at right angles, and I could pass my hand immediately over the old man's head but no lower. He smiled mockingly and waved his arm to suggest I circle him. I went left, sliding my palm along the surface, and felt it continue its regular curvature. When I had made the circuit, it appeared that he was surrounded by a cylinder.

I bent and investigated the bottom of the barrier to his front to see if it went all the way to down, since he looked to be standing on the soil and not another plane. There was no gap at the base; it followed the profile of the ground. While I was crouching, Mr. Bromfield stepped forward, and I was thrown off balance, falling. I rose and thrust back, with no effect. He stepped again, and I was able to halt his advance by bracing my feet and setting my shoulder against the moving wall, but I could not force him back.

The other two had come up, puzzled by my antics, which would have looked to them like a very gymnastic dance. I ceased pushing and hurriedly stepped out of the cylinder's path. The gentleman inside, the resistance gone, fell forward. I was mildly ashamed.

Mr. Graham's right eyebrow arched like a question mark. "What in damnation..." He moved forward to help the fallen man and came up against the barrier. I have never before seen his face wear such intensity of expression. "What in very damnation? Nick, what is this?"

Mr. Bromfield, having shifted himself painfully into a

seated position, pointed to his ear and moved his lips voicelessly.

Our own elder gave an "Eh?" and cupped his ear.

There was the barest suggestion of a stir in the air. The one on the ground said, "I cannot hear you when the shield is up."

"Shield?"

"Yes, you befuddled old mossback. A shield. This is a part of what I wanted to show you."

Mr. Selby was too late to have his own confrontation with the barrier, so Mr. Bromfield condescended to demonstrate it once more. The engineer had his composure back far sooner than I could manage. Rather, he accommodated himself to it a good deal more readily than I have yet. He was far from composed, and actually shook with excitement and delight.

"How does it work? What are its principles? Where did you obtain it?"

"I will entertain questions from its rightful new owner."

Mr. Graham cleared his throat. "All right, then. Where did you get this device?"

"In the course of my investigations, as I have said. This was near forty years gone. I knew of a community of self-styled 'adepts' in the Slovenian Alps. They passed for a papist monastery, but those who traveled in the right crowd knew what they were. What they were adepts in doesn't signify. There may have been more to them than I concluded by the end, but I never saw it.

"What they did have was something I haven't shown you. The stones aren't the meat of the thing. It's how you *make* the stones that's the captain's dinner."

"You can *make* the stones?" interrupted Mr. Selby.

"It was an isolated place—they chose it for that—but beautiful, and I could have stayed there just for that. As it was, I spent less than a year. I couldn't bear close quarters with people, even then, and it really was

monastic, after its fashion. I will grant that the food was
excellent.

"But they were what I've become. Failed mystics who
happened to stumble across this instrument. A sphinx
only needs one secret, I suppose, but this isn't a secret
that leads beyond itself. It's just a mechanism that does
something extraordinary and very useful."

"A mechanism!" I cried. "This is no machine! There
is the stench of sorcery here!" Was this excessive?
Possibly, but I was in a daze, which was only then
beginning to lift. The implications of this thing had
started to penetrate.

"Nonsense," said Mr. Selby. "Unknown physical laws
are at work, here, maybe, but laws nonetheless.
Sufficient study will reveal them." This earned him a
surprised and approving glance from Mr. Bromfield.

"I've learned next to naught about the laws that
govern it," the latter said. "I can tell you some things
about how it works, but not *why* it works."

"And the end of the tale is that they gave you a stone
as a parting gift," suggested Mr. Graham.

"Well, no. That was about the time that I left Europe
altogether. But, I say, the stones are not the main thing.
What I brought back was something they definitely didn't
want me to make off with. Come back in the house."

We complied, trailing politely while he hobbled inside
and over to the desk. He cleared a space and moved a
box forward. I had noticed this before, but made nothing
of it. It was not prepossessing in any way, simply a
scratched, nicked hardwood box that could have stored
letters or pens. In the front were two small doors with
glass knobs. The whole was about a foot and a half high
and as much deep, and two feet long.

"This can't be part of the original apparatus," the
hunchback observed. "It's just a covering that someone
built around it."

He opened both doors and unfastened some hooks,

which allowed him to raise the top of the box on a pair of runners. Within was a rounded case, of dull metal, with two stacked partitions that proved to be drawers that opened at a touch. The top of this box also raised, and stayed in whatever orientation it was given.

"Exquisitely balanced," he commented. "I've been unable to sample or identify the metal. It has resisted all my attempts. Its density appears to be less than any metal's I've heard of, but I have no way of knowing how solid the inaccessible parts are. I can't disassemble it, either, except for this one article, here."

In the topmost compartment, exposed by the lid, was a strip of metal about three-quarters of an inch by four that stood a *ligne* or so out of the surface. He pried this out with his fingernails and showed us two prongs on its underside, near the opposite ends. These had fitted into holes in the box.

"I've probed the holes, and they just close up maybe half an inch down. This thing is lighter than lithium, if you know what that is. Or measures that way—I don't trust that there's not something odd going on that disguises its weight. I haven't trusted anything much for a long time."

To the right front of the holes was a slot. "This is where you feed in the raw material. I have no idea where it goes then, but, if there's carbon or silicon in it, those are separated out and end up in the section immediately below, I think. You can't open it when it's in operation. But everything else ends up in the lowest section, and I've experimented to see what's missing from what I've fed in, and it seems to be carbon and silicon."

"Silicon," Mr. Graham repeated, as though it were unfamiliar.

"Like glass," our engineer explained.

Mr. Bromfield nodded and went on: "At the monastery, they seem to have figured that out, over the years, by trial and error. At least, they only put in

143

charcoal and sand. You could put anything in, I reckon, but the box won't open again until it has enough of what it needs. With fairly pure material, it finishes almost immediately."

"Finishes what?" I asked.

"Making another shield. This was their big prize, and what I came away with. Watch, and I will demonstrate its operation."

He replaced the strip and directed our attention to two indentations in the first drawer. "I will place my shield in one of these. It doesn't matter which. Then, close it," which he did.

"The bottom drawer should be closed, too, though it's just a receptacle for the dross. It won't work unless you do. I don't understand why, but the thing seems designed to defy peeking.

"Now we add the mixture of carbon and silicon in a three to one ratio, as my analyses have specified. And the process begins."

I saw and heard nothing, but, after a few seconds, he added, "And ends."

He tapped the middle drawer, and it opened upon two identical stones.

"Then, there is cleaning to do, but I'll leave that for one of you." He wiped his blackened hands on an old towel. "Just empty out the bottom tray and wipe out the top. None of it adheres to the metal if there's something else near, like cloth. Or skin."

He handed Mr. Graham one of the stones. "*Et voici.*"

The other old man examined it, passing it from hand to hand. "Now what?" he inquired.

"Now we turn to our next lesson. You may find a number of stones distributed about the property, by the way. I couldn't say where, exactly. Mostly in the laboratory. But, let us go outside, again."

He directed Mr. Graham to stand in the spot where he himself had been shortly before, then gave him his instructions. "You must be in immediate physical communication with the stone if it is to do what you want. Hold it in your bare hand whenever you want to use it. The shield itself will be adapted to your height and extend around two and a half feet in all horizontal directions. I have no notion *how* it conforms to the body's height, but it does.

"That and the necessity of bodily contact lead me to believe that the phenomenon is purely corporeal. I suspect that the stone receives impulses from the user's brain through the animal spirits in the nerves."

"Or electricity, as they now think," offered Mr. Selby.

"That's as may be. My point is that, when finally there is an explanation for this, it will be in terms of physiological causality. There is no need to introduce sorcery into the discussion."

This was a slap at me, of course, but I did not want to gratify him with a reaction. I noticed that he had succeeded in smearing his cheek with carbon, and I decided to take my satisfaction in not calling that to his attention. Perhaps it would spread.

"Whether the shield is up or down is entirely dependent on your volition. You don't have to say or do anything beyond wishing it up or down. Its response is instantaneous, for all my measurement has been able to establish. You'll want to take it down periodically in order to refresh the air. The supply trapped inside with you lasts a long time, but not forever. Also, it becomes uncomfortably warm. I have reason to believe that some heat is radiated away, but not all of it, apparently."

"But you can wait until your breathing is labored, presumably," said Mr. Selby.

"That might be too late. You can get to feeling pretty good breathing bad air, and your judgment goes. When you passed out, the shield would come down, but that's not very helpful when you're surrounded by enemies. Not to mention you'd probably be simple the rest of your life. Or simpler, anyway."

"But, you say that air is trapped with you. Does that mean the shield doesn't expand outward?"

"It just appears at its given distance. That is another reason why I think it's instantaneous. There's no propagation. Anything within two and a half feet of you is trapped inside."

"What about..."

"Please allow me to finish giving Hugh his instructions. We can talk about all this, afterwards."

He addressed himself again to Mr. Graham. "Never leave it up longer than you have to. You can have it up and down in an eye blink if you must, so it's not a major disadvantage. Besides that—let's see—you won't be able to hear because your air is sealed off from the outside. By the same token, it doesn't do to make much noise in there.

"Light comes through, however. I don't know why— nothing else does, including bullets."

"That suggests..." Mr. Selby started.

"You can walk, because there's something anomalous about the bottom of the cylinder. Another thing about which I haven't a clue. No external force affects you, otherwise, though your ability to push against things is limited by your own strength.

"That may be everything. Do you want to give it a try, now?"

Mr. Graham's *insouciance* is as impenetrable as any shield. "Stand back, and we'll let her rip. So, how do I go about making the wish?"

"It helps, at first, to imagine the shield up as you're wishing. That seems to focus the will intently enough to stimulate the stone. It'll get to where it's more instinctive."

Holding the stone at the end of an outstretched arm and closing his eyes, Mr. Graham visibly strained to erect the barrier. His face turned red with exertion.

"Hughie," said Mr. Bromfield. "You don't have to work that hard."

There was no sign that he heard and, seized by a thought, I put out my hand. The shield was up. Until he opened his eyes, though, there was no way to let him know.

"The damned fool's going to give himself apoplexy," said his old associate.

At length, he did open his eyes, and we made motions to signify that he had been successful. He tested his ability to walk and to take the thing down again. "No weight to it at all. Makes me wonder even more what it's made out of."

"That's the central question," Mr. Bromfield said. "I have a theory that it's not made out of anything—that it's some sort of distortion in the luminiferous ether. I will explain my reasoning later. First, though, put the shield up again."

When he was confident that this had been done, he picked up a rock and hefted it to ensure that Mr. Graham saw. Then, he threw it at him. He could not put strength behind it, but it reached the barrier and stopped, falling straight down. The man inside watched impassively, without a flinch.

"Very peculiar," observed our engineer. "It didn't rebound at all. It is as if the energy were drained from it the instant it touched. Does the shield absorb it?"

"I think so. I can make a more compelling demonstration that there is no bounce."

He went into the house and reemerged with the revolver. "A good day to hunt fowl. Shield up, you old buzzard?"

It must have been, because Mr. Graham, who was facing half away, did not hear. He detected motion, however, and turned. His eyes narrowed when he saw the gun, but he merely drew his shoulders back.

I started forward when the man raised the weapon

and aimed. He cocked and fired, with astounding rapidity, until all chambers were emptied. I seized the gun, too late, and spun to see what damage had been done. There was none. His target was unharmed.

We found all six balls in a neat cluster directly in front of Mr. Graham. There had been no *ricochets*.

"You want to have a go at it?" the alchemist asked Mr. Selby.

"I trust your aim. It looks like it was a tight grouping."

"I mean, in the shield."

Mr. Selby raised and lowered his barrier without dramatics, and had me use an axe on it. The sensation was bizarre in the extreme. The blade simply came to a stop with no shock to my arms or shoulders, no matter how vigorously I swung.

I was not asked if I wanted to make a trial of the device myself, and I did not request to do so. I did not want to believe its principles were natural, and, if they were not, all the better reason not to meddle with it. I felt remote from the place and happenings, and the people, and myself, as though I were viewing a Chinese shadow play, and there was such tightness in my chest that I could scarcely breathe.

While Mr. Graham sat musing on a log, and the others discussed "ethereal waves" and something Mr. Selby had read on "potential energy," I drifted aimlessly about the property. Dim as was the light around the buildings, the natural realm beyond the cleared area was darker yet. Little more than ten paces into the trees, it was obscure as night.

I returned to where the two interlocutors sat. "But does it have definite thickness?" the younger was inquiring. "That would seem to be a...."

"Where did the box come from?" I asked. "And when? How did the monastery obtain it?"

The old man, intent on the conversation, had not seen me come up. He gaped for a moment, then said, "They stole it from somebody who stole it from somebody else. That's why I didn't feel too bad about pinching it myself."

"Ultimately, what is its origin?"

"I was told that, if you follow the trail of thefts back a couple of decades, it leads to a farmer in northern Italy. How he acquired it is not clear. That is, the story is clear but short on specifics and plausibility."

"Still, what is the story?"

He took a breath. "The farmer was given it by men who arrived in a flying machine and then left. Those are all the particulars I was given."

"A flying machine?"

"A machine that flew. Not a balloon, apparently. I have only that negative description: 'Not a balloon.'"

"Twenty years ago?"

"About."

"What manner of men were they?"

"The kind who fly without balloons and give things to Italians. I repeat: the account I received lacked detail. I already had designs on the contraption and didn't want to seem overly interested, so I didn't press them too much. I don't think they really knew much more, anyhow."

"They were not suspicious that you showed so little curiosity? A normal man..."

"I showed a well-calculated curiosity. I must have played my hand well because I have the box and they do not."

Mr. Graham had emerged from his rumination and was listening. "In that twenty years or so, how many stones do you reckon were made?"

"I would imagine many. Strewn about the world and finding useful employment. But, a finite number—I have obstructed their production."

"In the way of policy?"

"Not at first. I took it because it seemed a good thing to have. I had no more defined motive than that. Later, I made the mistake of thinking about it. I never could decide what should be done with it. What would be the effect if this got loose? Millions of shields in millions of hands. Whatever that did would be big. So, I didn't decide and I never did anything with it at all. Outside of some bushwhacking in self-defense.

"And now it's not my problem, anymore."

He looked down and examined his hands. "I'm tired, of a sudden. This is more than I've moved in weeks. I can't get up."

We helped him back to his bed, where he suddenly demanded that we restore the will and the gun to him. "And don't take the stones. Come back in another week, and we'll see."

"Changeable old stick, isn't he?" Mr. Selby muttered as we made our way back down the creek. "You might have occasion for a shield where you're going."

"I would not have one if he tried to present me with it." I could say no more than that.

Pulaski County, Kentucky, U. S. A., 26 September 1861

I am, if not wholly regenerated by my travels, somewhat renewed and out of the lowest depths of my funk. I rode a saddle-horse, partly for speed, if necessary, and partly as a return to younger—if not happier—days. She was the best I could hire, a decent, good-natured sorrel mare, but not the prancer of my Kenilworth adventure. We got along capitally once I accepted that she had no tolerance for sport.

My kit was meager. I did not expect a long trip or stay, and had not planned to sleep out of doors as often as I did. Having done that once, on my first night out, however, I found it so bracing that I looked for (or invented) pretexts to do so as often as possible.

Even the news that Lincoln has rescinded General Fremont's emancipation order has not disheartened me. The slaves of Missouri are back in their chains, and I am back in my habitual, healthful cynicism. I am even ready to brave the shields again, with all their nihilistic terrors. Or, at least, Mr. Selby's report on his examinations—I have no desire to touch one of the accursed things.

When I was not in the field, I stayed at an old tavern in Barbourville, a town on the banks of the Cumberland in Knox County. The hills about the town better suited my humor. August's rains relented with the new month, and I could sleep without a shelter, though it was cold some nights.

As I write this, it occurs to me for the first time that we have entered true autumn since my return. I have been preoccupied.

I have mentioned Barbourville as a rallying point for Tennessee Unionists. They trained at Camp Andy Johnson, a Home Guard station north of the town commanded by a Captain Isaac J. Black. I would estimate that the camp quartered one hundred to two hundred men, though this was hard to judge, since uniforms were so rare. I saw no artillery.

As it chanced, I reached Barbourville on the very day that the Confederates issued from the Gap into Kentucky. They set up a base of operations—subsequently "Camp Buckner"—at Cumberland Ford, ten miles north of the Gap and twenty miles below Barbourville on the Wilderness Road. I had planned to continue south the next morning, but the sudden invasion made me cautious —it was impossible to tell what their immediate intentions were.

For days, there was no new intelligence, and the men at Camp Andy Johnson were increasingly on edge. I was an object of suspicion from the start, with my unwelcome questioning and my foreignness, and, in the end, I was officially declared *persona non grata* and unofficially threatened with confinement.

My recourse was to resume my progress south, trusting that an open approach by an unarmed civilian would suffice to keep me out of trouble until I had tried the limits of the tactic. The limits happened to be very constricting, in the event: I was stopped by pickets before I could observe anything of significance.

This gave me, however, my first encounter with the rebel forces. I could have taken them, at first sight, to be a party of mountaineers out searching for a lost animal, were it not for the occasional pieces of military uniform. Some these were the anticipated grey, but much seemed to be old bits of United States Army issue in dark blue, and some seemed to be of home manufacture from cotton cloth dyed brown. They carried all manner of arms, but mostly elderly smoothbore muskets.

In speech and features and bearing, they would not have been conspicuous in the streets of Somerset, though I have only an outsider's discernment. Still, the ones who forced me to turn about had the Westerner's tongue, not the coastal. It stuck me what misfortune it is that the conflicts here in the center of the continent will pit like against like—truly brother against brother. A man from Massachusetts and a man from Georgia share merely a contractual nationality; there can be no civil war between them. That can only happen here and in like places.

In France, I will concede, there is not even a common language—certainly not French, which the majority acquire only as they need it. But France is an ideal that transcends its people. Civil war there has a different and deeper meaning.

I took to the hills to see what was to be seen, tethering my horse in a secluded gully and hiking hours through the pines and poplars. At last, I gained a brushy eminence and crawled to where I felt I could have a reasonable view without being detected in my turn. I was aware that I was engaged as much in espionage as journalism from the Confederates' standpoint. I was attempting to gather detailed information on troop strength and composition, and I intended to convey the information to Northerners. That the Northerners were newspaper readers would probably avail little in my defense, were I caught.

I was also aware, now, that I should have brought a glass. At my distance from the camp, my unaided eyesight told me little I had not known on setting out from Barbourville. I could ascertain that the troops numbered in the thousands, and I could see that they included cavalry. I counted six pieces of ordnance, two of which looked like howitzers and four of which did not. That was the sum of my observations. I could make out nothing to help me identify individual units. If any special preparations were taking place, they were not evident to me.

Yet, I was satisfied with what I had done. It was material enough for a dispatch, and more than most stringers would dare seek. Appearances were that nothing would occur soon—the Southerners were establishing themselves in their new territory and would be occupied with that for the near future.

Most of the walk back to my horse was spent debating whether or not to pass on my report to Captain Black before returning to Somerset. I was nettled by my treatment and had no responsibility, moreover, to assist the Northern cause. On the other hand, I had developed a listing toward that cause for a very Kentuckian reason: it was the Secessionists who posed a danger to Stirling and Susannah.

Distracted by this, I was skidding down the slope of the gully toward my horse before I noticed the two men standing next to her. They raised muskets when they heard the clatter of dislodged rocks and ordered me to stay where I landed. As they approached, I perceived that they were clad in Confederate diversity, and I felt stirrings of nausea.

"Who are you?" one demanded. He was a well-built gentleman in a red, woolen shirt and blue army trousers held up by braces. Corporal's chevrons had been sewn onto his sleeves. The other man, taller and leaner, had a uniform of the brown cotton but no insignia, and sported a mutilated straw hat. Both wore unfriendly expressions.

"A traveler," I responded. We were far enough from the camp that I might have innocent purposes.

"A traveler doing what?"

"I am a naturalist. I am studying the regional flora."

"What the devil does that mean?"

"I am a scientist. From France. I am writing a big book on all the plants of North America, and I am now studying southeastern Kentucky."

He stared at me as though I were feebleminded. "Do you know there's a war going on?"

"Yes, but I shall be here only a short time. I am starting back to France tomorrow."

"Well, we'll just have a look through your gear and see if that holds up."

This was not good. Carrying so little at the outset, I had packed it all with me on this journey, including the notebooks in which I composed my dispatches. These I wrote in English, since they would otherwise have to be translated, anyway. There was the possibility that these men were illiterates, but I could not assume that.

I smiled as like a cretin as I thought believable. "I will unlade the horse for you."

"Let's start with you first."

He seized my shoulder and pulled me to face him. The other rebel stood a few feet back. As my soldier began to pat my torso, I snatched his weapon with my left hand and gave him a boxing blow beneath his ribs. It had only enough effect that I was able to step back out of his reach and aim the gun at him, but that was an adequate result. We three stood in a line, shielding me from the man who was still armed.

"Do not move!" I shouted. "Hold your positions exactly!"

The man with the musket stepped to his left, despite that. I adjusted to keep his comrade between us and said, "If you insist on moving, I shall simply fire."

"Then you'll die, too," the armed man said.

That was a credible result. I could not think myself around this *impasse*. We stood like that for more than a minute.

"What I have told you is true," I said. "All of it. But I have reasons for protecting my possessions. Reasons that have nothing to do with your war. I am not your enemy. If you will place your weapon on the ground, I shall mount the horse and leave. I shall drop your musket at a safe distance."

After another minute, the man in front of me said, "Hob, do what he wants. Put the gun down."

I almost collapsed as blood flooded back into my brain. "Move away from the gun, both of you."

Keeping the musket pointing in their direction, I

untethered the animal and clumsily mounted her. I dug my heels into her flanks to make her gallop. She began to wander slowly out of the gully.

Neither of the men had tried to regain their weapon, fortunately, by the time I swiveled and aimed at them again. I kicked the mare more sharply and got no better reaction.

Then, I had an idea. I had planned to discharge the musket, anyway, to prevent them from shooting at me when they recovered it. I decided to fire it into the ground, now, and startle the horse into a faster pace.

It was much louder than I thought it would be. The mare reared up, nearly spilling me. When her hooves came down, our speed was all I could have hoped, but in the wrong direction. She headed farther into the ravine.

I pulled forcefully on the reins and headed her properly, only to see the taller man drop to the fallen musket and raise it at me. All I had was my empty weapon, so I threw that at him with a whipping motion and lay as low as I could. It must have been effective—by the time he fired, we were too far for his unrifled bore to have any accuracy, I think. In any event, neither of us was hit.

The horse quickly slowed to a trot, but the men did not pursue, and soon I let her control the pace again.

Mr. Selby thinks this experience should reconcile me to the existence of the shields, but my instinctive abhorrence is not softened. I was never blind to their advantages. Those are not the crux of the matter. It is the world they imply that unnerves me.

There is yet more to the tale, but it must wait for tomorrow.

Pulaski County, Kentucky, U. S. A., 27 September 1861

I did not try to talk to Captain Black. In the end, it would probably have made no difference. I spent that night and the next in town, the 17th and 18th, and, early on the morning of the 19th, I was awakened by the voices of many people in the street outside my window. I rose and drew on my day clothing and stepped into the hall, where the proprietor informed me that the seseshes were attacking.

The best account I have been able to piece together is that a force of approximately eight hundred men, including one or two companies of cavalry, had been sent to raze Camp Andy Johnson. At a bridge on the Wilderness Road only a mile east of the camp, the vanguard of the cavalry encountered Home Guardsmen who had been posted as guards. Both sides retreated after a minor clash, in which, however, some Confederates were wounded. This, within the scope of my knowledge, was the first blood shed in this war on Kentucky soil.

I could not sleep, of course, so I performed my morning ablutions and dressed in fresher clothes. One of fogs that will be what I remember best about this land had fallen over us all. In that dimness, men were moving like armies of ghosts. Both sides returned to the bridge later that morning, but the Southerners now had their entire force and succeeded in driving off the Guardsmen. Camp Andy Dick was torn down after further fighting, and, their enemy having fled north, the rebels turned their attention to Barbourville itself.

We knew of their approach before they arrived, and the town was a confusion of writhing lights and shadows as the citizens ran about in the enveloping mist to secure their goods. Daylight had prevailed by the time the troops were in the streets, however.

They made no attempts to interfere with the exodus that began, but, as the morning progressed, they helped themselves more and more to the contents of the passing wagons. I took my own leave when they fell to arbitrary, meaningless vandalism and destruction. I did not like the trend in their temper. At the last house on my way out, a fence was being ripped apart and burned.

While I was on the road back to Stirling, the Confederates withdrew to Camp Buckner. Nevertheless, their way is clear, now, all the way to London. If they can take that and then Camp Dick Robinson, they will have taken the east.

I had a hero's welcome from Susannah merely for surviving. It gained fervency when I gave her an improved account of my adventure with the muskets. We read and reveled far into the night. I was in transit to Somerset, though, and left the next day.

There is great disturbance there. It is the next obvious target for Zollicoffer after the east is cleared. Bowling Green has just been taken by the South, and Somerset would make a pretty link in the chain that stretches from Columbus to Bowling Green to Camp Buckner. The nearest Home Guard bases of any size are in Monticello, some thirty miles away. A Colonel Hoskins organized a regiment of our local Guard, but has taken them away to Waitsboro. It is not far, but it is not immediate, and the unit is not large, in any case.

But now I have fulfilled my duties in Somerset and am back to my cabin at last. How long my fragile *otium* can endure, I decline to contemplate.

Pulaski County, Kentucky, U. S. A., 28 September 1861

Susannah has a bobcat. It looks like a type of lynx to me, but smaller, with almost no tail. She has it only in the sense that it is willing to let her watch when it comes to investigate the chickens. It has a regular route and visits the Armstrongs' poultry at dusk (at which time, coincidentally, the dog always begins to whine to be let inside). This evening, Susannah secreted me behind the woodpile so that I could see.

It is a beautiful animal, and I know that Susannah believes she can tame it, though she will not admit that. I doubt both the likelihood and the wisdom of such a project. She has convinced her mother not to shoot it. She played on Mrs. Armstrong's guilt over the killing of a pair of foxes her daughters used to watch. Susannah was teary for a week and may still be brought to sobs by the mention of a fox.

She is infatuated with wildlife, which is plentiful. Her store of minutiae on the habits of elk and deer and beaver and otters and raccoons (a species like a skunk or badger) is impressive, and much of it comes from her own observations. No bears have been in evidence during my time here, but she has spied upon those in the past. It is fortunate that the puma has not been seen in the county in recent years.

I cannot determine if there are wolves. There is no agreement. To ask about this in a group is to risk bringing its members to blows.

Susannah has seen none in Pulaski County, but has related a curious anecdote about one of the counties bordering Tennessee: There was a tract of forested land straddling the state line, half of it belonging to a Tennessean and half to a Kentuckian. The Kentuckian set traps on his property and, one day, found that a wolf had been caught in one. He informed his neighbor that "one of your wolves has been caught in a trap on my side." The neighbor asked why he assumed that it had come from his side of the border. He was told that it had already chewed off three of its legs and was still trapped.

My understanding is that a wolf will only gnaw away the leg holding it in a trap, so something singular was going on in this instance, but Susannah would only sigh when I urged her to expand on the story. The salient fact is that the only reported wolves in this part of Kentucky are in the southernmost counties. Otherwise, there are no large beasts of prey in our woods.

"Thank you for showing that to me," I told Susannah when the bobcat had abandoned its efforts to get through the chicken wire and gone away. "He is a strikingly fine-looking gentleman."

"She's a lady," she said. "I can hardly wait until next summer when the kittens come around."

"Do you think she will bring them?"

"They accompany their mothers on the hunt."

"What if she should become frustrated by the wire too many times and stop visiting?"

"I've considered that," she said, looking wicked. "But sometimes people forget to fasten the door to the coop. It happens often."

"You would not!"

"Not intentionally, certainly. Still, one is not always as careful as one should be."

"You should have a kitten of your own by that time," I said. In the past, I would never have been first to bring up this topic. It is much easier, of late.

She smiled and folded her hands across her abdomen. "With hardly any longer tail than hers."

"My son will not have a tail," I insisted.

"Daughter."

"No, it will be a son. In my family, the firstborn has always been a son, all the way back to the time of the Conqueror. At the latest. Probably before that."

"I do not believe that for a second."

"Nonetheless, it is true, and you had best resign yourself to it."

Pulaski County, Kentucky, U. S. A., 29 September 1861

I had agreed to meet with Messrs. Graham and Selby to talk about disposition of Mr. Bromfield's estate, so I collected the old man this morning and conducted him to the house on the creek. The young engineer has been staying there, making an inventory.

While I was away, the two had made their scheduled visit. The old alchemist was nowhere to be found. There was only a note on the desk, held down by a corner of the box:

> *I am now resolved to make my departure. You will only lose your time should you try to find me. My testament and the pistol are in the desk. All arrangements are as we have discussed. I have only taken the one additional measure of gathering and removing all existing stones. It is best that you be made to give deliberate thought and effort to their production and distribution. I felt that, after all my vacillation, I should make one intervention in the course of things as I bowed out, and this seems delicate enough. Express my friendly feeling to anyone who may inquire about me.*

Mr. Selby has explored the property and effects in a desultory way and thinks the most of it may as well be destroyed. There is little of value except the laboratory equipment. There is nothing of a personal nature in which the family might be interested, even if we could hunt them down.

He will persevere in the search, but has been dedicating most of his time to the stones. He has made four so far: one for each of us and one to examine. He tried to give me mine after we had lunched on what Mr. Bromfield left of liquor.

"I do not want it. You may test mine to destruction, if you will."

"That I've already done with one. I learned nothing about any internal organization—it resisted all my efforts to slice off a piece, and it held up to pressure until it just shattered into powder. I could analyze that, though. The laboratory is well rigged up for chemical studies. It even has electrical apparatus—as good as I've seen anywhere. Lord knows what he was doing with it.

"It's not true that they're just carbon and silicon. I found a dozen trace elements. His raw materials must have been slightly contaminated, or the things couldn't have been made. Or, maybe—and this is the interesting possibility—the box took them from the atmosphere. But, why not take carbon, too, then? There's plenty of that in air."

We confessed our own bafflement. (I tried not to show my lack of interest.)

"Maybe these 'trace elements' *are* just contaminants, and don't do anything." Mr. Graham said.

The young man looked embarrassed. "Well, yes, I suppose that could be the answer."

He thought about it and, I suppose, set the question aside. In a subdued voice, he said, "Mostly, I've just got measurements and calculations and speculations. For one thing, the volume of air trapped inside will last you for hours. Probably still a good idea to replenish it when you can. There is heat being radiated out, somehow, but your body pumps it out at a tremendous rate, so the greater part is heating the air inside. Another good reason to take the shield down, occasionally.

"I've been wondering what the shield itself is, but I've been fought to a draw there, too. I don't even know if it's material. It might be something like a magnet's field. If the barrier has thickness, I can't gauge it. There's no refraction of light, as far as I can see.

"I constructed a wooden framework so that I could get inside and the shield would manifest inside the solid timber. It sliced through it, but I can't measure if the slice itself has any width. Not much, if it does."

"Where does that leave us?" asked the old man.

"It leaves me coming up with conjectures and not being able to test them against observations. For instance, the fact that light and some heat can get through is a big puzzle. They think those are pretty much the same kind of thing, these days. Anyhow, one kind of radiated heat is. But what is light? There're two main notions: it's little corpuscles or it's waves, like waves in water."

Mr. Graham looked over at me to see how I was taking this. I kept my expression empty, but I could not look Mr. Selby in the face. He was trying to extort enthusiasm from us by staring at us with eager eyes.

He went on: "If it's waves, then it has to be waves in something, isn't that right?"

I grunted. Mr. Graham swirled his fingertip on the table.

"So, there's this idea of 'ether,' which is just to give light something to be the waves in. Ether pervades everything, so there's no reason to think it wouldn't be inside the shield. All that has to happen is for the light waves outside to set up light waves inside, and that's pretty plausible, especially if there's no thickness to the barrier. Even if there *is* thickness.

"Some people think now that light doesn't need a medium like ether, and that would make things even easier.

"The wave theory's winning out, lately, as a matter of fact. But if it's corpuscles, then it gets more complicated. If it's corpuscles, they have to be a lot smaller or a lot faster than molecules of air, which don't get in. Either there are tiny interstices—pores, that is to say—in the barrier, or it takes a certain high speed to get through.

"What would account for the latter, you ask yourself. Well, it happens..."

Mr. Graham broke in. "Bob, could we put that part off for a later time? You're giving us such fascinating new ideas that it's taking me time to take them all in." He did not quite wink at me, but one eye squinted.

"Yes, surely. But you can already see the repercussions this will have for electromagnetical science."

"Without a doubt. I've been considering, though, what these things would do to the country if people laid their hands on them. We don't have to worry about Nick's millions of stones, given how slowly we can make them, but there're going to be more and more over time. Assuming we don't keep it to ourselves. Even then, we've got to die someday."

This was a matter on which I had not been able to prevent myself thinking. It is, in some way, connected with the profound anxiety any other thoughts of the shield produce in me. "It will be a thieves' jubilee—a festival of criminality."

"How so? Their victims are just as likely to have the things."

"I don't know about theft," said Mr. Selby. "But it would mean the end to crimes of force. It is specifically force that they negate."

"And with force, government," Mr. Graham appended.

"Wait, wait," I protested. "How can you possibly you arrive at that?"

"Government is basically force, isn't it?"

"So, all use of force is an act of government?"

"You could say that, if you wanted to divert the discussion. But, all I'm saying right now is that all acts of government involve use of force. If only tacitly."

"That is preposterous!"

"It's what I've been saying to you all along."

"I see that now. And since you have set it out so baldly, I understand why we have never agreed." I felt unaccountably warm.

"What, then, is your notion of the connection between government and force?"

"Government uses force when necessary. No one would gainsay that. But that is the smallest fraction of its function. It is certainly not definitive."

"Give me an example of something governments do that doesn't involve force."

"Easy enough. They adjudicate use of property."

"You could go to anyone for that."

"Who might not be taken as the authority by all parties involved."

"And the government is accepted as the authority, why?"

"Because it *is* accepted as the authority. That is a part of what government is."

"Now, you're just dishonest. It's because it has the power to enforce its judgments. Note the etymology of 'enforce.'"

"It has that power because it is recognized as necessary that it have that power."

"Again, you're taking us along a side track. I'm not denying—for the present—that governments are given that power. I just want to establish that it couldn't operate without it."

"Roads, then."

"How do they pay for roads?"

"Tolls. The users pay for service, just as in a shop." But, I was aware of the speciousness of this as I said it. It is always my way in sophistical debates, where my opponent will use any fallacy he can to win. I am drawn into his deceit. It is why I hate such exchanges so. And, hating them, I have never learned to be good at them. It is one reason, among others, that I left the law. Would that there were men in our times who valued truth over victory.

"There are toll roads, yes, but anyone can build one of those—it doesn't have to be a government. And if the government claimed a monopoly, it would have to enforce it. But, mostly, it's taxes that build roads."

"And?"

"The taxes must be extorted from the populace."

"*C'est absurde*! Citizens pay taxes because they want that for which the taxes pay. And out of duty."

"Spoken like a true representative of the *Ancien Régime*. Some people pay voluntarily. Some people will do anything voluntarily. But not everybody. And some people want what the taxes pay for. But not everybody. Otherwise, tax laws wouldn't have to be enforced. Notice how that word keeps coming up."

"It is juvenile of you to keep repeating it. It is true, in a system like the Old Regime, that taxes were an aspect of oppression. In a free republic such as you have, there is implicit consent."

"Only to what's been consented to explicitly. My people fought a war against the United States government over taxes. That was..."

"Save it until later! Save your maundering lesson until the same time we have to hear about Selby's imbecilic corpuscles!"

Mr. Selby was wounded, naturally. I am losing my mind—I am sure of it now. I cannot think how to heal the injury of that unrestrained, hurtful remark. Possibly, there is no way.

"I am sorry. I cannot apologize satisfactorily. I am beside myself, recently, and I do and say things without cause and beyond explanation. Let me gather myself."

After several moments, I said, "My only point is that man is a political animal. He does not associate merely under threats. We have government because we have a social nature."

"You're mixing up two things, and you can only do it because you're quoting Aristotle. Aristotle meant that men by nature live in a city-state. A Greek city-state was both a governmental body and the kind of community that people were members of, part and parcel. For him, it made sense to connect government and society. Do any of us live in a city-state?"

"No. What..."

"So, for most people, being social doesn't mean being political. Besides, human nature is whatever people do when you leave them alone."

After my false step, I had lost any desire to pursue the conversation. I rose and said conclusively, "Most of them live under governments."

"By nature or by force?" He does not acknowledge hints.

"To protect themselves from force, if nothing else."

"And the government has to use force to protect them."

"That is bad?" I located my hat and walking stick.

"I'm not saying it's good or bad. I just want to get things clear so we can talk about them intelligently. Then we can worry about whether it's good or bad. Taxes might be the best thing in the world, for all I know, but we'll never figure that out unless we're clear about what we're talking about."

"I do not choose to talk about it."

"You'd better. There are two ways to test what I'm saying. We can disarm the government and see how long people take it seriously. That's not going to happen. Or we can let the shields loose on the world. And that's a decision that's really facing us."

"Not me. They are not my shields, and I want nothing to do with them." And I left.

Pulaski County, Kentucky, U. S. A., 30 September 1861

Mr. Selby had planned to return to Somerset this morning but was stopped west of town by a squad of Confederate soldiers. We have been occupied.

He was carrying a stone—was, in fact, taking it to the city to do further testing at his own place—but did not want to demonstrate its existence. The squad's leader, a sergeant, told him to appear in front of the post office at 3:00 and to pass the word that all local residents were to do the same.

Mr. Selby had not gone through the town on his way out. He returned that way, however, and found it under ostentatious rebel control. Men were stationed at regular intervals, intercepting everyone unwary enough to show himself. The post office had been converted to a headquarters and flew a Southern flag. No one was especially harassed—as far as he could tell, they were merely being given the same instructions as he.

He dutifully informed those he knows well. The Armstrongs were persuaded not to attend, though the two youngest Armstrongs pleaded with their mother to allow them to go. Mr. Graham asked us to convey his regrets and explain that he had a previous engagement. (As it happened, we neglected to do so.)

Mr. Selby and I went. A sizeable number of others also made an appearance, to my surprise. I recognized many whom I would not take as people given to easy compliance with commands. I think they were drawn by curiosity more than anything. Still, I missed more faces than I saw.

At 3:00, precisely, a lieutenant mounted a podium they had placed in the middle of the street. He—and all the soldiers, in fact—wore a complete, professional uniform of genuine grey. These were a different class of troop from those I encountered at Cumberland Ford and

Barbourville.

"I'm Lieutenant Joseph Edgcombe, commanding the second platoon of Company L of the 11th Tennessee Infantry Regiment," he began in the coastal accent that Susannah calls "mush mouthed". "Our company's guarding the approaches to the Wilderness Road, and my platoon's been detailed to guard the way to London. No loyal son or daughter of the South has anything to fear from us.

"I have here a proclamation by General Felix Zollicoffer, our brigade commander:

> *To the People of Southeastern Kentucky:*
> *The brigade I have the honor to command is here for no purpose of war upon Kentuckians, but to repel those Northern hordes who, with arms in their hands, are attempting the subjugation of a sister Southern State. We have come to open again your rivers, to restore the ancient markets for your produce, and thereby to return to you the accustomed value of your lands and labor.*
>
> *They have represented us as murderers and outlaws. We have come to convince you that we truly respect the laws, revere justice, and mean to give security to your personal and property rights. We come to take you by the hand as heretofore—as friends and brothers.*
>
> *Their Government has laid heavy taxes on you to carry on this unnatural war, which is openly avowed to be to set at liberty your slaves, and the ensuing steps in which will be to put arms in their hands, and give them political and social equality with yourselves. We saw these*

things in the beginning, and are offering our hearts' blood to avert those dreadful evils which we saw the Abolition leaders had deliberately planned for the South.

How long will Kentuckians close their eyes to the contemplated ruin of their present structure of society? How long will they continue to raise their arms against brothers of the South, struggling for those rights, and for that independence common to us all, and which was guaranteed to all by the Constitution of 1787?

For many long years we remonstrated against the encroachments against rights, and the insecurity to that property thus guaranteed, which these Northern hordes so remorselessly inflicted upon us. They became deaf to our remonstrances, because they believed they had the power, and felt in every fiber the will to 'whip us in.'

We have disappointed them. We have broken their columns in almost every conflict. We have early acquired a prestige of success which has stricken terror into the Northern heart. Their 'grand armies' have been held in check by comparatively few but stern-hearted men; and now they would invoke Kentucky valor to aid them in beating down the true sons of the South who have stood the shock, and in bringing common ruin upon Kentucky and her kindred people.

Will you play this unnatural part, Kentuckians? Heaven, forbid. The

*memories of the past forbid. The honor of
your wives and daughters, your past
renown, and the fair name of your
posterity, forbid that you should strike for
Lincoln and the abolition of Slavery
against those struggling for the rights
and independence of your kindred race.
Strike with us for independence and the
preservation of your property, and those
Northern invaders of your soil will soon
be driven across the Ohio.*

"It's signed, 'F. K. Zollicoffer, Brigadier General.' I
will have copies posted."

He folded the document and placed it in his breast.
"I'll just add that my unit's not looking for recruits. Our
Company's made up of volunteers from all over the South
who think that these western states are the key to
Confederate victory. We're in a Tennessee brigade, but
we're mostly from Virginia and the Carolinas and
Alabama. Any of you Westerners who want to join up
had best make your way to Cumberland Ford and enlist
there.

"The important thing for you people is that any
interference with my troops will be treated as an act of
war, and you'll be shot or hanged until dead. That is all."

There were questions from the crowd, but they were
not entertained. The officer returned to the post office
and shut the door behind him.

Pulaski County, Kentucky, U. S. A., 1 October 1861

When Mr. Selby asked me to meet with him and Mr. Graham at the latter's house, I assumed it was more of the estate business. I would have preferred to be quit of it, but I was regretful over the offense I had given him and wanted to avoid further estrangement.

I was surprised, therefore, to find Mr. Moffat present as well. I cocked an eyebrow at Mr. Selby, who said, "It seems to me that we have a problem and need to deliberate solutions."

"If that is what this is," I said, "then we are doing a very dangerous thing. They will consider this conspiracy. I know, from experience, how this sort of mind thinks."

"Well, but it *is* a conspiracy."

"Why am I being drawn into it? I am the subject of a foreign power. It is no proper concern of mine."

"I thought, perhaps, through personal loyalties and an interest in self-preservation. These rebels are no respecters of person or property. They've shown that wherever they've encroached. You are in as much peril as we, and Susannah more so."

I started to disagree but remembered the warnings I myself had given Susannah on the hazards of general warfare. Even the most disciplined troops are volatile, and much depends on their commander. I did not trust this one.

"Have you discussed our... discovery...with Mr. Moffat?"

"No. That is a part of what we must discuss."

"What discovery is this?" asked the denominated individual.

"We cannot tell you yet," the young man told him. "It is a matter of confidence."

"And what are my reasons supposed to be for being interested in this?" Mr. Graham asked.

"As a champion of freedom. I do not appeal to your self-interest but to your principles."

"You are not appealing to me at all at the moment. A big part of freedom is leisure, and a good way to lose that is to fight for freedom. It's a balance—you don't want to shoot yourself in the foot by being a slave to an idea. I'll just wait here till they're gone. That always happens in time, one way or another, with this breed. If I were young, I might do it for fun, but I'm not."

"Josh, do you, at least, care about this?" Mr. Selby asked, exasperated.

"Surely. Tell me where to shoot, and I'll do it in a heartbeat." He slapped a holster at his hip, which I now saw carried a revolver identical to Mr. Bromfield's.

"Mr. Graham," I inquired, "did you give that gun to Mr. Moffat?"

"He showed me that he's the best one to handle it. I'm willing to do that much for the cause. It didn't cost me anything."

"Then," said Mr. Selby, "the time has come to consider the other issue, to speak like a lawyer. Josh, would you mind leaving us? I thank you for coming. I will be by to see you shortly."

When the constable had left, Mr. Selby put the question of the shield to us bluntly.

"I have decided not to decide," said the old man. "I've tried to point out what I think the consequences of this thing might be, so you know what the choice is about, but I can't say if those consequences would be good or bad. I think the world would be a better place with a stone in every hand, but I don't know it would. I leave it up to you young fellows."

I said, "I do not agree with your assessment of the consequences, as you know. But I want nothing to do with the things, as you also know. That leaves it up to you, Mr. Selby, to make the determination. I'll only state that I believe you are risking a titanic disruption in the order of the world."

"But not politically, according to you," Mr. Graham said. "It can't harm your cherished governments, if you're right."

Mr. Selby coughed, unnaturally loudly. "I'll leave you two to sort that out. Since it's been left up to me, I'm going to start distributing the stones to men I trust. I'll show Josh how they work, and then we'll judge who we think is suitable to recruit."

My part in everything to do with Mr. Bromfield was finally done, so I went to the post office to request an interview with the lieutenant. I had no hopes that he would volunteer anything I could use—and I had no way to communicate with the newspaper in the event he did— but I wanted to establish my identity with him as a disinterested foreign journalist. At best, I might be given leave to come and go.

The door was ajar but guarded by a private. "The lieutenant's not seeing civilians," he told me.

"He might be willing to see me," I said. "I am a French subject who has been inadvertently trapped here by the shift in the lines. I am also a member of the press and am interested in hearing the Confederate perspective on this move into Kentucky. So far, I have been unable to talk with anyone from your side." I smiled winningly.

"Why would the lieutenant want to talk to a foreigner?"

"Well, as I say..."

"Private Wilsher!" a voice called from inside. "What is all the jawing about out there?"

"A French reporter to see you, sir!"

"That's different, anyway, I reckon! Send him in!"

The office had changed only in losing the passionate tidiness the postmaster always maintained. The desk behind which the officer sat was a litter of papers. By one wall were the piled remains of mail, apparently torn open and discarded.

Lieutenant Edgcombe, from near at hand, looks far too young for his rank. I expect that is deceptive. He squared a sheaf of documents by striking it against a vacant section of the desk and looked up.

"A French reporter, are you?"

"Yes. I am here to observe the situation in Kentucky. Thus far, I have only been exposed to the perceptions of Unionists and neutrals. I have not been able to get a fair view of things—a view from all sides."

"Neutrals, huh? Where I come from, there're only two sides."

"That may very well be. All the more motivation for you to give me your take on the subject."

"Which side are you on?"

"It would be presumptuous for me to take a side. I am not an American."

He became aware that the private was still inside. "Wilsher, take your post!"

To me, when the man had exited, he said, "Now, I just told you that where I come from, there are only two sides. I'll ask you again: Are you for the North or for the South?"

"If I am compelled to choose, then, since I have a partiality for the people around here, and they do not like your presence, I am temporarily anti-Confederate."

"Meaning, a Unionist. That makes you my enemy."

He leaned back in his chair with his hands laced behind his head. "What do you suppose we should do about that?"

"Since my sovereign may very well be open to an alliance with the Confederacy, it would probably not be wise to do anything at all, unless you suspect me of working against your interests."

"If I ever do, I won't have any trouble deciding what to do about that." He straightened, and the front legs of the chair clattered. "For now, it would be just as well for you if I never see you around. In fact, tell all your Western trash that the fewer people we see on the street, the better it's going to be for everybody."

He went back to the papers, and I was evidently dismissed. My honor would not abide such arrogant treatment, however. "Western trash?"

He continued what he was doing for a few seconds, to demonstrate that he was in command of the situation. Then, he almost snarled. "We have this sort in Virginia. Not so many, and we know how to handle them. Used to have more, but we suggested they move out here. A bunch of drunken, whoring rowdies, profaning the Sabbath with their gambling and swearing. Most of them missing an ear or a nose from fighting. And their harlot women, half naked and throwing their eyes at everybody. We didn't put up with them at home, and I'm not going to put up with anything here.

"Any disorder's going to be treated as rioting and insurgency, and you can tell them that. You Frenchies may think that sort of thing's all right—you're not much better, from what I hear—but I'm going to have decency. If they can't manage that, they need to stay out of sight."

He had taken on the frozen, unblinking gaze that I associate with the brainsick. Louis-Napoleon sometimes has that look. "I shall be certain to inform them," I said and walked out.

The private grasped my arm as I went by him. I tore it away and faced him.

"I heard what the lieutenant was saying to you. You ought to know that we all agree. We aren't putting up with any trouble from these crackers. We had more than our fill of them coming up through the Gap—long-legged, long-haired men with squirrel rifles shooting at us whenever they got sight of us. And those mountain girls with their bare feet and uncombed hair, spitting at us if we tried to talk to them. You tell them we're not going to put up with much. You tell the girls, especially."

"I shall be certain to inform them," I repeated.

Pulaski County, Kentucky, U. S. A., 2 October 1861

People can get around the soldiers on the road to Somerset, so we are not entirely isolated. I may make the experiment myself. In the meantime, the news is that no one is coming to rescue us. They are fully aware of our predicament, but dare not commit the troops. Colonel Hoskins' men are at Albany, twenty or twenty-five miles southwest of Monticello. A Confederate force from Tennessee recently captured the town. They have been expelled, but it shows the vulnerability of the area.

Any help from the Home Guard in Monticello is therefore out of the question. It is not believed that our Confederates have any immediate designs on Somerset, so Colonel Hoskins' men, who are returning, will remain in their camp, ready to move in either direction as necessary. The campaign against Zollicoffer's forces in the east will be conducted from Camp Dick Robinson.

This I had from Mr. Selby, who had it from returning blockade runners. He also brought bad news about his designs for a *guerrilla* organization. (I have suggested it be called Robert's Irregulars or Robert's Rangers.) He exhibited the shield to Mr. Moffat and nursed him through his initial disorientation. When they began to manufacture more stones, they produced only three before the box apparently stopped functioning. They have only five altogether, in addition to the one given to Mr. Graham. Five will give them a definite advantage, but not the invincible army for which they hoped.

I have tried to dispel his pessimism by pointing out that Lieutenant Edgcombe has only fifty men. Each Irregular need only kill ten, and that seems entirely feasible to me from what I have seen of the shield's workings. This also means that they need only three more recruits, and there is security in small numbers for clandestine undertakings of this sort.

Mr. Selby is afraid that my plan will take too long and that there will be retaliation against civilians in the intervening time. Maybe. What they really need are more revolvers so that all may be settled in one unanticipated pitched battle. I have seen a couple carried by the Southerners themselves—Lieutenant Edgcombe has one, though of a model with which I am unfamiliar—so there is the possibility of targeting those men first and obtaining their weapons. Surely, others can be smuggled in from Somerset.

I suppose I am acclimating to this new world the shield has imposed on me. Or, perhaps I am angry.

The rest of Mr. Selby's news concerns the conduct of the rebel troops themselves, who have taken possession of private homes near their headquarters. They are using them for billeting and cooking, except for the postmaster's house behind the post office. That has become a stable.

The owners have been evicted, but their possessions and provisions stayed with the new tenants. Those who have seen inside the buildings since the confiscations say that they have been ruined. Carpets have been torn up and furniture smashed. Dirt covers all. Stores of food, of course, are all being consumed. Clothing has been a particular focus of casual destruction. Some is worn as a lark; most is simply shredded.

I must talk to Mr. Selby about moving the Armstrongs to the old Bromfield property. It is the one place I know that offers no intimations of its own existence. What we cannot take of value, we can bury.

Pulaski County, Kentucky, U. S. A., 3 October 1861

Mr. Selby is not to be found. I have walked for hours only to establish that no one has seen him.

It is imperative that we move the Armstrongs as soon as possible. In the town, it is worse than the reports led me to picture. There are actually holes in the walls of the houses. How they were made is beyond me. I do not ask *why* they were made—that, most likely, has no answer. Why the soldiers would not consider that cold weather is approaching, and that these are to be their own quarters, would be an equally idle question.

Fences have removed from private dwellings and reassembled in the street to hold pigs and cattle. These and all manner of fowl are being rounded up methodically.

All households in the town have now been expropriated. Every garden has mattress or two, slit open and gutted. One I saw was partially burnt.

There are not above seven homes or so in Stirling proper, and the circle of wreckage must expand.

The churches have not been damaged, though Susannah's has boards nailed across the entrances. The Elder Bell's holds daily services for the soldiers who are not on duty. I have no explanation for this. I had looked forward to the Elder being executed the moment he opened his mouth in the hearing of a Confederate. Instead, I have seen him strolling with Lieutenant Edgcombe, chatting and smiling. The smiles evaporated when they saw me, and the clergyman muttered something low to the lieutenant. I waved, but they kept their stone faces until I was out of sight.

I have met one rebel with whom it is possible to have a civil conversation. Corporal Guildford was an apothecary in his civilian life and is relieved of all other duties in order to see to the platoon's medical needs. There are many of these due to fighting among the men—they have discovered what stores of liquor there are to be had here. It is enough for him to patrol the street to hit upon patients.

When not immediately occupied, he talks with all and sundry, military and civilian. His fellow troops do not like this, but he has a special status because of his work. He is also interesting because he has brought along his own slave to assist him. Anthony, the slave, insists that his surname is also Guildford. This is common in the Southern slave system.

The corporal was unusually inquisitive about everything to do with me. I think he is more intelligent than the run of his platoon and is dying for stimulation. I may have been more candid with him than is prudent, but I detected no slyness or, at any rate, no treachery, there. He was interested, most of all, in my views on the war and the conditions that gave rise to it. Because I am officially a Unionist, I suspect, he interpreted my every utterance to be from that standpoint, and I had constantly to correct him. These people—even the clever ones—really do believe there are only two sides to questions.

I could not spend as much time with this pair as I would have wanted. I can, it seems, be seen in Stirling without being arrested on the spot, but I should not "push my luck," as they say. Also, I had taken the route through town originally only as the shortest way to the Armstrongs, where I expected to see Mr. Selby. I now had the additional purpose of persuading them to move. Susannah would be my biggest challenge, given where I wanted to move them.

No one was home. This is peculiar, since five people live there when Mr. Selby is around, and they have frequent callers, but it is not unprecedented. The locked door did disturb me. I continued on my rounds to find the young engineer and, unsuccessful, had another try at the Armstrongs. Things were as before.

I came back here to rest after going to Mr. Moffat's and have gotten lost in writing. There is still the store on the London road to visit.

Pulaski County, Kentucky, U. S. A., 4 October 1861

The condition of the store should have distressed me much more than it did. I must have expected it, in some sense. It was to be predicted that it would go early, the biggest attraction the town had to offer for such holiday makers as these. On the main road, filled with every essential and every comfort a brigand army could hope to pilfer. The pickets are not far beyond it—they would have known about it from the first.

There was nothing there. It was as thorough and perfect a pillaging as ever was. Something may have been hidden by the debris, something small, a nail or thimble overlooked in the rush after greater prizes, but I saw nothing. The shop itself cannot be used again. Apart from damage to the structure, it has been used as a latrine.

Of Mrs. Armstrong and the boy there was no sign. I now began to worry in earnest. Where could everyone be? I did not believe that the whole family could be in the hands of the soldiers. Their house was intact and I had seen and heard nothing in the town to suggest that any civilians were detained.

Could they have slipped through to Somerset? There would be no way to know. Had they elected to hide? If so, their choices were too many to investigate.

I had to assume they were still around and had gone to ground someplace obvious to me. This could only be the Bromfield place, as I had planned for them myself. With the decisiveness that comes from having no other course, I set off down the creek.

When I found all of them there, I would have sat and wept but for the presence of Mr. Selby. It was he who greeted me, with a stone in one hand and a long rifle in the other.

"You found the note, then," he said.

"Note?"

"Held under a rock on your porch." The rifle was no longer pointed at me but at the approach behind me, and swung back and forth as though seeking a scent.

"I saw no note. It does not mean it was not there. I was agitated and running all over the county looking for you. I had better return and recover it before it is taken up by unfriendly hands."

"You figured it out!" shrieked someone from just inside the trees to my side. It was Ella, togged out in buckskin, and shedding twigs and leaves from her hair as she came. Her leggings were muddy to the knees.

"You worked it out. I spent ever so much time on the clues."

"Clues?"

"In the letter we left at your door. The poem." Her face fell as she realized I had not seen the note. "Shit and damnation! I spent hours on that!"

"But it is a cryptogram? If it tells too plainly where you are, I must go retrieve it at once. How did it run?"

She brought her heels together and clasped her hands over her heart. "It went:

> *Son of Gaul, we all will wend*
> *Where the tickling waters end.*
> *Dark as Egypt, old as night.*
> *In the gleam of lantern's light,*
> *I, Susannah, wait thy tread,*
> *Dreaming in the wizard's bed.*
> *O, Ned, I need thee dreadful quick.*
> *Thy voice, thy arms, thy lips...*

"Ella!" cried Mr. Selby. "That will be sufficient."

"But there's lots more! I haven't even got to most of the clues!"

"*Ned?*" I queried.

"That's you, I take it," he said.

"The reference to waters might be too plain," I said to the girl. "Is there more like that?"

"But the waters don't actually end here. The big part of the creek starts here. It's only the end if you're walking up it." She was frowning.

"Do I need to leave immediately? That is my real question."

"I don't think so. I was almighty smart about it. If I could finish it, you'd see."

I was moved to delay my return more by thoughts of the walk back than of safety. "Where are the others?"

I noticed, then, however, that the door to the dwelling was open and the curtain taken from the window. Inside, figures moved.

"They're cleaning up the place," she said. "It was horrid. I am not sleeping in that bed, whatever the others may do. I'm sleeping in the laboratory."

"You are not," said Mr. Selby. "I'm working there at all hours. It's dangerous, anyhow, and probably not healthy."

"The old man's house is what's not healthy."

Toodie came through the door with a bundle that looked to be clothing. She dropped it on the ground and rubbed her arms against her dress. Her nose wrinkled with revulsion. When she caught sight of me, she waved and called Susannah to come out.

Mother and daughter both emerged. Susannah ran to me unsmiling and embraced me as urgently as if I had been the one missing.

"How did he talk you into this?" I whispered.

"It was the only reasonable thing to do," she whispered back.

"But this is the center for all evil in the valley. Or, so some would have had me believe."

"I don't like it. But it's the only way to keep my family safe, and I can endure it for that. Besides, Bob has been telling us about Nick Bromfield. It all seems more sad than anything."

"What has he been telling you?"

"Just what he knows of his life. I'm ashamed of the way I was carrying on. It's just that we've been hearing stories for years. I still feel a dread of the place that I can't shake, but I'm trying to be rational about it."

"Just about his life?"

"What else is there to tell? What do you know?"

"Nothing, nothing. He had an interesting accent—just like Mr. Graham's. Otherwise, nothing. There is the laboratory, though. Have you been in there?"

"No longer than I had to be. Oh, yes, there's the invention. Is that what you're trying to be subtle about? Bob's been tinkering with it, trying to get it to work."

"What has he told you about it?" I was cursing myself for making her more wary with every question I asked, but I could not seem to stop.

"Some new sort of electrical engine. Something no one else has. Is there more to it than that?"

"No, that is it. I thought you might be afraid of it."

This met with the purest scorn I have seen human features assume. "I know all about electricity. Or, as much as you do, I bet you. Bob has been lecturing us."

"That has been fun. I bet you." How to change the subject? "Did Ella let you read her poem?"

"Do you mean the clue poem? Toodie read it and pronounced it a masterpiece. Bob said that it would do, and there wasn't time to write another. We had to pull foot too quickly for me to look at it."

Her mother had come up behind her. "Do you know what's happening in town?" she asked. "Have you heard anything about the store?"

"I was there not three hours ago," I told her. "It is lost. The merchandise is gone and you may not wish to restore the structure."

She showed nothing. "I knew that would be the way of it. I've told John Foster not to come in, and I've only been in because it wouldn't matter whether it was locked or open. I thought I would get some last selling in before the taking started."

"Were you there when they came?"

"For awhile. More and more came in, and more and more left with things, saying they were just borrowing. Finally, I took the money and some supplies and left."

"Will you be able to live?"

"We could have done with what was on the stead if we had to. But, now, we can't use the gardens and can't get to the animals. Will you help Bob look after them?"

"To the limits of my expertise."

"We brought everything we could carry, and Bob is making trips. If you could do the same, we'd be much, much obliged."

"But, of course."

"There's a big new lock on the front door. The key's under a rock right next to the well."

"I will do what I can."

"Now, we're just cleaning this place up. I don't know if it can be done. It's worse than Hugh Graham's place, and we always said we'd burn that when he went. But we need somewhere to live."

I saw Mr. Selby heading around to the laboratory, shooing the youngest daughter away as one would a lonely stray dog.

"Is Ella not helping?" I asked her mother.

"Oh, yes, she's worked all afternoon. We're giving her a respite. She likes to run around in the woods looking at plants. Since her sisters are plighted, she's too much by herself."

Despite my decision about Susannah, this cool, easy reference to betrothal stopped my breath for an instant. I felt pent in and airless. The family, and the slopes of the tiny hollow, and the close-ranked trees, and the darkness, and the grey-clad men were suddenly walls ringing me round, confining me. How had I become so trapped? I could not remain passive.

One wall, at least, I could breach. Then, first, I began to consider a serious role in Mr. Selby's insurgency. What I could accomplish without resorting to a shield, I did not know. I would do much for the cause, however, if I only spurred him to act. We had five stones. It was enough for a start. And he spent all his energies trying fruitlessly to make more. We did not have the time.

"I must speak with Mr. Selby," I said abruptly and walked off unceremoniously.

He had attained the laboratory door and was easing it shut against Ella.

"If I might have a minute of your time," I said.

He ushered me past the girl and barred the door. "That should hold her. What is it, Monsieur Grimouville?"

"It is essential to move at once against the seseshes."

He shrugged. "We've talked that to death, and I don't judge that anything has changed. We do not have the men or the stones or the weapons. If we were better off on any one of those counts, I would say good, let's go."

"What have you done to improve our affairs?"

"*Our* affairs? Do you mean to say you are with us?"

"I see no alternative. The situation is too dire."

"Welcome then, sir!"

He straightened and thrust his hand at me. I took it, diffidently, and we shook.

"But, I ask, what have you done?"

"I have spoken with all the men I trust and deem capable. They were all prompt to throw in with us. We are seven, with you. I have located another revolver besides Josh's. I have asked for more from Somerset, but that hangs on many contingencies. And we have yet but five stones."

"You have made no progress with the box?"

"Notional progress. Promising, nonetheless."

"Will we have the substantial variety soon?"

His eyes twitched sideways. "Perhaps. I would explain, but I wouldn't want to burden your patience."

"Mr. Selby, I truly desire to make amends for my rudeness. I have never had the social graces that seem to come without effort even to the common man, let alone those expected in one of my rank. I can only plead an indisposition that rendered any communication tedious to me at that moment. You know that I share your fondness for the sciences."

He took my hand again and clapped my back. "I didn't feel slighted. It's just that I'm apt to go on about the things I'm interested in and forget about the poor people listening. It hasn't done me good, and I've tried to rein myself in, but I always end up talking to Bunkum. It pains me."

"I am ready now to hear all."

Here I will leave it, however. It will be an effort to set down faithfully all that he then said, and the shadows are growing short. I am to be busy today as agriculturalist and spy and nurse.

Pulaski County, Kentucky, U. S. A., 5 October 1861

The Armstrong place is burned to the ground. Small ribbons of smoke still curled up from spots when I was there, but the destruction is complete. The gardens have been stripped and the animals are gone.

I am not yet expected at the dark house on the creek, and I will not hurry there. When I go, I will take all that I have of importance with me.

Stirling is now a camp. No one save the Elder Bell and I will go there, and the atmosphere is so poisonous that I would not go by preference. Soldiers follow one's every step with hostile, porcine eyes.

It is not safe—all restraint is going. Corporal Guildford told me, shamefaced, that a girl has been violated by several of their men. I learned from Mrs. Taylor, whom I met on my way to Mr. Graham's, that it was young Rachael Halliday, who lives with her aged aunt east of the town. The corporal continues to probe me with questions. What he wants to find, I cannot guess.

I learned nothing in the town beyond that. That left only one errand on my list—to look in on Mr. Graham. He was not well the day before yesterday when I went there to ask after Mr. Selby. He said nothing, but it was evident in his manner and speech. But, I could not tarry then.

He strengthened in the night, it seems, like all bad things. He was as hale as ever when I first arrived. The call turned merely social, an echo of the old days of summer.

I informed him of all that has happened. "Well," he said, "now you're seeing government in the raw. They're not doing anything a state doesn't do every day. They're just not being as discreet about it."

"Most states also provide some benefit."

"Well, these fellows are protecting you from the Yankees, aren't they? Have you seen any of them around here, lately? Pretty good service, in that regard, I'd say."

I was too fatigued, in body and mind, to rise to the bait. "Are you still to sit here, unconcerned, while this goes on around you?"

"If I've never even bothered to shoot at a politician, why should I muddy my hands with this little lieutenant of yours and his jackals?"

"Should you not, at least, look to your own security?"

"You see the guns. If they choose to involve me, then I will get involved."

"A primitive's philosophy." But I smiled resignedly.

"Not philosophy, as I've told you. Part of the heritage and tradition of my people. We leave other people alone and we expect the same courtesy in return."

"Unless the other people have land that you want. Indians or Irishmen, say."

He sighed. "We could stand more consistency."

"But then you would have a political philosophy, like it or not."

"Maybe." He pulled the jug toward him. "I always thought of a philosophical problem as one that goes away if you don't think about it."

We drank quietly.

"I have given thought to what you said about the beauty of greatness," he said after some minutes. "It seems to me that my folk always have had a philosophy of beauty. It's just that we admire freedom more than power. It's a manlier take on things, I would argue."

He was slurring his words. I have never known alcohol to affect him in a perceptible way. Perhaps it is a mark of the illness.

"Manlier? What is more masculine than striving for grandeur and ascendancy?"

"For who? Or, whom? Unless you're sitting at the top, you're just making yourself more a slave the grander and more powerful you make your leader."

"But, the greatness of the leader redounds upon the nation. I am a Frenchman—I have a share in the greatness and glory of France."

"If you say so. It seems to me that fighting for another man and helping him get power is just a way of looking for a master. Do you feel more a man with this Napoleon of yours on the throne?"

I spat a mouthful of the whiskey on the table. "Do you feel more a man with this Lincoln of yours?" This made a sort of sense to me at the time, although, at the present moment, as I write this, I could not say how.

My host was certainly puzzled. "I don't see..."

My fit of temper passed as suddenly as it had come, and I smiled again, weakly. I waved away the question. "It is no matter. You touched a wound."

"I'm sorry. If you think I was casting aspersions on France..."

"No, no."

"But, if you did, I have to admit that Americans have developed the same taste for servitude."

"Or, always had it. You have not convinced me that your Westerners are the true soul of America."

"Who, would you say, early on, was fond of strong central governments meddling in their lives? Not us, not the Puritans, not the Quakers. There's been a change."

His speech was growing swiftly less distinct.

"It doesn't matter, though," he said. "Maybe we're the soul or maybe we're not. But we were here before the United States or the Confederacy, and they can deal with us on our terms or have trouble. They can't just change the conditions we agreed to when we accepted the Constitution. They can't just start a war and use that as an excuse to do away with freedom of speech or assembly, like they've done, or lock people away whenever they want. We didn't back down at Londonderry, and we didn't back down for Hamilton's whiskey tax, and we won't keep backing down now."

"*You* may not back down. I fear, with the change of which you speak, that you may be alone in your defiance."

He vomited.

"Mr. Graham, are you ill? You did not seem well yesterday."

"I'm not any sicker than usual. Just got started on the drinking early."

"Is there anything I can do for you?"

"No, but I think you'd better go. I'm not going to be much company till I get my legs again."

So, in the end, I was useless as stockman and farmer and nurse. I do not know that my *reconnaissance* duties yielded much beyond a sense that the town should be avoided.

I know what Hamilton's whiskey tax was, and I know of the war against it. What my books have is this: In the early 1790's, Alexander Hamilton, the Secretary of the Treasury, managed to get an excise tax passed on alcohol. The ostensible purpose was to help pay the national debt, but Hamilton is known to have wanted it more as an instrument of social discipline than a source of revenue. The tax was designed to spare large Eastern distillers as much as possible—they paid a flat fee that was small in comparison to their incomes. It fell heaviest on small home producers on the frontier in Pennsylvania, Kentucky, and the southern states, as was intended. These producers were to pay a higher tax based on volume. Firms with connections to the new government were thus favored in competition.

Settlers in the frontier regions had great difficulty in getting their grain to market except by distilling it into a relatively portable form. Lacking money, they also tended to use whiskey as a medium of exchange. Apart from the burden the tax imposed, however, excise taxes had been a traditional target of hatred both in Britain and the Americas and had a role in the discontent that led to the Revolution.

Though protests were common in all the affected areas, only in western Pennsylvania were attempts made to collect the excise. This is because only in Pennsylvania were there wealthy individuals willing to act as tax collectors. When the protests became armed rebellion in western Pennsylvania, federal troops were sent to suppress the uprising and enforce collection. However, no one outside of Pennsylvania ever bothered to pay the excise.

The rebellion helped in the decline of Hamilton's Federalist Party. Jefferson repealed the tax in 1803.

Given the time and places concerned, I have to concede that this was a war between the Ulster Scots and the federal government. And the Scots appear to have won, in the end. I knew a little of this, and I knew the importance of whiskey in the lives of Mr. Graham's people, but I had never seen the tie between the two. Whiskey is not simply a drink—it is a sacrament.

Susannah holds that the offense in drunkenness is its abuse of a gift. She says that this is the common view. A gift from whom? Around here, it is an article of faith that Kentucky whiskey—"bourbon"—was invented by a Baptist preacher. Mr. Graham tells me that Virginians had the same beverage and ascribed it to an Episcopal priest. He is of two minds about this.

Of Londonderry I know nothing. He could very well mean the one in Ireland, but this is no aid.

I could not write last night. I was tired but, more, I think I was afraid of leaving further hostages to fortune (to steal from Bacon). My notes and the earlier installments of this journal are hidden, but they would vanish, all the same, in a general conflagration. All will go with me to the hiding place on the creek.

Pulaski County, Kentucky, U. S. A., 6 October 1861

Our sanctuary is full to bursting. The cabin that barely housed one inert old man must make do for five people and a hulking hound. Susannah and I are lodged in the laboratory over Ella's appeal to priority. After so much time alone, I cannot sleep in a crowd. The barracks at the Quai d'Orsay afforded more solitude.

The innocent indifference to nudity also distresses me. It inducts me into a private and domestic world of which I am not yet happily a part. It is like an unwanted embrace. Mr. Selby has accepted his fate and does not mind a particle, but I still feel the itch of independence.

The younger girls and Mrs. Armstrong sleep on blankets beside the bed, which has been reserved by unanimous consent for Toodie and Mr. Selby. The family will stay warm in these cold nights even without the fire. Susannah and I sleep near a stove that must have been used more as an apparatus than a source of heat.

We have gathered all the readable books that were found and keep them with us in the laboratory. Mr. Bromfield's tastes or opportunities were indiscriminate. We have Cooper's *Last of the Mohicans*, a French edition of *Manon Lescaut*, Elizabeth Barrett Browning's *Sonnets from the Portuguese*, a ragged and greasy copy of *Frankenstein*, and four volumes of Josephus.

I shall have to translate the Prévost. I have told Susannah that it is a cautionary and improving tale, particularly fitting for her. The Shelley book I have told her was greatly admired by Sir Walter Scott and that she should read it by herself when alone. The poems I have glanced through just now but never read before. The Cooper I have read but would not mind reading again. And we have the Josephus, which will fill time if I can overcome my abhorrence of the man. The collection as a whole is not the worst with which we could have been enisled.

Taken all in all, our situation will not be disagreeable so long as our supplies hold out. That is the rub. We have a store of salt pork and apples and whiskey and alcoholic cider and such vegetables as still grew when these people last saw their gardens. It is only such a store as Mr. Selby could lay in, however, before he felt pressed to move the family. They carried some possessions on their backs in their flight. It was assumed that the young man and I could bring more little by little, but this hope has been incinerated. Nevertheless, we have sufficient unto a number of days.

Still, despondency reigns in our tiny commonwealth. When I informed them what had become of their home, Mrs. Armstrong merely remarked that freezes would soon have put an end to growing, and that mostly roots and pumpkins were left, anyway. She will not talk about the house, though, and she wears her face like a mask. The girls are not so stoic.

Susannah is bearing up the best—in the presence of the others. In private, it is clear she is heartbroken. She has never spent more than a night in any other house.

She is sleeping now, at last. She did not rest well last night.

"And everything is gone?" she asked before her weariness finally overcame her. She has asked more than once. "Nothing at all was left?"

"Perhaps there is something in the ashes," I answered yet once again. "But it is not safe to search yet."

She misses the animals, not all of whom were destined for the table. Most had names. That she knows they are to be killed makes their theft infinitely worse, of course.

"And I'll never see the bobcat again. Or its kittens."

"There will be other bobcats."

"But I had looked forward to them so. I knew how my life was to go, at least for the near while, and now it's just disappeared. It's like losing a part of my self, a part of my body."

I had nothing to say.

She cried for a time, her face hidden in her palms. Then, she said something too muffled to hear.

"What?"

"I said, we need music. Bob has his guitar. I saw it. It's all that will pull us out of this."

"I do not know that the others would welcome that, right now."

"No, they wouldn't. Perhaps by tomorrow, though. *I* need it, of a certainty."

"Is Mr. Selby that good?"

"He's terrible," she sniffled. The coincidence of words and emotion made me laugh despite myself, but it had a good effect. She slapped at me with a frail and teary smile.

"So," I said. "Very, very terrible."

"No, not that terrible. But he makes mistakes and he can't keep time by himself. Someone has to sing or dance or stamp on the floor."

"If it will help, I am sure he will volunteer. The three of us can draw in the others."

"It would almost cure me, I think. It's like liquor to me, or henbane, or church. But so much better."

I looked at her quizzically, but she did not see.

"When it's right, I feel almost part of God, and everything mean and silly about life falls away. And never quite comes back."

"Then we should talk to Mr. Selby, by all means."

The thought consoled her sufficiently that she was willing to lie down on the layer of blankets and close her eyes and drowse away. I have put out all lights except here in the colder reaches of the laboratory. My fingers are stiff, now, and my toes are numbed, and I think I shall join her.

Pulaski County, Kentucky, U. S. A., 7 October 1861

Mr. Selby left before Susannah awakened, so we shall have to await his return. It is his turn to do intelligence work, scouting out Stirling and assembling news from townspeople he can still find. He will also try to learn how things stand with regard to food generally. Someone may have concealed a stock they would be willing to share.

He has been "stumped," as he puts it, by the box. His guess as to why it does not operate is a very likely one, but it has not cleared the path to a solution. But, I realize I have not given the account of his reasoning that I promised.

His discourse ran thus: "My error has been to wonder why the device no longer functions. I should have been wondering how it functioned to start with. It does something, and that takes energy. Energy has to come from somewhere. I missed that, somehow—I think I was so dazzled by it that I was willing to suspend my scientific expectations. I was approaching it like some sort of magical phenomenon. Your influence, perhaps."

I smiled indulgently.

"The way I got on to this was that I was thinking about how the shields would have to work if light is actually little corpuscles, little bodies. Why do some bodies get through and others don't? As I was telling you and Hugh, it has to be either size or speed. Molecules of air don't get in, so either the barrier filters out anything that big or it's the high speed of the light particles that gets them through.

"So, how would that last one work? Well, there's this new notion called 'potential energy.' Say you have something moving against a force. You throw a rock in the air, maybe, and gravity is pulling it down. You give it kinetic energy—energy of movement—but that seems to run out at a certain height and the rock stops going up. Where did the energy go? It can't just disappear. Well, it's stored, in a way. It's stored as potential energy, the energy that will make it move back down."

"Stored where?"

He pursed his lips. "Well, in the whole arrangement."

"But where in the arrangement?"

"That question doesn't make any sense. The arrangement's one thing."

"No, it's not. It's me and the rock and gravity and space."

He thought. "Then the arrangement is that collection of things, and a collection is one thing."

"In what part of the collection is the energy stored?"

"It's not in a part." His sibilant fairly sizzled, and he stopped, embarrassed. He does not often display a temper.

"Never mind," I said. "I think I take your meaning. When you say it is stored in the arrangement, you just mean that it is not showing for the moment, but is not gone and has the possibility of reappearing. Oh— *potential*—now I see."

"Exactly. And it reappears as kinetic energy when the rock falls."

"But, how does this help?"

"I got to thinking. What would stop things that are moving a certain speed but not things moving faster? Well, something like gravity that doesn't actually put up an obstruction to stop things dead but does drain away kinetic energy. If you had enough momentum to start with, you could get through. I would think the energy would be restored on the other side of the barrier.

"But, then I got to thinking, why don't things that are stopped by the barrier come back with the same velocity? They should look like they're bouncing off, and they don't. They just drop. The energy has to be going somewhere.

"I tested it and it's not going into heat, as far as I can tell. The shield has to be storing it, I thought, the way a voltaic pile or a Daniell cell stores electricity. Why, though? Then, the obvious finally occurred to me: the shield needs energy to function. It doesn't have to be storing it—it just has to be using it. I don't think the stones are big enough for anything functional to be inside, so I don't think any storage is going on. But the shields could power themselves from the energy they take from objects hitting them."

"And they would get enough from occasional impacts?"

"I wondered about that. Probably not. They are, however, being struck by molecules of air the entire time they are operating. That might very well be sufficient."

He stopped and smiled in pure, proud joy.

"You believe this is the key to reanimating the box?" I said to nudge him along his way.

The joy abruptly gave way to embarrassment. "Not exactly...this was just the train of thought that led me to consider the matter of power. If the stones must have power, so, too, must the box. And the box does not receive it immediately from its surroundings, else there would be no reason for it to cease functioning. There has been no noteworthy change in its environs. The box is large enough, though, that something like a battery of cells may well be concealed in its interior."

"Which you cannot reach."

"Which I cannot reach."

"Could you recharge the cell through the material of the box?"

"It is nonconductive. Besides, I have no cause to believe electricity is involved—I am only using that as an analogy."

He has advanced no further since that conversation. He may, I am afraid, already have capitulated. If so, our purposes are vain if I cannot win him to my strategy.

Pulaski County, Kentucky, U. S. A., 8 October 1861

Mr. Selby returned in the evening uncommonly agitated. "They have been capturing and shooting blockade runners," he informed me. "Harry Carruthers and Tom Fenwick are dead, at least. I was told there were others. We're now cut off completely unless we're prepared to use the shields and brazen our way through."

"That could well betray our one advantage," I said. "I am afraid we have no choice but to use the stones we have in a surreptitious campaign."

"You're as eager for them now as you were afraid of them before."

"I am still fearful of what they represent. I shall not be wielding one."

"Then you may not be much use to us."

"We shall see."

This voiced more confidence than I felt. To be frank, I have still no clear idea of what I might be able to do. If he had demanded anything specific, I would have made a feeble showing.

Instead, he looked sad. "We may have to see, for certain sure. It's going hard for everyone hereabout. I asked after provisions, and no one has any to speak of. We're better supplied out here than most families near town. Our visitors have scraped this country clean."

"So, something must be done."

"Yes, and your plan is the only one we have. I'll muster the men we have tomorrow and instruct them in how to use the shields. I don't look forward to that—who knows how anyone will respond to the things."

"We shall have to retrieve Mr. Graham's."

"I already have." He pulled it from his pocket. "He was willing enough. I was afraid he wouldn't be, but he's tickled by the idea. He's in one of his nastier moods. I think his health may finally be broken for good."

"We should bring him out here."

He laughed. "You may broach the subject with him. And good luck. Though, if anyone has food cached somewhere, it would be him. He might do it for the girls' sake if you can appeal to the less bad part of his nature."

"Speaking of the girls," I began, then explained what Susannah wanted.

"That would be nuts to me. Any diversion would be agreeable right now. Have you suggested it to the others?"

"Let us find Susannah, and the three of us together should be able to bring them around."

And we did bring them to a dejected compliance, adequate for our purposes. After dinner, we moved the furniture to the walls to clear a space.

"Who will go first?" asked Mr. Selby, tuning his strings. No one put herself forward.

"Then I will take the lead," he said. "This is something I had forgotten about until I heard one of the soldiers in town sing it just recently. I haven't practiced it, but I believe I can give it a fair shake."

He experimented with chords, then sang a song about a yellow rose of Texas, which everyone seemed to recognize.

"And she is yellow because she is blonde?" I asked.

"No," he said. "'Yellow' means mulatto."

"Why would a Southerner sing that?"

"I haven't a suspicion. Except that it's a pretty tune."

"Well, then," I exclaimed with labored jollity, slapping my palms together. "I *do* have a song about a blonde."

I had spent much time pondering what my contribution might be. My cello is in France, and that left only my voice, which is not up to songs I would have liked to try on them. I had decided, at last, to give them *Auprès de ma blonde*. It succeeded better with the audience than I had hoped, if only for the novelty. Mr. Selby was able to accompany me before the end, and Ella even made a decipherable attempt to help with the chorus.

"Me now! Me!" the latter insisted when I had essayed a translation.

"Fine," said Mrs. Armstrong. "But go outside and spit out that wad before anything else."

When the girl returned, she struck a pose and was about to start when her mother interrupted again. "And not 'Sweet Betsy from Pike.'"

Ella pulled a face. "I know lots worse songs than that."

"And you needn't demonstrate the truth of that."

"Then I'm not going to sing at all."

"You may suit yourself on that."

"I'll go," volunteered Toodie. I believe I was the only one to see the furtive grin she gave her younger sister.

"Susannah says you're interested in the old songs," she said to me as she rose. "This has always been one of my favorites:

> *The maid went to the mill by night.*
> *Hey, Hey, so wanton!*
> *The maid went to the mill by night.*
> *Hey, so wanton she!*

Her mother glowered at her, but she drove on:

> *She swore by all the stars so bright*
> *That she would get her corn ground,*
> *She would get her corn ground,*
> *Mill and multure free!*
>
> *Then out and came the miller's man...*

"Mr. de Grimouville," said Mrs. Armstrong in a very loud voice. "I'm sorry, but I'm going to have to put a stop to this before it goes beyond all bounds. I know my daughters—it will descend into a competition to see who can be the crudest."

"Not all your daughters," objected Susannah. "Not anymore, anyway."

"Then you do something."

"I will." She thought for a moment.

"Do the lover's grave ballad," I requested.

"That's the last thing I feel like singing at present," she said.

"I hate that one, anyway," Ella said. "The idea that she wants to be left alone and unfeeling forever. It's too sad."

"I'll do 'Lorena,'" Susannah decided, and delivered another very sweet song I had not heard before but that Mr. Selby apparently knew well.

The mother then performed a song called "Aura Lee." She sang with the nasality that is favored around here. Susannah seems deliberately to avoid that, thankfully, but even she barely skirts its edges when she is caught up by the music and forgets herself.

Mr. Selby did several instrumental pieces, and, as his dexterity and quickness grew with the playing, the others began to dance. I would not participate at first—I was colder than the others since I had not done anything after my one early offering. I much preferred to sit and wonder again at Susannah's celestial abandon. Soon, however, alcohol (which had made its appearance) allied with the music in seduction and drew me in.

I recall much four-part harmonizing at the end, in which I joined. How, since I did not know the songs, I cannot say, nor do I remember precisely which part I filled. Possibly all of them at some point or another.

As Susannah and I supported each other on our way out to the laboratory, she breathed, "That was it. It exactly."

Pulaski County, Kentucky, U. S. A., 10 October 1861

Perhaps I share the same constitutional resistance to the obvious for which Mr. Selby criticizes himself. I do not intend for the rebels ever to come into possession of these journals, but, should they, there is already enough in them to hang us. I shall bring my account up to the present with this entry. Then, this volume and its predecessors will go into oilskin and a hiding place in the woods. I shall write thereafter nothing but domestic drama until the danger has been removed for good and all.

I started toward the town this morning more to weigh my welcome there than anything else. All useful news would come in my rounds of houses and cabins. I did intend an accidental encounter with Corporal Guildford, if that could be managed. Finding him would be easy—it was the fortuitous aspect that had to be carefully staged. He could not feel that he was being used for information.

Picture my astonishment, therefore, when I encountered his slave Anthony on one of the lanes that leads to the main road. He looked as shocked and pleased as I.

"Mr. de Grimouville!" he cried. "I've been all over these parts trying to find you. Hardly anyone is any help, though—most won't talk to me and the others have sent me on to empty or burnt houses."

"Probably the right houses, then. But, I don't frequent them anymore. Is there something with which I may be of service?"

"Well, first, don't go near the town. You would be risking your freedom or your life. There've been killings."

This was said in a carefully neutral tone, but I caught the appraisal in his eyes.

"I heard about those. People trying to make their way

around to Somerset."

"No. These are our people. Southern boys. The squad guarding the Somerset road was slaughtered to a man and others have been picked off nearer to town. It's happened in the last couple of nights."

Still the same question in his gaze, not quite successfully veiled. A few days later and I might merit that, but Mr. Selby's Irregulars are still being sorted out. The killings were as much a surprise to me as anyone else.

"Was there anything strange about the incidents?"

"Strange? I would say they were strange, all right. Fourteen men gone in the night without a warning. Do you mean stranger than that?"

"Well, I am just wondering how it was done. There are no witnesses?"

"None living."

"Then it is very strange, to be certain. And they are all on the alert, now?"

"On the alert, but that isn't all. The lieutenant is making a list of Union men and bringing them in. You're on the list. You'll be grabbed as soon as you show your face."

"I? How am I a Union man?" This was a waste of words, I knew, but I grudge being placed in easy categories.

"Because you're on the list. Though, I imagine they don't care who they pull in—they're out for blood."

"Who else is on this list?"

"All manner of people. I only recognized Mr. Selby and Mr. Graham because you've talked about them."

"Mr. Graham? What would he know of Mr. Graham?"

"That preacher is telling him who to put on it."

"Elder Bell?"

"That's the one. And you're not safe even here. Patrols are going all over."

"Then I had best go to warn Mr. Graham. Thank you

very much for informing me of this."

"I've already been to his place. He says he knows some place to go. And it's Master Geoffrey who's had me looking for you all." This is Corporal Guilford's given name.

"Give him my thanks as well, if you will be so kind. He is running an unreasonable danger."

"And he wants you to meet with him. Tonight, if you can."

"Where?"

"That's up to you."

"Then..." I remembered a ruin of a cabin, one of those that had fallen into Mr. Graham's hands in the passage of the years. It would not show a light with the windows covered and would give no clue to where I was staying. I gave directions and set a time.

He made to leave, but I saw an opportunity for something I have long wished. "Anthony," I said. "I need to talk to you about something. Unrelated to all of this. What do you know of the slaves in Kentucky?"

"I haven't seen any except me."

This was a disappointment. "Then, would you favor me with an interview on your condition and your experiences?"

"Now? Mr. de Grimouville, it's no time to be out talking with the patrols all around."

"Some time, at least. I am making a study of the American nation and its folk, and I need to know more of your institution."

"Maybe you should talk about that with Master Geoffrey tonight. He can decide."

Mr. Selby was in the laboratory suspending something over a burner. I told him what I had learned and what was arranged

"It isn't our people. I've only just finished demonstrating the shields—and lost some men by doing so—and we haven't even begun to make plans."

He looked up suddenly. "But, I know who it has to be. I've been trying to replace our defectors by going farther afield. Fellows out in the hills that the older set are willing to vouch for. A lot of them saw the elephant in Mexico, and the others all know how to shoot better than they know how to piss. We're up to eight, now, if they all stay by us.

"A couple mentioned that Johnny Elliot's been talking up the idea of forming a company to hunt down and kill rebels one by one or in small groups. Pretty much our proposal, without the shields."

"Perhaps we should discuss alliance."

"He's not reliable. Though, if it *is* him, he's making a bully job of it. That's a quarter of the platoon out of the way. I'd prefer to keep our outfit small and secret, though. Too many already know of the stones—we will have to act hastily enough as it is. It sounds like the Reverend Elder Bell may deserve first honors. I must say, I don't understand how one goes from abolitionist to chief Copperhead in a little over a week."

"I understand it perfectly. It is an old theme on which I observed many variations in my political days. For some men, ideas are only clothing for indecency of the soul. If one wants most that others be controlled, one will don whatever rags best cloak that aim. Abolitionism served him for a time; now, he has found better."

"If that's the truth of it, we should make sure to give him some attention. Tell me tonight what the corporal has to say and we will, at last, form exact plans. I may, as well, have accomplished something here to tell of." He nodded at the box. "Or not."

Susannah and I passed the rest of the day in the woods, searching for a high and open spot from which to view the autumn. We chanced on a slope that took us above all the surrounding hills, into the sunlight. The town was hidden from where we finally stood. The trees have been turning all along, and I have not had time to spare for them.

There must be more varieties of leaf here than all the places I have been. Some leaves were still green. Some were merely yellow. But all glowed in the sun, and, together with the maples' gold and the dogwoods' burgundy and the sumacs' crimson, they made the little hills a tossing, iridescent ocean.

We watched until evening, when the slanting light of October muted the colors. We both felt it as a foretaste of winter. Autumn came early for me this year—earlier than it came to the land. I have been feeling an emptiness in my chest for weeks, as though I have suffered some loss. It is gentle enough that it half pleases, like the bitterness of food or drink. It wears after a time, however. I look forward to the winter, now, and the end that it brings. I think my loss is only the slow dying of things, and that will, at last, be over.

I remember that I like the spring as well, but I have no present desire for its coming and the rebirth it brings. That seems like a cruel promise. The seasons will continue on their way. Still, I know that I shall be ready for spring long before winter ends. I suppose it would be best to stand outside the change and watch it roll by with a dispassionate eye, but each stage in the cycle is too alluring by contrast with the last.

That only leaves acceptance of the changes in all their outward and inward consequences. And making myself content, as the song goes, 'til death calls me away.

Pulaski County, Kentucky, U. S. A.,
12 October 1861

The advantage of being an official enemy of the regime is that there is no point in restricting my writing. The notebooks will remain in hiding in the forest, but I am free to jot down whatever thoughts I please. I would be hanged or shot no less for composing idylls or sermons than the account that is to follow. No one will be named who is not already proscribed or, sadly, dead.

I arrived at our rendezvous early, partly from caution and partly to prepare the place. I found the corporal and Anthony already on hand. The former gave me a scare by clearing his throat in the darkness as I stood in the doorway. I was standing in *silhouette* with the moon more than half full behind me.

"I have a pistol, and I can see you well enough," he said. "Identify yourself."

"Edouard de Grimouville, at your service."

"Sorry for the precaution, but we are engaged in dangerous business."

I had brought blankets and a lantern. "Allow me to cover the windows and I believe we may make a light."

"Certainly. We too have lamps."

The flames showed treacherous looking furniture. We tried some chairs without incident and set the lights on the floor. I laid my hat and stick next to me.

"What have you to tell me?" I asked.

"First, I have done my best to reproduce Lieutenant Edgcombe's list of Union men." He handed me a sheet of paper. "You may examine it now, if you choose, or at better leisure. I offer it as a gesture of good faith."

I could not distinguish names in the shifting glow, so I folded it and put it in my breast. "Thank you very much. They shall be informed."

"They have already—those Anthony could find. Those who are not already in custody."

"Who has been taken?" I queried, alarmed.

"No one I can recognize. There are, though, no less than six, men and women."

"What is to be done with them?"

"I could not say. I fear they may be hanged in reprisal for the Southern dead."

His face was skeletal, the hollows of its gaunt lines filled with shadows that flickered eerily. "There may be time to save them, if you are prepared to act."

"How?"

"That, I must leave to your company."

"My company?"

"Your fighters or troops or however you care to designate them. Those whose hand we have seen at work recently."

"I have nothing to do with that. I do not know whose work that is."

"That is for you to say. But if I have been of use to you at all, I have a favor to ask in return."

I waited, since I could not read his face for cues.

"Anthony has been of more service to you than I," he continued, at last. "It is he who has warned those in peril. I am not free to come and go as I wish, but he can, unregarded. I tell them he is searching for herbs.

"I wish to pass him to the north. This was all my purpose in enlisting—to bring him as near to freedom as I might, to circumstances where he might escape."

I looked at the slave, whose form was as spectral and unfixed as his master's. "But, he is yours to keep or loose. Why not emancipate him in the customary way?"

"He is *not* mine. He is my father's."

"And you disapprove of slavery?"

"Yes, but that is not my motivation." His face was obscured entirely as he bent his head. "Anthony is my natural brother."

He lifted his face again, but it gave me no better sight of his expression.

"How am I to help?"

"You can deliver him to the care of your Northern associates. Tell them how he has assisted the cause."

"I have no Northern associates. We are isolated here."

"Your group is wholly independent of the regular military?"

"Why do you insist I have a group? I have said nothing to suggest that. I am a citizen of France and have no stake in the affairs of other nations. I have, indeed, no right to meddle."

"But you are a Unionist. Sufficiently Unionist to be on that list I have given you. And you have confirmed that in our conversations."

"I have said nothing that might be construed in such a way." That he was right, in every practical sense, was less important to me at the moment than my anger at being catalogued so offhandedly. I fully intended to help him in his venture, but not until my position was made fully clear.

"You are not for the Union?"

"Do you hear me only now? I have said as much every time we have talked."

"Then, you are a Confederate!"

"I am not a Confederate. I cannot be a Confederate. It would be meaningless for me to be a Confederate."

"You are a Confederate, and I have betrayed myself!"

He leapt to his feet, overturning his chair. Anthony, as startled as I was, rose and backed away. My attention diverted by that, I did not see that the corporal had drawn his pistol until it was almost too late.

I fell, attempting to get up too quickly, my leg entangled in the chair, but this put my walking stick in reach. I grasped it and swung at his legs. He evaded me and fired. I felt no pain, but my left arm was jolted. I made it to my feet, only distantly aware that the limb was hanging slackly at my side.

His weapon empty and useless, he threw it at me. I

dodged and assumed a position *en garde.* I supposed that both men were threats. Anthony was farther from me, so I went for the corporal, cutting at his head. I scored and, while he was stunned, moved so that he was between me and his brother. Then, I simply clubbed him, inelegantly and brutally.

He did not go down, but I did not know what weapons the other might have on him, so I took the opportunity to dash for the door and out. I did not really expect them to pursue, but, looking back as I reached the dirt lane that would take me downhill, I saw first Anthony and then the corporal emerge and begin to run after me.

I ran to where trees almost choked the path, thinking to turn into the woods and make my flight under cover of the vegetation. A long series of gun blasts doubled my speed. When I attained my goal, I hid behind a large trunk and glanced back again, puzzled by the number of shots. Corporal Guildford was lying prone, and Anthony had his hands in the air.

Figures glided from the forest. One placed a hand in Anthony's back and thrust him to the ground. Another knelt by the still body and felt its throat. "Got him," he said.

He stood and, facing the spot where I thought myself concealed, waved his arms as if signaling. I listened, without moving, for any sound around me. There was none. I withdrew as silently as I could into the trees.

"Duke!" the man called in a muffled shout.

They have mistaken me for a comrade, I thought, and continued to back into cover.

"Duke!" he cried more forcefully, and this time the voice sounded familiar.

"Yes, this is Duke!" I responded, still careful. "Who is that?"

"It's me, Johnny!"

It was, as I had hoped, Johnny Elliot.

I came out and walked toward the cluster of men.

When I was close enough to speak at a normal volume, I said, "I am not really Duke. I am Edouard de Grimouville."

"I thought you were some kind of Duke."

I did not take the time to disentangle the matter. "Is that gentleman alive?"

"He's cold as a wagon tire."

"Pardon?"

"He's dead."

I was torn between gratitude and horror. "Did you shoot him for a Confederate?"

"And to save your hide. But, we're out to hunt rebels and we would have taken him down, anyway."

I hated to undeceive them, but Anthony would tell them if I did not. "That man was no rebel. Not truly." I explained all that had happened.

They helped the slave up, and he snatched his arms from theirs and dropped to his brother's side, where he searched for signs of life. Finding none, he simply sat. He did not weep, but stared blankly into the night.

There were four men with Mr. Elliot, of whom I only recognized Mr. Daniel Shays Routledge, and he more by a missing piece of ear than anything else. I have heard that it was bitten away in a wrestling match.

Their leader introduced me with "This is the Duke. I can warrant him. He's the one who cleaned Elder Bell's plow a while back."

This brought radiant approval into faces thitherto closed and wary.

"I'm no end sorry," said Mr. Routledge. "I was the one who got in the killing shot."

This was disputed by a swarthy individual who appeared part Indian, but Mr. Routledge refused to be interrupted. "We didn't have any way of knowing. He's wearing a uniform and he was chasing someone dressed like one of ours."

I have submitted to wearing the late Mr. Armstrong's

clothing. Most that I have still presentable of my own is in the leather trunk in my rooms in Somerset. The engraving on the nameplate will suggest where to send them if I do not survive to recover them.

Mr. Routledge put his hand on Anthony's shoulder. "Not that that'll be any consolation to you. If we'd known, this never would have happened in a million years. I can't say how sorry I am."

Anthony shook the hand off and raised his head, but gave no reply. His face remained immobile, but I did not like the eyes he set on his brother's slayer.

"You're hurt," Mr. Elliot suddenly noticed. My coat was dark, but the left sleeve, I saw now, was darker still. I felt, and it was wet with blood, starting at the upper arm, where the wound showed through.

They made me take off my coat and shirt, and the aboriginal-looking gentleman examined me by feel, provoking shameful moans I could not suppress. "It's still bleeding a little, but it didn't hit the bone. Took out a chunk of muscle. It needs to be sewn."

"Does it need to be sewn *now*?" asked his captain.

"No," the other answered, to my relief. "We can wrap it and send him on."

While a piece of my shirt was being wound around my bicep, I asked about their plans for the night.

"Just going near town to patrol for strays," Mr. Elliot said. "We haven't been able to catch a group off guard since we did for the pickets on the road."

"You know that they have captured a number of people and plan to hang them in vengeance for that."

"Well, then, we'll have to do something. Where are they deposited?"

"Anthony there may know. They are from a list of suspected Unionists the corporal gave me."

"Who's on it?"

"I shall have to wait until I have the light to read it. I am, I am told. I shall make a copy and get it to you."

"*Anthony*, is it?" he asked the seated man gently. It seemed that Anthony would take no notice, but he nodded finally.

"Do you have any idea where the captives are?"

"They've strung wire behind the headquarters and watch over them there. There's a whole squad on that duty."

"We've handled a squad." He thought for a few seconds. "We're going to send you home with the Duke. Sounds like we have a night ahead of us."

I still felt no actual pain from my wound. It was coming, I knew, and I dreaded it in a distant way, not knowing how severe it would be. My emotions had been anaesthetized as well by the shock of my shooting and the death of Corporal Guildford. Yet, I was also energized by the events, and in a humor for action. Someone was doing something, and I was present to partake in it.

"If you have an additional firearm, I ask to accompany you. I am not a bad hand with guns."

"That's a bad hole you've got. You may not feel so keen in a few minutes. And where is Anthony to go?"

"He may come with us. They are as much or more his foes as ours."

"Can you shoot?" Mr. Routledge asked the slave.

"I can."

"Are you going to shoot *me*, if we give you a gun?"

"Not tonight."

"Then, let them come," he advised his leader. "And I think we have something that will keep the Duke on his feet."

The one who had bound my arm opened his pack and extracted a vial and a small, rounded metal case. From the latter, he removed and assembled what I could identify as a Pravaz injector (another French invention, it should be noted). He inserted the needle into the vial and screwed the knob at the end of the apparatus. Then, he stabbed my arm with it and reversed the direction of the twist. In a very brief time, I felt utterly marvelous.

One of the men sang, in a whisper, "Twenty-five cents for whiskey, fifteen cents for beer, twenty-five cents for morphine, going to take you away from here."

I was handed a musket pistol and powder and shot. To Anthony, Mr. Elliot said, "If you want to bury your brother now, we're going to have to leave you to it. Otherwise, let's hide him and set a time to come back. You take his gun."

"I'll do it by myself," he was answered. "Help me put him under just shallow, and I will see to the rest tomorrow. I don't want animals tearing him."

They were impatient to be off, but could not, in decency, refuse. There was no spade or shovel, so they used their hands and stacked as many rocks as they could find on the mound.

What transpired then, I will record in my next entry. Now, I must begin to fortify myself with as much strong drink as I can tolerate. I am suppurating, and Mrs. Armstrong has scant praise for "laudable pus." She is convinced she lost a brother to that teaching and is determined to cauterize my wound with a heated iron. I have heard of this being done with good effect, and I have lived long enough to know to avoid medical orthodoxy.

Pulaski County, Kentucky, U. S. A.,
13 October 1861

Scarring from the injury itself and from the burning may affect the extent to which I can move my arm. I cannot tell, thus far, because pain discourages the experiment. I am worried more by the difficulty I have even with slighter movements, like wriggling my fingers or bending my elbow. The response is slow and limited. Some conduit of communication may have been cut.

Then, again, I am a deity to all females in our household. I must remember, should I turn out a cripple, always to arrange that women know why. That— with an able right arm—may compensate.

I have had the leisure to read the corporal's catalogue. It contains most of those I know, if only through word of mouth. All in seclusion here by the creek are on it, down to young Ella. All in Mr. Selby's corps are listed. Messrs. Elliot and Routledge are on it, though not the others of their band whose names I learned. Their persons and residences were most likely too remote from the cognizance of the good and pious Elder. I will not name them—even the dead, lest they had families.

The Taylors' inclusion I would have guessed from their presence in the stockade (as I am about to tell). Toodie's friend Miss Percina Johnstone was also there. John Foster was not, but is on the register.

Of those I would not have known by sight and cannot say if they survive are Mr. Arthur Crozier and his wife, Toodie's piano teacher, and poor Miss Rachael Halliday, the victim of the soldiers' bestiality.

All other names are outside my ken. I would have seen some of their persons, though, the other night.

We forsook all open paths long before nearing the town. The others could go noiselessly among the trees. Anthony (perhaps I can say, now, Mr. Guildford) and I were not so skilled. We exasperated them, first, with the sounds we could not help making and, then, by the slower pace we had to adopt.

Messrs. Elliot and Routledge, frequenters of the town, knew how best to approach it, and took us where the forest crept down closest to the rear of the postmaster's old house behind the headquarters. I had been told this was used as a stable and barracks both, and it may still have been that, but the light of torches and of the waxing moon showed that the area in front was a prison yard. Posts had been driven at intervals between the two structures, and wire strung.

We stopped right before the ground dropped off quickly to the buildings below. Not many guards were visible, but we knew the whole platoon was at hand and could be called to repel an attack. Aside from the new squad that barred the way to Somerset, the troops had all withdrawn to this place as an encampment when it became clear that scattered groups could be murdered in the night. This held the sole benefit for us that we met no patrols—they were relying on lookouts atop buildings to guard the whole.

"This might be impossible, few as we are," said one of the men.

"We can't make an open fight of it," Mr. Elliot conceded. "But, if we can pick off the right sentries without rousing the others, we should be able to sneak a couple of men in to cut the prisoners out and lead them up here. The rest of us can fire to cover them. Once they're all in the woods, it doesn't matter how many come after us—we'll have the whip hand. And I don't think these rebels will risk coming in here in the dark, anyway."

I estimated we were three hundred English yards or more from the stockade. "Can you possibly hit anything at this distance?" I inquired.

"You haven't seen a long rifle spit, if you can ask that," said the man I thought part Indian. "I can hit a tree at twice this distance, with luck and calm weather."

I had not seen one fired, though I had inspected Mr. Graham's and the one Mr. Selby found in the old alchemist's house. They are monstrously long but beautifully and ornately fashioned, as much art as weapon. All in our party carried one, except for Mr. Guildford and me.

Mr. Routledge said, "I think I've got them all spotted—the ones on top. There's an even half-dozen, and they're all facing in different directions. Two on the near building, two on the post office, and two on that tall house on the other side of the street. I can't swear there aren't more, lying too still to catch, but, once the ones going down the hill start, we can manage those six and it'll give us a good chance."

"How are they to get through the wire?" I asked.

The man could not answer, perceptibly confounded, but my dark physician said, "I have snips. I've been carrying them just in case we met a fence that needed getting through."

He and another were sent to the edge of the trees. They were to signal when they were ready and race to the captives as soon as the remaining three fired. It was unfortunate that only half of the sentries could be eliminated at a time, but I was assured that the riflemen could reload and aim accurately in a space of seconds.

"If we had some covering noise, this would be just right," Mr. Elliot commented as he allotted targets. "We'll just have to act quickly and hope it throws them. Take your near men first."

We saw a hand glint in the moonlight. "Right. Get ready to lay the lead to them, at my mark." He paused. "Fire!"

The reports were almost coincident. As promised, another volley followed hard on the first.

I could see a figure dancing on the roof of the farthest house. "I didn't get a clean shot," muttered Mr.

Routledge. He loaded and fired again, but it was too late. The sound of the man's screams finished traveling the space between even as we saw him fall.

Our men were still trying to reach the buildings when a general alarm began. "Go!" hissed our leader. "You and Anthony go!"

We took our pistols in our hands and stumbled out of the trees and down the slope. I heard a shot somewhere to our front, but the two preceding us continued unharmed. I saw them attain their goal and disappear in the shadow of the postmaster's house.

"Go around the other way," panted Mr. Guildford, pointing to the right side of the structure. "I think they went around the left. We don't want to concentrate ourselves."

As we completed our own transit and crouched in the grass by an old, untended fence, we heard the shouting of several men and then a series of shots. We looked at each other and waited. "Let me fire first," he said. "I can't load fast, and we can't afford to both be empty."

More shots came from the far side, where we believed the others had gone. "Let us move forward," I proposed. "Our comrades have drawn their attention, and we may catch them unawares."

He nodded, surprisingly to me, and we eased our way slowly to the face of the building itself and toward the front. At the corner, I peered around and was dismayed by the number of grey uniforms to be seen. The civilians —perhaps eight in total—were there in their enclosure, grouped as far from the activity as the wire allowed. I noted Percina Johnstone and the Taylors.

I hissed, "Look, but be careful."

He did so, taking longer about it than I thought wise, then withdrew his head. "One of ours is down," he told me. "I can see him lying in a heap. I didn't see the other, but they seem to think he's still about."

"What shall we do?" I asked.

He shrugged.

There was another shot and a cry. "That is one of theirs," I guessed. I looked around again and verified this—a soldier was thrashing in the dirt like a landed fish. I also saw three Confederates run toward the street.

"I think some are coming around our way," I said.

We began to edge away when there were three cracks afar off. In a second came a loud groan, almost comical—like a stage ghost's—from the rebel position. Hurriedly, I moved up again and saw three more soldiers down.

I could not remark on this before there was activity on our side of the headquarters. The soldiers who had gone around were coming in our direction. We froze, but one of them raised a musket and fired, cutting a furrow in the wall by Mr. Guildford's knee. We fell back as promptly as we might, and they broke into a run.

Another triad of cracks from the hills, a delay, and two of our attackers convulsed and dropped. Mr. Guildford sighted his gun and shot. I saw the third rebel's cap leave his head, and his skull showed white for an instant through the tear in his scalp as he fell. He was not out of the battle, however, but rose again and trained his weapon on us.

I had expected to hesitate if ever life presented me with such a development. In the event, the drug still exercised its benumbing virtue, and I shot without a thought for the personality forever extinguished by that act.

The others were now aware of our presence. Seen, I threw myself behind a stack of wood a few feet from the house and in the open. Balls slapped into the logs but those protected me well enough. My companion remained in the spot by the corner. I could hear their reinforcements coming and knew that our mission would not succeed. We could not try to leave, however, without finding a way to inform our man.

Suddenly, Lieutenant Edgcombe's gelatinous voice

rose above the din. "Whoever you are, if you do not show yourselves and surrender, I will order that a prisoner be killed!"

We recharged and reloaded our pistols, not willing to make the decision, leaving it to our fellow on the other side of the house. There was no response from that quarter, however.

"I will give the order for execution!" the lieutenant shouted. "Sergeant, shoot one of the prisoners."

A sergeant rested his gun on one of the wire strands and aimed into the cluster of civilians. He pulled the trigger and Pastor Taylor's head blossomed like a red flower.

"I am not jesting! I will give you thirty seconds more, and then I will kill another!"

"I can get him," I hissed to Mr. Guildford.

"Not yet. You can't tell what they would do."

The time expired and Percina began to cry. "Shoot the bawler," the lieutenant ordered. The sergeant shot her quickly and cleanly through the heart, perhaps moved by a remnant of decency.

Three shots again sounded from above. The sergeant was thrown against a post and sank slowly, his fingers grasping and then losing hold of a wire. Another soldier sprawled backwards and lay quiet. I saw Lieutenant Edgcombe's coat twitch, but he stood unharmed.

"Kill them all, then!" he roared, and the men around him proceeded to slaughter the rest of the hostages. Mrs. Taylor raised her face, tight-lipped and defiant, to the one who took responsibility for her, and died with no mark of fear.

Mr. Guildford ran to the rear of the building and looked to where safety lay. When he came back, he said, "Mr. de Grimouville, I think I can see that gentleman who was here with us lying dead about thirty feet up the slope. He must have taken a ball early on and crawled there. They can't see him from their angle."

"*Merde.* We had best make our retreat."

Those above fired once more, and, not waiting to see the result, I used the distraction to regain the side of the house. Then we sprinted to where our man's body lay, unmistakably dead, and then up into the darkness.

We did not look back, but shots continued from ahead of us until we were back with our fellows. True to our leader's prediction, they did not pursue us into the forest.

Mr. Guildford is lodged with Mr. Elliot, who volunteered to help him with his brother. They have seen to that by now, I assume. By the time I made it home, the pain in my arm was asserting itself dramatically.

I have told the women some of what happened.

Pulaski County, Kentucky, U. S. A.,
15 October 1861

I am taking what little freedom I have to recuperate, both bodily and otherwise. The pain of the injury is abating, though the arm does not look healthy. Red streaks branch out from the wound, and I suspect we did not thwart the infection. There may be an abscess under the searing. Mrs. Armstrong promises to slice me open and burn me again if I do not heal.

The reaction to the killing has commenced. I am hardly anguished—and, certainly, I do not suffer from guilt—but, in this way, too, I fester under cover. I feel a bursting sadness, virtually physical, that never quite succeeds in breaking through. It will mend itself in time, I trust.

I use drink for an analgesic, and the days go quickly. In the evenings, I join the family in their amusements. Since we have been here, this has often consisted of one or another of the girls reading the Cooper book to the others, but, as often, they play singing and dancing games. One song concerns an Irish pig; another is called "Skip to My Love." One is about "Killiecrankie," which sounds Scottish to me. I have Toodie making a collection of lyrics and tunes.

Much time, day and night, has been spent making quilts and blankets. These are impressive in their workmanship. Some of the dyes they have manufactured themselves from trees and use in tartan patterns. These will be blessings as the temperature keeps dropping, but Mr. Selby and I have taken cigars and a pack of cards to the laboratory when this was all the evening's entertainment.

He is in there now. It is the middle of the afternoon, and he has been there since breakfast, alone. I was dismayed to find how much he has told the Armstrongs. They know of the shields. They know much about our plans. They have been insulated from most of what has happened outside our nest (he assures me). Susannah sees the shields as confirmation of her nastiest misgivings about Mr. Bromfield, but the other girls have been helping him with his inquiries.

"They would have learned all in time—they will learn the worst in time—and I need assistants," he offered in justification. "I needed to see, for one thing, what happened when barriers touch. Would they merge? If so, large areas could be protected—whole cities, possibly. They don't, unfortunately. They resist each other as they would any other object. But, I needed another person to test that, and you have been unwilling to step forward.

"I also wished to see how the shields conformed to the size of their occupants. They do, in fact, adjust to height. Ella also inadvertently answered a question I had not thought to ask: what happens when one lies horizontally? It turns out that the shield is actually fully symmetric. You see that if the occupant lies down—it follows his orientation and becomes horizontal, rounded at both ends, head and foot. But, again, only about half of the shape manifests itself above the ground.

"There's no difficulty in standing back up. It has no weight, itself. I think the shield may be only a distortion in the ether. It's strange, however, that it's not spherical, the simplest shape. It has obviously been designed, and designed for convenience. One can imagine walking in a sphere that enclosed one all round, as one could in a large glass ball, but it would not be easy. And, really, I don't think it could roll relative to the person inside—as I said, it follows his orientation.

"It could still be matter, though, and immune to gravity in some way. Gravity apparently penetrates it, which suggests that gravity has a nature in some way similar to light. Or, it's a..."

"It is clear we shall not succeed without the stones," I said. "But it is also clear that we must act soon. Unless you are on the verge of repairing the box, it would be best to desist from your experiments and speculation and use what you have."

"I didn't want to say anything, for fear of raising and dashing hopes. I may have the solution. If I cannot corroborate my thinking by tomorrow evening, we will begin to consider active measures at once."

This exchange took place before our meal last night. He ate and went to work at once and worked through the night, forcing Susannah and me to sleep with the others. He emerged only for the meal this morning, tired and excited and uncommunicative, and returned to his studies after a few ritual stabs at his food.

All of these females have experience with guns and want to practice their shooting. We cannot risk the sound of gunfire leading the enemy here. They have kept themselves happy by making short bows on the model of one with which their father hunted. This was an heirloom, passed forward to them through unnumbered generations. They tell me these are as common among their people as the ancestral long rifles. Theirs was lost in the fire.

I await the issue of Mr. Selby's labors. If there is none, I shall demand battle.

Pulaski County, Kentucky, U. S. A., 16 October 1861

Our young engineer came to dinner late last night, having had no lunch at all. I inferred from his absence that his results were not coming up to his hopes, and that he would stretch the connotations of "evening" to their furthest limit. However, he entered about ten minutes after we had started, so slowly and unobtrusively, and with such a demure smile, that I knew at once he had triumphed.

"You have something to tell us?" I asked as he seated himself.

"I've much to tell you if I may eat while I do so."

By fine degrees, porridge made from maize and sweetened with molasses has become the main course in our meals. Mrs. Armstrong wishes to conserve all else against the long scarcity she expects. Mr. Selby ladled an obscene quantity of this mush onto his plate and began to burrow into it.

"So. Victory," I hinted, impatiently, when I judged that he was beyond immediate danger of starvation.

"Such a victory," he gurgled, then swallowed and wiped his lips with the handkerchief that has to serve him for a napkin. "A victory beyond reasonable expectation. I had no luck with the box itself—there is no way to take it apart, and I haven't the means to cut into it. The only detachable component is that strip of metal in the uppermost compartment, so I have been directing my attention to that.

"It revealed no interesting properties in response to all my testing. I could not, to save my life, figure out what it was. Finally, in the course of things, I got around to examining its electrical properties. I connected it to the galvanometer and got nothing. More out of desperation than anything else, I decided to see if it would at least hold a charge. I ran wires from the generator to those prongs on the bottom and cranked away."

He stopped to help himself to some of the scraps of pork we are permitted, and there was a delay in the narrative that, I really believe, was partially for effect.

"Wonder of wonders, I now got a current. Not a strong one, but lasting. The thing is nothing but a storage cell, small as it is. I was on the right track with my analogy, all along, if only I'd been willing to pursue its literal sense. The stones' makers must have abilities I cannot begin to estimate. It's frightening that there are such people somewhere in the world."

"Whoever can they be?" asked Toodie.

"I do not know that we want to discover that," I said. I could see from Susannah's expression that she wanted to know as little on the subject as possible.

"When I replaced the strip in the box, though, it still didn't work," Mr. Selby continued. "That was as far as I'd gotten when I talked with you last night. But, I hadn't charged it for long. In fact, by the help of God and my good right arm, I have since succeeded in restoring function to the damned thing."

Two of the girls hurrahed.

"Wait. That is the least of it. I then ran wires directly from the generator into the holes in the box where the strip was attached, and I was able to duplicate a stone that way. Then, I accomplished the same feat using a small battery of voltaic cells.

"And that is still not the most amazing thing. I forewent the box altogether and placed a stone on a sheet of copper with silicon and carbon. I connected the sheet to the generator and cranked. That served the purpose just as well! As did the battery, when I tried that! It's most extraordinary, seeing the new stone come together!

"But, what this means is, that we may make the stones as fast and as many as we choose. We are not to be impeded by the capacity of the one device."

"Do the new stones work?" I asked.

"Yes, indeed."

"Does this not mean, too, that *anyone* may make a stone?"

"Anyone who has a battery. Or can make one—and that's trivial."

"Then we are faced with Mr. Bromfield's millions of stones in millions of hands. Unless we suppress the secret."

"I thought that was to be left to me."

"It still is. But, it bears much thought."

"And it will get it. Eventually. Now we have more pressing matters."

All applied themselves, in silence, to the food, thinking I know not what private thoughts.

"Bob, I don't understand," said Susannah, at length. "Why is there a box to begin with? Why wasn't the farmer just given a stone and directions?"

"I can't answer that. Maybe precisely to hinder production of the shields."

"Why that?"

"I don't know."

"Could it be that they're a bad thing?"

"Then, why give a way of making them at all?"

She shrugged and looked down at her plate.

Toodie spoke up, in a bright voice. "Maybe they just couldn't rely on anyone understanding electricity."

"Possibly. I suspect all such questions are vain, however."

"You will muster the troops now?" I asked.

"Tomorrow."

"Might I try to recommend Mr. Elliot again? And his remaining associates? They all did good service the other night. I think you can trust them."

"Can you find them?"

"I may know how. When will you meet? And where?"

"Late. Late afternoon. I think we must all meet here

—no other place is both commodious and secure. I hate to give it away to anyone, but we should be able to solve our problem in short order, and then it won't make any difference."

And, so, we are to move at last. I have risen today before the dawn and shall go seek Corporal Guildford's grave when there is light enough.

Pulaski County, Kentucky, U. S. A., 18 October 1861

I had thought it would be easy, in sunlight, to find where the corporal was slain and thence his grave, which could not be far from there. I quickly realized that running in a forest lane by dark can leave one with little sense of the distance covered. Trees closed in on the path from both sides more often than I remembered, and I had trusted in that to be my best sign. I had also recalled that the vegetation about the scene was pine, but, by day, the whole tract through which the road ran was revealed to be pines, still green when all else was blazing up and dying out.

As I was near to abandoning the quest, I found a likely spot in the road, much scuffed and recently. Broken branches a few feet onward were a clue that the wood had been entered there. I thrust myself through that rough passage, noisily jostling the brush and boughs that survived to bar my progress. A little ways in, and I saw a flash of movement to my left, unmistakably a human, for he or she wore something a brighter blue than any natural creature in these wilds.

It was no part of the uniforms I had seen, and this was not a place the rebels were apt to patrol. Still, rationality would have kept me quiet. I was so dedicated to the idea that Mr. Guildford would visit here, however, that I at once shouted his name.

"Mr. de Grimouville?" he called from some invisible place.

"Yes. Come out. I am alone."

"Wait." After much thrashing in the underbrush, he appeared from around a tree, brushing his hair and blue shirt with his hands. "Come on a little ways, and I'll show you where my brother is buried."

The mound had been covered over with rocks and tree limbs and cones and needles. I would not have noticed it except for evidence of fresh digging.

"I thought you would come here," I said. "I did not hope actually to meet you—I was going to leave a note."

"About what?"

I informed him of the meeting and, when he agreed to bring the other two men, told him how to find us.

"How do things stand between Mr. Routledge and you?" I asked.

"I can't bring myself to forgive him, yet, but I'm not out for revenge. I won't let it interfere. Johnny Elliot was as much to blame, and we are cordial."

"Mr. Elliot helped you dig this."

"Yes, and I guess I have spent more time than not sitting here since you saw me last."

"It is not an unpleasant place."

"Oh, it's fine and private."

I sat on the ground, and so did he. After a full five minutes of silence, he asked, "Have you lost anyone?"

"A number of friends and family. My father died some years ago."

"When did you get over the grief?"

I tried to think how to answer truly. "I do not know that I have."

He nodded and said nothing more.

After some time had passed, I rose, saying, "Well, there are preparations to be made before the grand assembly."

"I'll accompany you part of the way, if you don't mind. I have to go in that direction."

When we had negotiated a ridge that led down on its other side to the creek, I asked, "What do you plan to do? Once we are finished here?"

"I'm going to find the Federal army and join, if they'll have me."

"What are the chances of that?"

"I don't know, but it makes sense that they'd want to use those who have most stake in the fight."

"So, you are not wholly without an instinct for vengeance."

"You asked me before what it's like to be a slave. If you knew, you'd understand that we'd devour our masters raw if we could."

"That is from Xenophon, is it not? Something he says about the Helots."

"From the *Hellenica*."

"And you have read that?"

"My brother made sure that I could read. Even Greek. I think we spent most of our childhood sneaking around and hiding so that I could steal an education."

At that moment, I managed to spear my arm with a tree branch and dropped to my knees with the pain.

"Christ Jesus! Are you all right?"

"Give me a minute, and I can go on."

"You should have that looked at. That could become gangrenous."

"It is nothing. It is nothing," I said, valiantly. "Did you gain any military skill following the army? Something that you can use in the service of the North?"

"Only what I observed when Company L was at Camp Cheatham. That was their Camp of Instruction. They despised the Tennesseans who were training them almost as much as they despised me, but they were willing to make a show of it, and I picked up as much as I could."

"They seem proficient at shooting noncombatants."

He grimaced. "That may have come natural to them. Did you know any of those people?"

"Some. And some I knew of indirectly, friends of friends, like that Halliday girl."

"*She* wasn't one of the prisoners."

"No?"

"No. She would have been, but she hanged herself before they even starting rounding people up."

I went down from there, and he went south (and that

may have been misdirection, for all that I know). I was less than truthful, myself, about my arm, which stung terribly. It had hurt far worse, all along, than I had been willing to let anyone know—I could not risk being kept from the fight. I had been able, in fact, to inure myself to the pain simply by refusing to acknowledge it. This incident had brought it back to my attention, but I was confident I could force it back into the unseen corner of my mind that was its proper place.

More disturbing to me was his remark about gangrene. I knew this was a possibility, and this knowledge, too, I had banished from my consciousness. To have another bring it up, to hear it spoken of aloud, gave it the reality I had been able to withhold from it.

Like a valetudinarian who feels every symptom he encounters in a medical text, I began to feel the slow creep of death through my tissues. This was fantasy. More genuine, as the sequel has shown, was the feverish light-headedness I now first noticed. It was mild, but I knew where it would lead.

Mrs. Armstrong wants me on a regimen of whiskey, inside and out. She cleaned my wound with it before the cautery, and would have had me treat the burn by rubbing the healing liquor into it with a rag at set intervals. My first trial of this was my last, the sensation only slightly offset by the prescribed internal application of the same elixir.

She cites a well established consensus that whiskey has special curative powers. Despite her dislike for it, she will take it herself medicinally. The very name, she says, shows that it contains the vital principle—it apparently means "water of life" in Gaelic. However that might be, I decided as I descended into the valley, I would see what else she had.

My one task for the day had been completed with dispatch, so I had nothing to do until the late afternoon. After looking at the arm, Mrs. Armstrong wanted to do her proposed surgery at once. I was willing, but only if she could guarantee that I would be on my feet by the time the other men came.

"On your feet, I suppose," she said, "but not sober."

"I wonder if we might dispense with both the fire and whiskey this time. Do you have other remedies that would serve the purpose?"

"Nothing I have as much faith in. Sometimes these things take more than one treatment."

"But, you do know of other things?"

"Well, I suppose I could send Ella to get willow bark. You can drink a tea of that, and we can use it in a compress. It works well, if you don't have better—which we do."

"Let us try the bark. We can return to the more approved methods if nothing comes of it. I cannot afford to dull my senses in the present situation."

"You'll still need to drink some whiskey just for the cutting. And I want to use it in the first cleaning."

"I can endure the cutting abstinently. You may do as you deem best for the cleaning, but I would like to try the compress afterwards."

The operation will not bear detailed description. She bathed her hands and the razor in whiskey almost in the fashion of a ritual ablution, which, for her, I suppose it was. Foul discharge flew from the incision as soon as she began to slice, and a distressing amount was pressed out subsequently. After the cleaning, a cloth soaked in the tea Ella made was bandaged to the area, and I was given some to drink. I am to brew my own from the bitter powder that was left.

That out of the way, I slept until Susannah came to wake me and announce that men were arriving. The fever was worse, but I staggered to a vertical posture and went to greet them.

Of the first to appear, I was only familiar with Mr. Moffat. In my state, I could only smile and nod during each introduction, and I am not sure I have retained the names. When I am recovered, I will confirm those and list them here. There were, eventually, four who were new to me. Mr. Guildford and his party were the last to come.

"I should have explained that there will be an odd feature to this," I told him. "But, it would be better for the others to acquaint you with it. I am not at my most lucid, I fear, and it is not something with which I personally will have anything to do, anyway."

I watched their initiation into the mysteries of the shields and was vaguely annoyed by how readily the three accepted the existence of the stones and how quickly comfortable they were with their workings. It was not stupidity, certainly, but a cast of mind I do not possess—a willingness to take the universe as it offers itself. It is a freedom from preconceptions that I envy but cannot emulate.

"And you can make as many of these as you want?" asked Mr. Elliot.

"We have more than enough already in store," our engineer answered. "In fact," he added, turning to me, "we should return Hugh Graham's to him, now that we don't need it."

One of those I had just met looked surprised. "A little late for that, I'd say."

"What do you mean?" said Mr. Selby.

"Hugh Graham's locked up in the post office."

"When did this happen?"

"Yesterday. Old Miss Cessford, who does their cleaning, told Tamar Fenwick, who told my wife."

"So, we've had a source of intelligence in their bosom this entire time?" asked Mr. Moffat, greatly displeased.

"Not a useful one. You know what Keziah Cessford is like as well as I do."

"How did they seize him?" I asked.

"He came out of wherever he's been holed up to get

something from his house, and found it burned down. He went into town with that hideout gun he always carries and demanded to see the lieutenant. The lieutenant thought it was funny, so he let him in. Hugh took off the flesh on one side of his face, but didn't kill him and only got the one shot. I guess he's slowing down. They're going to hang him as soon as the lieutenant's well enough to enjoy it."

"Then we must rescue him without delay," I said.

"Soon enough," said Mr. Selby. "Let's plan this out so we don't get him killed."

"I shall go and see what I can accomplish while you are doing so."

"What do you think you can accomplish?"

"I can get inside, even as a prisoner. That would not be without its advantages. And perhaps I can temporize with them and keep Mr. Graham alive until you come."

"Sounds unnecessary from what we've heard. We'll be there in good time."

I was not thinking clearly, I am willing to admit, but I did not share his assurance that nothing could happen before they acted. "I am going, regardless. Without a shield, my role in this enterprise is uncertain. If I go, fortune may reward the endeavor."

"You shall not go. I'm not sure you're not sick from your arm, and it may be fever talking. Wait the littlest while, and we will save him."

"You are right," I dissembled. "I shall rest in the laboratory until you are ready. Come and get me when it is time."

Mr. Elliot caught me as I was leaving. "I have something for you." He produced a Bowie knife and put it in my hands. "It was my uncle's. You admired ours so much at the dance that I thought you should have it as a reward for the other night."

I had barely the control left not to weep, but I thanked him over-profusely and wandered off with the gift

gripped in both hands. In the laboratory, I found the
musket I had been given at the battle for the stockade
and slipped that in my waistband under my coat. The
knife went on the other hip.

Taking my walking stick—for I was increasingly
unsteady—I went into the woods behind the building
and, by a long circuit, reached the trees that bordered the
stream. I cut uphill from there, though following the
water down to the road would have been easier. The way
through the forest was just as sheltered and more direct,
and would bring me in behind the town, near the same
jutting arm of woods we had used a few nights before. I
had no settled thought on what I was going to do and
how openly I wished to approach the headquarters, but I
did not want to restrict my choices.

The fever was increasingly real and evident, while the
world was less and less so. My head was hot as an oven,
and I half believed my brain was cooking in my skull. I
saw movements on the edges of my vision and had my
gun out more than a couple of times before I resolved to
ignore all such, be they fanciful or true.

When I had nearly gone as far as the covering of the
woods would take me, however, I heard a crashing in the
brush so vivid and sustained that I could not but take it
for real. I hid behind a large trunk and raised the pistol
again.

A rebel walked out of the foliage not ten feet in front
of me, obviously alerted to my presence by some sound I
had made. His musket was up, and his finger on the
trigger. I did not move and scarcely breathed. He
stopped and listened for so long that I came near to
shooting him merely to relieve the suspense, but I
preserved enough understanding that I refrained. If
these woods were patrolled—as it would be wise for them
to do—there would be more than one soldier about.

Instead, I put the gun away once more and pulled out
the enormous knife. With one serviceable hand, I could

not hold both. He moved, slanting toward my right so far that I was forced to slip around the tree, and stopped to listen again. I waited, and, on his next move, he came directly toward me. For a second, I pictured myself revolving further around the trunk, like a child in a game, but the image was too unmanly. When he was close enough, I stepped out and rushed against him, swinging the blade up under his ribs. It penetrated very little—he had fallen backward in surprise. I threw my good shoulder against him and forced him against another tree, then swung the knife once more and, this time, drove it in. He made a noise like a tea kettle when it just begins to boil. I placed my palm over his mouth and stabbed a third time, then supported his weight as he sank to the ground.

Even now, I can view this killing with detachment. I was buffered against it by the fever, yes, as I was in my first by the drug, but I do not think that is the whole explanation. It was simply easier the second time. And became easier with each death, thereafter. One's sentiments only pay one penalty for homicide, apparently —only for the very first. After that, a boundary has been crossed.

There was too much blood on my clothing to wander into the town like an innocent, as had been one possibility. I considered removing my bandage and running to the Southerners for aid, as if I were escaping from their enemies after many injuries and indignities. As I stood there plotting the particulars of the fiction, my surroundings started to rotate and the light faded.

I awoke in what seemed to be a storage room somewhere, to judge from the size and empty shelves. Mr. Graham, his face swollen and bruised and scarcely recognizable, was holding my eyelid open with his thumb.

"You're back," he said.

"What happened?"

"You were found lying unconscious next to a murdered Confederate. They're being very narrow in their interpretation of the scene."

"It was not the ideal occasion for a faint."

"You're burning up. From that arm, I'd guess. Good thing we're going to be hanged, or it'd have to come off."

I heard boots outside the door. "Where are we?"

"In the back of the post office. They've been poking in, off and on, to see if you're awake. You've been here the better part of an hour. That may be them coming again."

And it was. But I do not have the strength to extend this narrative further today and, if I did, Susannah is being too distracting with her insistence that I rest. There is much yet to tell of that day and night, but I neither can nor may continue right now.

Pulaski County, Kentucky, U. S. A., 19 October 1861

Contrary to the expectations—or hopes—of some, I shall elude both the noose and the surgeon's saw. Thanks to the willow, or my constitution, or a chance swerve of atoms, my arm resembles a human member once again, and the fingers respond to my will (after a fashion). The fire in my head has been gone since the night before last, when I awoke in a very lake of sweat.

To resume my story: We were both taken from our cupboard and placed in chairs before Lieutenant Edgcombe's desk. He and Elder Bell sat behind it, side by side, like judges. The lieutenant looked half a mummy, the right side of his face swathed in bandages. On the desk itself lay my gun and knife and stick. Two armed soldiers remained in the room, one next to us and the other at the door. From the weak light penetrating the curtains, I gathered that it was near dusk.

"So, Mr. Graham," said the lieutenant. "Events have given the lie to your claim that there is no organized Unionist activity in the region."

"You see evidence of organization? I see a damned fool Frenchman who blundered into the middle of someone else's business."

"I see a Frenchman and a Corncracker apparently working together, and I don't think you two alone are responsible for all that's happened. But, we'll find out all we need to before we grant you your executions."

"I've told you why I'm here. You burned my house, you son of a whore. You burned my books."

The officer's face lost all expression, as though he had turned to waxwork. "You will have great cause to regret your choice of words," he said in a very hushed, smooth voice.

"I came here only to help a friend," I said. "There may be secret organizations, for all that I know. I can imagine that there are, given what you have done. But, I bear sole responsibility for my actions."

"No!" shouted Elder Bell suddenly. "That will not do! We know of which party you are—and with whom you associate. Your friend speaks of whores?" He was oblivious to the ominous look the lieutenant threw him. "These men have been told of your strumpet and her father's abolitionist ties. You are as much her partner in politics as you are in licentiousness."

I rose, and the soldier nearest us grasped my bad arm. I hissed with the pain and sat back down. But, I was able to say, "Now it is you who must be warned against his words. You have suffered for that once before. If you choose unwisely again, I shall knock you down, and no guard will stop me."

He smiled. "I have no fear of threats. They are the glory and the due of the godly as long as the prince of this world yet reigns. We shall have our recompense, by and by."

"Godly! The chaplain to drunken ravishers!"

"That very willingness to judge shows that you are no Christian," the lieutenant said, his face and voice still tight. "You do not understand the exigencies of war."

"*My* church does not have a horse's head buried beneath it," added Elder Bell.

I looked around at all their faces, but found myself alone in my bewilderment. Mr. Graham even snorted, as if it were a shared joke.

The others were not so amused. "That's neither here nor there," Lieutenant Edgcombe said. "Right now, our task..."

He could not finish his thought. Gunfire and cries sounded from outside.

"Private," the lieutenant told the guard by the door. "See what is going on."

As he watched the soldier leave, I leapt for the musket on the desk. I only succeeded in pushing it off onto the floor, however. I snatched the Bowie knife instead and started around the desk.

The other guard came after me, but was thwarted by Mr. Graham, who wrapped his arms about him and overbalanced him, taking them both down.

Elder Bell retreated to a corner of the room, while the lieutenant scratched at the flap of his holster, trying to unfasten it. Giving up the attempt, he glanced around and saw his saber hanging on a hook on the wall. He pulled it off and drew the weapon from its scabbard. I rammed the point of the knife into the desk to have it ready at hand and took up my stick. Behind me, I could hear the soldier on the floor begin to scream.

The lieutenant's saber play had no form to it. I doubt the American military do more with sabers than chop from horseback, and Lieutenant Edgcombe was no cavalryman. For him, it would never have been more than an article of costume. My closest training was in singlestick, but that stood me well at first against his wild slashing. An odd and distracting recollection of the rapier fight in Scott's *Kenilworth* began to run through my mind. I think it was because I knew my knife could be used for a poniard if only I had more than the one hand.

I did not and, though I scored many a hit, I was hard pressed and could not give them the force to do damage. Had my weapon an edge, as his did, the combat would soon have ended, but, as it was, I tired against his youthful vigor.

Then, it came to me—not in a sudden flare of insight, but rather late in the match—that I was being too sporting, too faithful to the rules. The next time he opened himself up with one of his broad swings, I jabbed him under his thigh (in the Biblical phrasing). As he was diverted with that, I had my first clear opportunity to strike the wrist of the hand holding the blade.

He released the saber, and I was about to stoop and

pick it up when the door to the outside opened and a pair of Confederates charged in, their pistols at the ready.

"Hold, or you are a dead man," one said, and the other crossed rapidly to take my stick and pull my arms behind my back. I lost awareness for a second and would have fallen had I not been held.

The rebel who had spoken stepped aside to allow the Elder Bell to flee the building, then came and helped the lieutenant to his feet. That officer faced me and was opening his mouth to speak when Mr. Moffat entered the door with a rifle pointed at us.

"Release the gentleman," he ordered.

They did not move. He said, "I guess this day's just used up my patience." He sighted on the man gripping me and pulled his trigger. I could see the flint spark, but there was no report. My man, who had laid his musket on the desk, moved from behind me to recover it, placing himself next to the other who was bringing his own pistol to bear on the constable.

Mr. Moffat let the rifle drop. More swiftly, in plainest truth, than my eye could see, he drew the revolver from his side and emptied it into them with a stroking motion of his free hand. It crackled like a packet of squibs. The soldiers died at once, while the lieutenant was spun around by, as it turned out, a ball in the thigh and came to rest back on the floor.

I stood agape. When I could speak, I said, "You must demonstrate to me, eventually, how you did that."

"It's easy enough, with practice."

I bent to unfasten the flap on the lieutenant's own revolver and slid it out of the holster, trying to attend to him and the door simultaneously. "I can see that it is a useful skill with a useful instrument. Your shield was down for only an instant."

He observed the old man and the guard lying in motionless embrace and walked over to them. "To tell you the truth, I forgot to bring my stone. It's back at the house, somewhere.

"Are these dead?" he asked.

"The one on the top is Mr. Graham."

He crouched and cupped his hand around the ancient throat. "There's a pulse," he said and rolled the bodies gently apart.

Both faces were coated with blood so thick they looked skinned. "You can't see from where you are, but the sesesh's throat's been cut. Look where it sprayed over to the side. Here's the knife. Hugh seems all right, but let's get him cleaned up to make sure. You keep watching the door."

I did so, and saw feeble shadows coalesce on the porch outside.

"Josh!" a man shouted. "Are you in there?"

"Come on in," he bellowed in reply.

Mr. Routledge and two of those I had only met that day funneled through the doorway. It was hardly wide enough for one at a time, encrusted, as they were, with armament.

"How's it going out there?" the constable asked. "I still hear shooting."

"We've killed a chance of them. Should be only ten or a dozen left, and we've caught most of those. We're taking pains to hunt down the strays—don't need any running around loose sniping at people."

"Can you take the lieutenant off our hands? He and the others should probably go in the pen out back."

The lieutenant could not support himself and had to be carried out, groaning. Mr. Moffat took off his kerchief and poured water onto it from a jug he found in another room. As soon as he began to bathe Mr. Graham's face, the latter opened his eyes and grunted.

"I don't see any damage anywhere," Mr. Moffat reported.

The object of his care spat something out and said, "Just on the back of my head, I think. I hit it against the floor when he started bucking. He thought he had his knife into me, but I distracted him and got hold of it."

"What is this?" asked Mr. Moffat, picking up the object. He examined it, then made a sharp sound and threw it from him.

"From the taste, I'd say a nose," Mr. Graham said. "It came off him when my head hit and my teeth clashed together."

Taking the kerchief and sitting up on his own, he completed the washing himself. He was at his most facetious throughout the procedure, but it was patently forced. When he made to rise to his feet, we tried to help and were shaken off, but he sat again immediately and vomited.

His balance was not good, and he confessed to a headache, yet we were unable to make him rest before he saw that all the prisoners were secured and was assured that few others had escaped alive. We coaxed him, in the end, onto the bed in the lieutenant's quarters, where he fell asleep straight away. Even then, he roused himself by the early morning and went off to make preparations.

Pulaski County, Kentucky, U. S. A.,
20 October 1861

For me, that night was spent back with the family, who could not be left wondering how the affair had ended. I was in everyone's bad graces. It had not been long before my absence was discovered, and it was obvious where I had gone. Strategy was abandoned in favor of a direct, immediate assault (which was, in point of fact, where all their planning had been leading them anyway).

There had been talk of trials for the rebels. Mr. Graham was the source and major advocate for the idea. I had never heard that Stirling had a judicial apparatus or any authority to try anyone, that being, to the best of my knowledge, a function of the county, and I was curious. It would, at best, qualify me as a witness to the political workings of one of these Western communities. At worst, it would provide spectacle.

I could not imagine that anybody, captor or captive, wanted the proceedings to start before noon, so I slept as fully and long as my sickness would allow. It was the last night of the fever and the most difficult. I passed it alternating between bad dreams and troubled wakefulness.

They were strenuous dreams, intense and terrifying, of most of which I retained only the emotional residue and not the particulars. One, however, stayed with me when I woke: I was in a dark place with Susannah, who was pleading with me to let her rest. The content may have mirrored actuality—I really was in a dark place with Susannah, who, in some watch of the night, could no longer abide my tossing and moaning, and moved her blankets to the far side of the laboratory. Why that would leave such a flavor of horror and sadness, I cannot say.

By the middle of the morning, I could no longer sleep

248

at all and rose to dress, more fatigued than when I had lain to rest. I equipped myself with the lieutenant's revolver and my knife, then, on an impulse, searched about for a stone. There was a hoard of them in one of the cabinets, and I tucked one into my pocket.

Susannah's nest of blankets was empty, and I considered that it was long past breakfast. I was vexed that no one had given a thought to my feeding. Food would not have sat well and, if I grew hungry later, there were better and more plentiful rations to be got in town, but I would have appreciated the gesture. I stood staring at the vacated bedclothes, flushing with heat as I perceived depth beyond depth of injustice in the matter.

When I could bring myself to leave the laboratory, I saw Susannah coming around the side of the main house with dishes and bowls balanced on a piece of board. I at once recognized my own injustice, but the anger remained, though it had no proper object.

She swept past me, saying, "Come on. You can have this in here. We thought you should sleep as much as you could, but we saved a breakfast."

The attitude of command rankled. "I shall not be eating this morning."

"You shan't, shan't you? I think you should try— you're not supposed to feed a fever, but..."

"There are things to eat in the town if I decide I can stomach them." I walked on, then turned and added, "Though I doubt that I shall ever be able to stomach 'corn' in any of its multifarious disguises again."

She looked dazed, as though I had struck her, and, I think, more because of my tone than my words. She tried to speak and could not, and I could see that she was trying to check her tears. As I left, she said something in a broken voice, but I could not hear what it was.

I knew the corruption in my arm and in my blood was acting upon me. This did not help. The anger was proof against all my efforts to will it away or reason it into

submission. I could not even temper it with remorse—
the two only combined in a particularly toxic compound.
I stumbled blindly and insensibly through the growth
along the creek, tearing my clothing and skin.

Were it not for the heat that threatened to bring me
down in another faint, I would have missed the sound of
men talking low somewhere in the trees. I had stopped,
wondering if I should not return and simply rest for a few
days until all trace of sickness was purged, letting events
run their course without my supervision. The voices
seemed to be on my right hand, and, from the light I
could see through the trunks that were elsewhere so
densely crowded, I inferred that the woods opened out in
that direction.

It was, in fact, a tiny glade much frequented by Ella in
her play. I had not come very far. When I discerned the
men's grey coats, I was almost cold for the first time in
many days. There were only a pair, and they were
huddled in a concavity under an outcropping, appearing
more prey than predator, but I could not have them here,
so close to the family's refuge.

My left hand could hold the stone, if it was good for
little else, so I placed that in its fingers and took the
pistol in my right. Then, I strode into the clearing and
proposed that they surrender their arms.

One drew on me, and, remembering the instructions, I
tried to raise the shield. The ball dropped at my feet. I
could not try Mr. Moffat's trick, which he calls "fanning,"
with only one hand, so—trusting that I had the shield
down again—I aimed carefully and fired. My first shot
took a man in the abdomen; he bowed and began to claw
the leaves in front of their shelter, emitting little gasps.
The next, I think, missed entirely, but the third caught
the other man in the throat. I approached and shot him
again, in the heart, to be certain. Then, I set the gun
against the back of the first man's head and conferred a
coup de grâce.

They could not be left for Ella to find, so I dragged them farther into the woods and gave them shallow burials of the sort we had given Corporal Guildford that night.

I was correct in my guess that the court would not convene early. The jury was just sitting when I reached the post office. Chairs and tables had been set up in the street in front of a new structure, a gallows, which showed signs of the pace of its construction. I would not have trusted it to stand on it, but we have since dismantled it. It displayed four ropes—this could not have heartened the four men who were brought out for the first bout of trials.

They were too overcome by it all to show anything but stunned perplexity as they were herded toward the seated assembly. Their hands were already bound behind their backs. Fear came only as they were taken past the judges directly to the gallows where the nooses were affixed, the constable superintending.

"Are we not to have a trial?" one shouted.

"Certainly," Mr. Graham answered over his shoulder. He noticed me and indicated an empty chair in the jurors' section with a stab of his hand. "Mr. de Grimouville, you may take a place if you wish."

"I do not have the rights of a citizen, I am afraid. Nor the obligations."

"Then, we will begin. Gentlemen of the jury, what color uniform are the accused wearing?"

Three or four answered, "Grey."

"Then, I find them guilty. Mr. Moffat, you may proceed with the executions."

I was able to watch as they dropped the length of their ropes. Their bodies jerked like the frogs' legs in demonstrations that were my only previous encounter with electric cells. This, too, I could endure. I had to look away at the sight of their faces, though—these were too grotesque to bear.

251

"Let us have the next defendants, please," called the judge.

These were met by the sight of their comrades hanging from the crossbar. One tried to run, but was tripped by an attendant and kicked in the back. The others gave no trouble, shuffling compliantly to the gallows, their eyes fixed on the suspended forms as though entranced by them.

"What color uniform are the accused wearing?"

"Grey."

"Mr. Moffat."

I did not watch this time. The faint cracks as the nooses stopped their descents were enough to tell me when the deed was done.

"We have one more candidate. Please usher him in."

Lieutenant Edgcombe was carried on a stretcher. I am told he had not spoken since the last time I had seen him. He did not now. Mr. Graham had the litter set on the ground before him.

"Gentlemen, what color uniform is he wearing?"

"Grey," they all roared.

With painful difficulty, Mr. Graham struggled out of his chair and around the table, and stood over the officer. "Lieutenant, I was doing my best to stay out of your war. I thought that if I didn't interfere with your affairs and you didn't intrude into mine, we could both get along fine, happy as crickets in a two-hole shithouse. But, you couldn't help meddling. Now, I'm going to put an end to that meddling."

The lieutenant had kept his face admirably under control throughout, but, as they draped the noose about him, two men supporting him, he began to weep.

The constable looked to Mr. Graham, waiting for his signal.

"Wait!" the old man said. "Don't drop him. Lower him gently—we wouldn't want his neck to break."

I went and sat in the post office as soon as I

understood what was intended. It was twenty minutes before they cut him down. Those with experience believed it took that long to ensure that his heart stopped beating.

When it was over, Mr. Graham came in and said, "And now you've had one of the most important lessons you're going to learn in your education about my people. It's an inherited reaction."

"It explains what happened to the Indians."

"Yes. I would never argue that it's just, but it's what happens."

"I do not object to it, in this instance."

They gathered the corpses of the executed and all they could find from the battle. There is a mound now somewhere in the forest.

The livestock will be returned to the original owners as they claim it. What little the Confederates left of other foodstuffs has been collected and will have to be doled out to those most in need of it. Everyone was most pleased about the stores of tobacco that have been liberated—what people kept from the Southerners has run low.

The hunt is on for Elder Bell. No one can be sure what he saw of the shield, and we would like the secret to be ours to disclose or not. So many know about it, however, that it may not matter. There are some, to be sure, who want the good cleric for other reasons.

I assume he has found his way to Somerset or east to Camp Buckner. I must go to the former as soon as I can to see what has become of my belongings and submit an account of the last three weeks to Mr. Greeley. Will it be the making of me? It would unquestionably if I did not edit out the part played by the shields. Sadly, I am probably too encumbered with honor and loyalty to seize the opportunity.

First, Mr. Selby and I must complete our repairs on one of Mr. Graham's cabins, into which we have moved the Armstrongs. After the executions, I returned to the Bromfield property with the happy task of informing the family that they could rejoin the world, and the burden of divulging, finally, what has become of their friends. I pray I never again face a like commission.

I had also to make amends to Susannah. But, at this moment, I am overlate to bed with her. How I regained that blessed state, I shall recount in my next chapter.

Pulaski County, Kentucky, U. S. A., 21 October 1861

I gave myself only one full day of rest after the emancipation of Stirling, and that was not enough, it seems. Though my fever is gone and my arm on the road to redemption—and though I have done little beyond walking and light carpentry—my strength has suddenly failed. I shall spend this day in bed and see what tomorrow permits.

My reunion with Susannah was neither sweet nor sour, but woodenly polite. Our *rapprochement* came after I called the household together and gave them an unabridged version of these last weeks. This blasted away all Susannah's other concerns. She sees herself as the shepherdess of the family's emotional welfare and has had to resort to me for her own support.

When at last we were satisfactorily intimate again, I made my apology and pled the fever.

"Oh, I know that," she said. "And knew it. I was upset, naturally, but I didn't take it to heart. It was a little thing, after all. And far from your character, so I worried more for your health than anything. Not that your character is without flaws."

"It probably distressed me more than you."

"I'm sure that it did. They say that the contrition of a blemished soul is its principal punishment."

"I thought we were agreed that my illness bore most of the guilt."

"We are, we are. Your faults may be many and weighty, but that was not like you."

"Perhaps we should change the subject. I think you have begun to show."

"I think so too, but I didn't know if anyone else could notice. I think I feel her move, sometimes. There's a fluttering, anyway. Thank the Lord I'm not sick all the time, anymore."

"I did not know that you had been feeling sick."

"We are back to the subject of your imperfections. I thought you wanted to set them aside. I've *always* been more than willing to pass over them in silence. I've always felt that it was the mark of a charitable heart not to draw attention to someone's failings, no matter how grave and numerous those might be."

"Then, let us make another attempt to leave the topic. Who will handle the birthing if we are still here?"

"My mother has enough experience. We could bring a doctor from Somerset, though."

"God forbid!"

"The important thing, people think around here, is to have a sharp object under the mattress. We can use your new knife."

The thought froze my blood.

"Seriously, though," she continued, "how are you feeling? You were so ill for so long."

"My body is on the mend. My mind may not be. It has not been right since...I do not know when. It started before the fever. I would like to say it started with the killing, but it goes back before that. Perhaps to the discovery of the shields? But, I think, before that."

I faded off into reverie. How long had it been since I had felt whole and part of a whole?

She watched my face and would not let it last. "Back to the 'twenties, at least, I would imagine."

"I do not think that is correct. I was passably sane when we first met, was I not?"

"I don't know a kind way to answer that."

"I remember I did not spend every moment regretting an unrestrained word or action. Of late, that is all I do. I used to have control of myself. And let me say: I do not mind maize at all, or the many fine things one may make from it."

"Good, for your sake. Whiskey is made from corn."

"I realized that later and repented my apostasy."

And just in time. We had Selby's Irregulars over with Mr. Graham the day before yesterday to discuss what was to be done about the shields. Elder Bell has still to be apprehended, but that is only one consideration.

"It will mean the end of slavery if the technique is disseminated," said Mr. Selby.

"The involuntary kind, anyway," said Mr. Graham. "I expect that people will pay every cent of taxes they're told to for awhile. And, when conscription comes, some people will answer the call. It will take a while for people to free themselves from the habit of obedience. Some never will—some people are flunkies by nature."

"Some people will also see the advantage of contributing money for public purposes," I suggested.

"If it's a contribution, it's not taxes."

Mr. Moffat rumbled in his throat. "You know, oddly enough, it'll mean both victory and defeat to the South. The slaves will shake them off, but they'll shake off the North. There'll be no way to stop secession."

"*If* we loose this thing on the world," I qualified.

"Oh, it's going to get loose. All we're here to talk about is how long we try to sit on it."

"And you all see no danger in this weapon?" asked Mrs. Armstrong.

"That's just it," responded Mr. Selby. "It's not a weapon. It's purely a defense. We were able to use it in conjunction with weapons, but that was only because we had it and the rebels didn't. If both sides have it, weapons don't mean much."

"It only allows what Sir Walter Scott calls 'passive resistance,'" I elaborated, pointlessly. They looked to me as if expecting more. "It's a policy he ascribes to an old Hebrew in *Ivanhoe*."

They kept looking, so I busied myself with a jug and tumbler until they gave up on me.

"Secession," Mr. Graham pronounced, as though tasting the word. "It won't stop with the South. And there's no reason the South will hold together, itself. You may get your townships back, Mr. de Grimouville—your city-states."

"Perhaps." I had not taken my thoughts so far. "And the civic virtues—and the freedom—that go with them. Freedom in a profounder sense than you use the word. Not just a negative freedom, but one that elevates the person and ennobles the spirit."

"We have to make sure everybody knows how to make the stones," said Mr. Routledge. "Or things will start off like the fight in Stirling. Everybody has to have an equal chance right at the start, North, South, or slave."

"Good thing it ended up in the hands of folk without any partialities," said his friend, Mr. Elliot.

"Good thing this is a war where no decent human being can take sides. Kind of like your average Presidential election."

I let Mr. Routledge enjoy the laughter he had won and, when it died away, said, "I cannot help but wonder if we are ending all order. The shields protect persons, yes, but they do not protect property. Property is protected by compulsion, Mr. Graham, if your theories are right. But, no one can be compelled, any longer."

"That's not my experience. The farther I've gotten from organized legal systems, the more people seem to respect rights. They have to—precisely because they know everything would break down, otherwise. Then, government catches up with them and the courts move in, and everything goes to hell. It becomes a game of seeing what you can get away with."

"That is fine if there is 'enough, and as good,' as the saying goes. What happens when that obtains no longer? When one man's possession debars others from the necessities of life?"

"There's always been enough, and as good, somewhere. People can always move if they don't like a situation. The clever ones always have."

"Until the earth is filled."

"What's the likelihood of that?"

"You are not aware how greatly populations have grown just in your lifetime."

"If it comes to that, we will have trouble, shields or not. Or, *they* will—I will not be around."

"This was not my main point, in any case. I simply meant that there are villains in the world who steal regardless of need or simply destroy for amusement. Were there never such in your frontier Edens?"

"Not many and not for long. But, I take your argument: our traditional solution to the problem—a bullet in the head—won't be possible. Then, again, those types of people are around even where there are governments trying to deal with them. If the old system couldn't eliminate them, it's unfair to expect the new system to do it. And the new system won't encourage it like the old did."

"And, then, there's the matter of fraud."

"Same reasonings hold, I think. And, without government courts to make you feel protected, people can only cheat big once unless they move on. It just means you don't trust strangers."

Then, it occurred to me what the real problem should be from his standpoint. "There is one entity you have forgotten: the government itself. If your general view of it is right, it would direct all its effort into organized pilferage. Not just from avarice, but with an eye to control. Hunger can compel as well as arms."

"So, government would no longer be based on the threat of violence, but on sneak-thievery? I don't think they could manage it. Think what all they'd need to do."

"Bob," asked a man named Jack Douglas, one of the original Irregulars, whom I still did not know well, "can more than one person get inside a shield?"

"Yes. We tried up to three. The shield adapts to the volume of meat inside. I don't know if there's an upper limit to the size. I'm sure that someone will try to find out."

"But, if there's no limit, or a big one, you could hold quite a bit of ground. Maybe even a city."

"Only if everyone holds hands all the time."

"What happens if two people with stones stand next to each other and put up the shields?"

"They bounce apart. We tried all this."

"Does that not mean that the shield propagates?" I inquired.

"It could, but..." He brought himself up short and raised his hand as if swearing an oath. "Gentlemen, let me ask, how do each of you stand at present on disposition of the shields? Do we let everyone know or not? I'm not asking for your final verdict, just how you're leaning right now."

No one in the room, in fact, stood anywhere. Some denied they had an opinion, some denied they cared.

"It seems to me," he said, "that there is only one way to put the issue: do we spread the secret of the shield immediately and lose the advantage it will give us if the war comes again to our gates, or do we hold onto it and risk its discovery by one faction before the other? That would make us culpable in much, I'm afraid."

He got no better response. Nor did the two hours of drinking—before Mrs. Armstrong drove us gracefully away—yield anything more helpful.

Pulaski County, Kentucky, U. S. A.,
23 October 1861

Mr. Graham is dead. I have sat here for thirty minutes, holding my pen above the paper, and I do not know what more to say about that.

I felt well enough today to transfer my personal effects back to my old cabin. I anticipate the privacy as I would a cold bath after a day in the field. The old, accustomed views are the same, however much I know what changes they conceal.

Afterwards, I walked down to Stirling. It is not returning to what it was. I did not expect an instant resurrection, with happy townsfolk singing to the sound of busy hammers, but I had hoped for more than is there. It is little more than a supply station, which people visit only for the supplies Mr. Moffat apportions to those who come seeking them. The animal pens are the liveliest quarter of the town—most of the animals remain unredeemed, I think because no one yet has anywhere to keep them.

I talked with Mr. Moffat for a time, with infrequent interruption, sitting on the steps of the post office, until first Mr. Graham and then Mr. Routledge happened by and joined us. Our conversation did not verge on recent events until the constable requested to look at my revolver, which he pronounced a Remington and wished to trade for his own. I did so readily—superior tools belong in the hands of superior craftsmen.

He held his new acquisition in both palms, admiring it. "Bob Shelby's right," he said. "The shield's not a weapon. But, this is, and if it weren't for the shields, this would transform the world all by itself. Just its luck, it came along just at the wrong time, and it's going to lose its place in history. You should get one, Daniel Shays, before they go out of fashion."

Mr. Routledge mumbled something about sticking

with the tested and true.

This gave me an opening to put a question to him I had wanted to ask since we first met. "Mr. Routledge, if you do not mind my asking, why do you go by both your names?"

"Because I'm proud of them. My great-some-odd-grandfather fought alongside Daniel Shays."

"I am ashamed to say that I do not know the name," I admitted, as deferentially as I could.

He smiled patronizingly. "Well, you're a foreigner. After the Revolution, Massachusetts decided to pay its war debts by taxing poor farmers and then confiscating their land for not paying. A lot of the farmers—like Daniel—couldn't pay because they been away fighting in the war and then hadn't been paid themselves. They organized an army called 'Regulators" and fought the state and lost, but it showed they wouldn't roll over and play dead. They were mostly Scotch-Irish. Daniel always said they were fighting for the same principles that made them join the Revolution."

"They didn't make up that name 'Regulators,'" said Mr. Moffat.

"Now we'll have to listen to this," Mr. Routledge told me in a low but purposely audible voice.

"He's heard your story. *My* family is as Scotch-Irish as his, and we fought the same kind of war, but it was a quarter-century before—and before the Revolution. We were in both Carolinas, and we lost in the north and won in the south. The northern branch moved to Tennessee with other Regulators and set up their own government, and the southern branch joined them later. We set the style for the Revolution—we weren't just copying it like some other families."

"Tell him why your family had to leave South Carolina after they won."

"Due to a misunderstanding."

"Which had more to do with cattle than Regulation, if

I remember the story."

"Which is far off to the side of the point."

This went no further. We had attracted the attention of a group of men, women and children who came into the street from the direction of the main road with a pair of wagons. Nearly all went on foot, since the wagons were filled with what appeared to be their worldly belongings.

As they approached, Mr. Routledge said, "Passing strange—I've never seen most of them, but that's John Foster in the front."

It was. The boy walked ahead of them like a guide, bringing them up to us and then standing wordlessly and pointing as though they would not otherwise have seen us.

One of the men introduced himself and explained that they were fleeing London for Somerset. General Zollicoffer had attacked a forward base the Union established on Wild Cat Mountain between Camp Dick Robinson and London. The Southerners were handily repulsed and were retreating back down the Wilderness Road to Cumberland Ford. (This may be, as far as my knowledge goes, the first Union victory of the war.)

"There's already a joke that they marched up there to the tune of 'Dixie' and left to the tune of 'Fire in the Mountain, Run Boys Run,'" the man added. "They weren't happy when they came through, and we thought we'd get out before anything else happened. We met this lad on the road, and he told us that you might have victuals to spare."

We sent them on their way with food from the common larder, judging that no one would take it ill.

"Why is the town so empty?" I asked. "Why are the citizens not reclaiming it?"

"Just caution," answered Mr. Moffat. "They're all settled in safe and don't see any reason to come out yet. Most of them got food the first couple of days, and they won't be back till that's gone. No one wants to take more than they have to. But, it was busy at first."

He sighed a weary sigh. I noticed, for the first time, how old and drained the constable and Mr. Routledge looked. I was, of course, in the condition I am. Mr. Graham's color was not good, and he was atypically silent. Only John Foster seemed untouched, and I never believed he was wholly intact. We were not a healthy gathering, and we sat there long into the afternoon, long after we had run out of words.

We all looked up languidly at the sound of a horse, hoping for some diversion. It was a Confederate, a sergeant, in a soiled uniform. All who had weapons felt for them.

He hailed us and rode his horse to the bottom of the steps. "I am looking for a platoon of the 11th Tennessee Infantry. They were supposed to be posted in this location." His manner insinuated that we somehow shared in the dereliction of duty. It was also evident that he did not see us as threats.

"They left," said Mr. Graham.

"They were to remain until they received orders to the contrary."

"You'll have to take that up with them."

"Where did they go?"

"That way, more or less." The old man pointed to the east.

"Toward Camp Buckner?"

"If that's that way."

The sergeant swung from his horse and charged the porch, grasping Mr. Graham's collar before we could react.

"You will give me a civil response, you old bastard, and a useful one, or I will see your brains on the wall behind you."

We would have moved, then, but Mr. Graham turned a bright blood-red and began to bleat unintelligibly. His pupils rolled up into his head, leaving only white. Only John Foster acted, seizing the rebel's sleeve and trying to pull him away. The soldier cuffed him, and he fell.

Mr. Graham half rose, the side of his face flowing down as if it were melting. Then, he sprawled backwards. We were on our feet by then, and the rebel drew his pistol and menaced us with it.

From the ground, John Foster said, in strangled derision, "I hear you got yourselves whipped all to hell up on the Rockcastle. I hear you went up there to the tune of 'Dixie' and came back to the tune of 'Fire in the Mountain, Run Boys Run.'"

The sergeant stopped, stock-still, as though working out what had been said, then used his gun on the boy. I leapt at him and we toppled off the steps into the dirt.

I remember next to nothing of what came next, only that I tried, at some stage, to drive my thumbs into his eyes. They pulled me off of him and Mr. Routledge put a ball into his head. For a long while, I was conscious only of a throbbing in my temples and a coppery taste in my mouth. When I was sufficiently back in my senses, they told me that Mr. Graham and the boy were dead.

"Do you know," Mr. Moffat asked, "that you tried to bite his throat out?"

I looked at the soldier's body and saw that the skin on the neck had been torn. I leaned against a column on the porch and gagged, but nothing would come up.

I was led inside to a chair. "You rest, and we'll dispose of this one, too. We're getting good at it." I do not know who said that.

I waited alone while the room darkened. Finally, they returned with lamps and brought me out. "We may have a whole new problem," the constable said.

Spaced along the street I could see the gleam of brass and boots. More men with uniforms and rifles. But, in the sparse light of lanterns and torches, I could see that these uniforms were blue. The Union is here.

Pulaski County, Kentucky, U. S. A.,
24 October 1861

It was thought by everyone to whom the question was presented that we could not defer Mr. Graham's funeral. Captain Arnim had informed us that the main body of his troops would enter to the martial airs of a full band, and the irony would be too perfect for the occasion to be let slip.

For a company to have its own band is no more usual here than in Europe. It has to do with the circumstances of the unit's creation. The 11th Independent Infantry Company was recruited and mustered in Cincinnati, Ohio, almost before the war was an assured thing. Captain Johann August Ernst Arnim himself took most of the initiative. The band was originally a militia band, funded by private donors. The captain contrived to have this arrangement continued. They are, therefore, I take it, practically private employees, as pipers in the British army used to be.

The company is attached to the 38th Ohio Volunteer Infantry, and may be fully assimilated in time with another change in name. At its inception, it was "Arnim's Independent Company," purportedly by decree of the general will. The musicians will be taken from them with the incorporation, I imagine.

No more than fifteen were in attendance to view the parade, all there for the funerals. Mr. Shelby's corps and the Armstrong clan made up the largest part of that number. John Foster had no family and lived with a man and wife on a farm in return for chores and what rent he could pay from his work in the store. Mr. Graham was Mr. Graham. Everything considered, fifteen was a respectable total.

"Will they play pieces by request?" Susannah asked me, threading her arm through mine as we took a position on the side of the street. "I've tried to think of what Hugh would have wanted played. He always liked "Dance All Night with a Bottle in Her Hand," though I think he liked the idea as much as the music."

"I doubt they will know that one. And this is for their purposes, not ours. You should enjoy this—I suspect it will be Austrian military music. It is sprightly, almost like dances. The captain was born in Hungary and attended the Vienna Military Academy."

When the music came, however, I was proven false. It was heavy and Prussian.

"I can see how you might be mistaken," my companion observed, sweetly. "It reminds me of the way you dance."

The ranks came into view around the turn at the end of the street. "Look at them," she said. "They're like a machine."

They were, indeed, better drilled than any I have seen in this country. A century of men marched past us as smartly as any professionals in my experience, as synchronized as the power looms I saw in factories in England.

"How long did it take them to be able to do that?" she asked.

"You will have to ask him. We are to dine with him as soon as he settles in. He knows that I am a fellow continental and is convinced I am an aristocrat on slum holiday. I tried to disabuse him, without success."

We assembled with the others and began to walk toward the churchyard, but the captain saw us and called out for us to wait. After we explained where we were going, and why, he requested to join us with his two lieutenants.

He is about my age, I would estimate, of middle height and well-favored after the towheaded, Teutonic fashion.

"Who were the deceased?"

"An elderly man and a young boy," I said.

He paused for a decent interval as we walked along

before taking his questions up again. "Were their demises related in some manner?"

"No. It is a sad coincidence. The older man died of a head injury, we believe. He had not been well as it was. The boy was shot by a Confederate as they withdrew."

He shook his head. "Such incidents are all too frequent. It is why we fight this war. One reason among many, I should say. What sort of man was the older gentleman?"

I thought. "A man."

"Take him for all in all," Susannah said.

He addressed me, ignoring her: "That is good. We are here in the service of all such. Our main purpose is to protect the approach to Somerset, but we will let nothing happen to your Stirling." Then, abruptly, he turned to Susannah and patted her on the head.

The services were longer than I felt seemly, especially the singing of hymns, which did not display the district's musical talents to good advantage. Everyone felt compelled to say something, and there was much talk of the grave loosening its wintry hold and the putting on of incorruption. I endured by picturing Mr. Graham on hand to listen and respond.

Pulaski County, Kentucky, U. S. A.,
25 October 1861

I am unable to leave for Somerset. A guard has been posted at the very same spot in the road where the Southern pickets used to be, and prevent all passage beyond. They were very polite and apologetic, but faithful to their orders. Captain Arnim was also very civil when I sought him out, and promised that it would be temporary. He would not give his reasons for it, however. I have also been refused the use of military channels to correspond with the newspaper, but that is understandable.

The constable has been evicted from the post office, and his function turned over to a sergeant. The captain met all objections with stiff affability and a refusal to yield.

"Your people are destitute, you tell me, and near starvation. I must ensure that the food is distributed fairly. It must be done by a regularized method."

I pointed out that the animals, at least, had identifiable owners.

"That is immaterial under present conditions. We cannot allow private interest to govern while so many are hungry."

"I don't believe," Mr. Moffat said, "that any of the owners will refuse to share. We are all family and friends and neighbors around here, of long standing. We've always helped those in need. It's always been how we are."

"I am pleased to hear that. But, that way of doing things does not have the objectivity that is required. We are the ones best suited to the task, and we will ensure that no one is treated unfairly or goes without. Our entire reason for being here is the welfare of your citizens. I will see that things are handled properly and to your satisfaction."

I stopped by the Armstrongs' new residence on my way back to my cabin and found the mood much improved. Having a place of their own, near their old property, has done that. They are planning to rebuild their former home—an exact reproduction, to hear the girls talk—on the former site. Ella, though, seems taken with the new because it is new. Mr. Selby and I were worthy of our pay, it appears. "It's spandy nice, really, and you don't notice that nothing goes straight unless you look too long."

I am doing well enough. I am finding the loss of Mr. Graham increasingly difficult. It is made harder by my tendency to forget he is gone. I think of something I must tell him and then remember I cannot. He dies anew for me each time. But this, I know, is common and not worth reporting. Thank God he was such an "old bastard," or it would go much worse for me.

I drank with him head to head for the last time only three days ago. He admitted to a headache, which, in retrospect, was not normal. He held that one's body was one's own affair and was as little interested in complaining about his health as he was in hearing about anyone else's. This day's drinking was dedicated to analgesia, which I still needed as much as he.

He could not be drawn into talk, too intent on dosing himself, though I baited him with every topic I thought might do. He was well into his jug before I found something to bring more than a word out of him.

"It does not bother you, really, that there can be no protection of property when anyone may have a stone?"

"No protection?" He watched the flames in the fireplace for so long that I assumed I had failed again.

He continued to live in the hut to which he had retreated when the Southerners were about. It is not far at all from his old lair, but connected by no plain or easy path.

I was thinking of leaving, but he turned, the flames

still dancing in his eyes, and said, "What protection would you need besides what you've always done? You put your rubbish in some place and then you lock it up."

"What if it is the place itself that is stolen? How do you remove someone who refuses to go?"

"Haven't I already addressed this? The other night, I thought. The best I could, anyway. But, you leave, or you think of something, or you don't. It's not going to be my problem unless they want this place, right now, and no one does."

"It is not any particular bit of property with which I am concerned. I am wondering how rights survive. One's rights to the labor one has mixed with land, or with a mine, or what have you."

"They survive if others respect them, the same way as now. The big problem will be when people start questioning your right to mix your labor with a piece of land to begin with. And they will. All land's stolen from somebody if you trace it back far enough. From a person or a group."

"So! I have discovered a commonality between Dr. Marx and you!"

"That writer you had me read."

"Yes. It was the only thing he ever said to me with which I could altogether agree. It is how he believes the original capitalists obtained their original capital. Actually, he thinks government force has always been the cardinal factor in the important thefts, so you really are kindred souls."

"As far as that goes, maybe. I'd think you'd bridle at the linking of government and force."

"It is the reduction of one to the other that is the stumbling block. Although, it may be my prejudices are softening."

"I did not see myself in that article of his."

"Well, you lack his predilection for the commons."

"If you mean the common people, I'm one of them. I

just don't like them around me in a group. And I don't trust democracy any more than I do anything else. I always said, having a thousand masters isn't any better than having just one."

"It can lead to tyranny, unquestionably. Not just in the political sphere. I am afraid your Andrew Jackson may have sent you down that road irretrievably."

"I didn't have much use for him. A good Ulster boy, but he did as much harm as good."

"You do not have much use for anybody, as far as I can tell."

He looked back into the hearth. "He should have died in the battle of New Orleans. The story of my folk culminated there. A grand climax, and we could have dropped out of history with everything wrapped up. Instead, we began to rot and leave a stink in everyone's nose. New Orleans was where we finally got our vengeance on the English after all those centuries. And finished off the Federalists. All in one blow."

I waited for him to enlarge on that, but the flames had him. "Because they had opposed the war?"

He escaped his abstraction with a perceptible jolt. "It made them look all the more like traitors when Jackson showed how easily we could win. It was the only war after the Revolution that we've needed to be in, and they tried to undermine us at every bend. You know they were plotting to give the wealthy states back to the British, don't you?"

"Some of them were. Not all of them, I think."

"A lot of them. And everybody was ready and willing to believe it was the whole lot—that's the interesting aspect. It was because everyone recognized that they were traitors in their principles and in their hearts right from the beginning. From before the beginning."

I looked into the fire to see what kept pulling him to it. It was burning well, blazing tall with flames that bent against the clay at the top. They flowed in the ordered turmoil good fires always show, almost in patterns and never quite. I could not help but see shapes, but shapes with no essence that outlived the instant—faces and forms that dissolved as soon as I distinguished them. There were living things in there, and architecture, creatures and constructions, but they were never still and they were never separate. Their identities streamed and merged and transformed. I could not hold them, and the fire would not. All that endured was the fire itself.

He said, "The Republic was sick from its birth because of them."

It was my turn to be snatched from the flames. It took an effort to remember what we were talking about. "The Federalists?"

"Hamilton, especially. He was a seed of cancer in our vitals right from the beginning."

"But, you think that ended at New Orleans."

"Just its first manifestation. It bought us time. Too late, though, as it turns out—the disease is in us too deep."

"The shield may change that," I said, but he was not listening.

"Let me say this for Hamilton, though," he continued. "He was sincere. He fought in the Revolution. He wasn't like most of your centralizers, who are just looking for strong men to take care of them and protect them and tell them what to do. He wasn't like his admirers. His only problem was that he didn't grow up here, so he put different values on things."

He stood and moved his chair so the back was to the fireplace, then sat again. "It is very sad, *Monsieur*, to outlast one's country."

Bending his head, he chafed his temples roughly with his knuckles. "I have fourteen children. Did I tell you that? Fourteen who lived."

"That poor woman."

He laughed, the first true laughter I had heard from

him in a long while. "I had more than one wife. Three, in fact."

"So, Margaret, and Lydia, and who?"

He laughed again. "No, Lydia's one that got away. All of them were named Margaret. My oldest boy, Charlie, lives in Pope County, Illinois. He was named after Margaret's father. He'll be the one to split up the property when I go, or sell it and split up the proceeds. Should be easy to get a letter to him."

"Me? I shall not be around here that long."

"Well, whoever. Josh Moffat or the Armstrong woman."

I would take that as prophetic, but I had noticed all along, in the relief the jumping firelight gave to the angles of his face, how thin he had gotten. I do not know precisely what killed him, hemorrhage or seizure or what you will, but it did not cheat him of many days.

Pulaski County, Kentucky, U. S. A., 26 October 1861

"Your friend the captain is being very sparing in his distributions," Susannah said to me this morning.

"What do you mean?"

"His sergeant gives out so little it's more an insult than an assistance. Old Miss Halliday is having to get help from her neighbors, and they don't have enough themselves. Nobody does. And the Yankees are sitting on that pile of food."

"It is not precisely a 'pile' anymore."

"Still, much as I hate the shields, we may need to send people to Somerset."

"We shall, if circumstances worsen. But, we would risk advertising the shields' existence."

"Then, you need to talk to the captain."

"Shall we walk down together? Sunny days like this are becoming rare."

She consented, and I collected my coat and stick, and slipped a stone into my pocket.

"Why are you taking that damn thing?" she asked.

"Because it is no trouble to carry and might be useful."

"For what?"

"I cannot say ahead of time, obviously. Who knows what may happen in the course of a day or an hour?"

"Why don't you wear your gun and new holster, too? That at least makes you look flash."

"Weapons make military governments uneasy. So would the stone, if they knew what it was, but they do not. You should carry one yourself."

"I'll never touch one of the things."

"But, one may touch you," I said, pulling the artifact out again and making as if to brush her with it.

She ran, giggling, and I pursued until I caught and kissed her. She held my wrist to keep the stone away from herself.

On our way down, she filled out my brief on the state of affairs. The situation is not good.

Apart from the post office, these soldiers do not use the town but have pitched tents in careful rows in a field nearby. They are building breastworks and fencing the perimeter, and have begun to construct tiny cabins to replace the tents for the winter. It is not difficult to gain admission to the camp—one need only alert a guard that one is entering so that he may give an official nod.

Captain Arnim administers from a table in front of his tent. We were directed there by a cheerful private with what may have been an Irish enunciation—my ear is not sufficiently educated to tell, and Susannah could not identify it. A great number of these soldiers are what the Kentuckians call "Dutchmen," but there is the mixture here one would find around any contemporary American city like Cincinnati.

I was not, therefore, surprised that a black man was in attendance at the captain's table until I saw that it was Mr. Guildford. The officer and he had been introduced at the funeral, but did not say a great deal to one another that I recalled.

"I'm getting advice on how to join up," he told me.

"With this company?"

"Probably not."

"Where is he?"

"Oh, he was called away for a minute on something to do with supplies of tobacco, if I understood correctly, but he promised to be back shortly."

Indeed, he returned at that moment, and bade us all sit after taking our hands and bowing. "I have been consulting with your Elder Bell."

We inhaled audibly and in unison, and the corner of his lipless mouth flicked up and down. "It appears everyone has shaded the truth about the rebels' departure. Why? You have accomplished a glorious thing."

"What did he tell you?" I asked.

"That you rose as one and cleansed your land of the subversionaries. Why did you wish to hide that?"

"What more did he tell you?"

"What more is there to tell?"

I heard no guile in this. I said, "It is for my benefit that we hid the truth. I took an active part, and neither of our governments would take a sympathetic view of that."

"That need not appear in the reports. *I* sympathize. You are an aristocrat—the promptings of your noble heart would allow no other course."

He lifted his chin. "My line was Prussian, long ago. It is said in my family that we are of Junker blood."

"It is said," I repeated.

"The *von* was dropped from our name in the passage of the years."

"Are you aware," I asked, "that this Bell cooperated with the Confederates while they were here?"

"He has explained that to me. It was a ploy to learn their designs."

"He did more than that. He identified people as Northern partisans and drew up a list. They were arrested and killed."

"That was unfortunate, but he tells me he chose only the unreliable—those with no loyalties either way. He did not foresee the killing, and would have acted otherwise had he known."

"Percina Johnstone was as keen a Unionist as anyone could be," Susannah said in an estimably steady voice. "And she wasn't the only one. The only thing those people had in common was that they'd gotten on Elder Bell's bad side."

"There are human costs to war, my dear. If this individual was as ardent a patriot as you say, she would not mind the sacrifice."

"I was on the list myself," I said.

277

This nonplussed him so, I nearly laughed aloud. He strove desperately to find an acceptable response, his mouth open the while.

I took pity on him. "The Elder is not worthy of your trust."

"I have talked with him at length and found his political views to be correct in all regards."

"As did the Southerners, I am sure. Do not place your confidence in anything he says. But, let that be. We are here on another matter. The feeling of the townspeople is that the distributions of food are inadequate. Many of them are in severe distress."

"I am sorry, but the reserves must be stewarded if they are to last. We are doing the most we are able."

"What about the livestock and fowl? They have not been rationed out at all."

"They will be. We are giving out the more perishable supplies first." He laid his hand on mine. "It is hard, I know, to watch the suffering. But, the seemingly most merciful remedy is often the least. True, rational compassion looks to the whole."

"The tobacco," Susannah whispered.

"Yes," I said. "I understand that you are as economical with the tobacco as with the rest. Would it do any harm to allot that more generously? It is not a necessity and it does help to relieve the pangs of hunger if nothing more substantial is to be had."

"I am afraid that our policy will be the contrary of that. Elder Bell has been very persuasive about the opportunity presented us to improve the morality and health of your citizens. The tobacco is to be destroyed."

We, now, were the ones at a loss, and the symptoms were much like his a moment before.

"Might I inquire," I finally managed to ask, "under what authority you are doing any of this? Neither the provisions nor the tobacco came to us from the army."

"I am the sole effective government in this district. As

such, I have the authority of the State."

It was clear from the emphasis he gave this last word that he had a doctrine and that discussion would be futile. "Then there is little more for us to say. I would only caution you that the population here has traditional views on liberty at variance with your aims. There will be disputes."

"Then they must be taught that true freedom is only found in alignment with the will of an ethical community."

He set his arms on the table and straightened, in the manner that indicates a meeting has ended. "We can discuss this further over dinner, however. Would tomorrow evening be acceptable? At around 7:00, perhaps, and we shall dine at 8:00? You are all to come, of course. I am also inviting Elder Bell and my lieutenants, so I will have this table replaced with a larger."

We thanked him and got up to depart.

"Anthony," he said. "We shall also talk further about your plans."

Mr. Guildford thanked him again, and we left together.

"What was that all about?" Susannah asked. Mr. Guildford laughed in commiseration.

I smiled as well. "It is a way of speaking increasingly popular in Europe nowadays. Our warrior is an *idéologue* too, it seems."

"It will not stand him well around here," said Mr. Guildford.

"Not once people go without smoking for a few days," Susannah said. "He's going to get himself shot."

"You might keep your voices down until we are no longer surrounded by his troops," I suggested. "So, what is his advice on joining the army?"

"He says that I would be welcome in his outfit, but Lincoln doesn't like the idea of us serving as soldiers.

There has been talk of organizing 'Colored Volunteers' companies, but the proposal's not going well. The captain's trying to think of a way around the problem. I could sign on as a laborer pretty easily." He shrugged. "That wasn't my plan. I'd rather just head into the south with bags full of stones and electrical batteries."

"It is difficult for a man of spirit to stand about idly while great enterprises offer themselves. The captain is right about that. I can esteem that in him—and you—and his men, I suppose. Even in the Southerners who were here."

"No matter what they're fighting for?"

"That is the difficulty. Captain Arnim, I much suspect, is fighting to give a shape to things where neither freedom nor honor will have a place. I would be satisfied with either, at this point, but he would banish both. It is a monstrous vision."

We were beyond the gates and Mr. Guildford kept pace with us, though I had assumed he would head in the opposite direction.

"You've changed, then," said Susannah, "if freedom alone is good enough."

"I am still not convinced that your notion of freedom can sustain itself with no shared ends beyond itself. Force is not the only enemy of freedom, whatever Mr. Graham may have thought. But, my one passion has always been the love of liberty and human dignity. I have a predilection for great events, though—if civilization remains stable at all in the coming age of shields, I worry that it will be a little, democratic, bourgeois pot of soup. That would tire me more than I can express."

"It's equality, then, that's your real adversary."

"No, I can accept that too. It is the way the world has been going, anyway. I love liberty by taste, but equality by instinct and reason."

"But, you don't think they sit easily together," Mr. Guildford said.

"No. And equality does not sit well with grandeur or glory, though liberty may."

"Is there a solution?"

"There is no need for one. Or, no point to one. I spent much of my life constructing polities in my mind that would reconcile them all, but the shields have swept that all away. What will happen, will happen. We must wait for the dust to settle before it will make sense to theorize again."

"Still, what did you conclude? It would be a shame, after all that work, just to scrap it without showing it to anyone."

"My thinking limited itself to the case of France, which is an exceptional case."

"Still..."

This theme had been so far from my mind of late that it was not easy to push my thoughts into articulable order. "First, understand that I can only see all governments as more or less effective ways of satisfying the passion for liberty and dignity, which I believe most men share with me unless they have been so perverted that they are scarcely human. It is the only legitimate— the only sacred—aim of government. All else must be referred to it.

"I find that my prejudices are more democratic or aristocratic as I observe a government that veers too far to the other extreme. I might have had only one of these predispositions had I been born in another time or place. As it is, I am comfortable with both. I was born in the wake of a long revolution that had destroyed the old but left nothing new and enduring in its stead. Aristocracy was dead by the time I came into the world, and democracy was a not yet more than a dream. I have, therefore, no prejudice toward the one or the other.

"I have no nostalgia for the Old Regime and no natural love for democracy. I am clear-sighted enough to see the good and evil in both. A republic would not do for France. She needs a monarchy, and not an elective one—she needs a monarchy by birth. Only with that will she be strong enough, especially in foreign affairs. France must have a central government vigorous in its proper domain of action."

"I knew it!" said Susannah. "You want a queen. An Elizabeth you can play courtier to."

"That says more about your fantasies than mine. I think I am the man in the world least suited to be a courtier. To be serious, though, an Elizabeth is precisely what I do not want. The central power needs to be restricted to explicitly limited functions—primarily war and whatever is external, though not entirely limited to that. It should not be involved with everything in general and it needs to be subordinate, ultimately, to the legislature and the public will. It is not impossible to vest it with great powers and still assure provincial liberties. The greatest part of the decisions of life can still be left in the individual's hands where it belongs."

"You think this is possible?" asked Mr. Guildford.

"I was convinced it was. It is not now. To be honest, I am no longer certain that the grand accomplishments for which I wanted a monarch have ever been more than uniformed thuggery—butchery exalted by opera costumes. Yet, I shall mourn for that world and the beauty of its illusions."

"I think you're always mourning something or other," said Susannah. "If it weren't that, it would be something else."

Pulaski County, Kentucky, U. S. A., 27 October 1861

Sunday, and Susannah spent most of it in church, again. They have a new pastor, promoted from the ranks of those considered qualified, which seems to be almost everyone.

I asked her before she left if she understood Elder Bell's allusion to a horse's head. There is, in fact, such a thing buried in the foundations. Susannah says it was an animal that did good service in the building's construction. I do not doubt he earned the distinction in that way. I also know that it was the custom in Europe, for many ages, among the peoples of the north and west, to bury animals under large structures and bridges. Not always the lower animals. It happens still, and is a token of the pagan past, like the bonfires they will burn on the hilltops here in a few days. I appreciate (even relish) Elder Bell's ire.

When I stopped at the Armstrongs' to collect her for the dinner, Susannah was tired and irritable. "Who eats at 8:00? I'm starving and I can barely stay awake."

"You are supposed to have something small to eat in the afternoon to fortify yourself. Eat something now."

"It's too late, now. It would spoil the meal."

"Just something small enough to last you."

"I don't want to eat!"

"Then, do not complain."

It did not augur well for the rest of the evening. She was more fetching than usual in a dress I had not seen before, but that caused its own problems when Toodie teased her about "trying to be fine." I hurried us out of the house before my companion's humor worsened irreparably.

We met Mr. Guildford in the town. He was not of a mind for socializing either. "We need to work to convince our host to moderate his policies. People are talking about taking up the guns and shields again."

"Who is talking?" I asked.

"Who do you think?"

"That is madness. These men have done nothing of the same order as the Confederates. Besides, they are twice as many and better secured."

"Then we'd better work on the captain."

One of the platoon leaders, Lieutenant William Robson, was waiting for us at the gate and took us to the captain's tent. As promised, a large table had been substituted for the other, spread with a linen cloth and costlier tableware than I have yet seen on this continent.

Captain Arnim introduced us to another officer, Lieutenant Carl Fiedler, and had us seated by a genial butler in civilian clothing whom we learned to be his private servant. Elder Bell was already seated and did not acknowledge our arrival beyond giving us all a guarded nod and a frown.

"I must apologize for my dress," I told the company as I sat. "The only appropriate clothing I have is in Somerset."

"I, too, must apologize again for that," said the captain, "and reassure you that the road will be opened as soon as feasible. You see, for our part, that we do not have dress uniforms. This will be a field dinner, though I hope the quality will compensate for the setting."

Before he could take his chair at the head of the table, his butler came and whispered in his ear. "Good," the captain said and, sitting, said to us, "We are all here, and it has been a long day, and I am told that it is unnecessary to wait until 8:00 to dine. Shall we anticipate our schedule?"

We were all eager to oblige and gave our consent. Susannah's was, perhaps, a slight bit too enthusiastically given.

"But, first," Captain Arnim said, "I have a treat for Monsieur de Grimouville. I have had sherry carried with us for just such occasions."

Susannah's face wilted, as did Mr. Guildford's and, possibly, mine. Alcohol we still had in plenty—it was food that we most craved. But, when the sherry was brought out, it was accompanied by platters of pickled oysters and herrings, gherkins, and little sausages with parsley. We took dutiful sips from our glasses when they were filled, then set them aside for a time while we paid court to the *hors d'œuvre.*

Lieutenant Robson was from a family that had moved to Ohio from Pennsylvania. "The name is Scottish," he told us. "But the family came here from Northern Ireland with a lot of other families. We stuck together, through the years, all the way to Ohio."

The other lieutenant's parents had come from Bavaria. I tried to speak German with him, but he knew none. "My father refused to use it, even with my mother."

The butler managed to make little jokes with us the whole time, without seeming to be overfamiliar. It was an impressive exercise in poise and balance, but was to be attributed, I think, more to genuine good nature and humility than artifice. He was especially obliging to me throughout the subsequent meal, since my arm is still impaired and I had difficulty with the utensils.

"Mr. Jones will be leaving us soon," Captain Arnim said, indicating this servant. "His wife is about to give birth, and he is rejoining her in Cincinnati. I hope to have him back, once things are in a settled condition." The man nodded.

The food and drink made me feel light in the head and playful. "You are not drinking?" I asked the Elder, who was as attentive to the food as we. He looked up at me sourly for a second, then returned to his feeding without responding.

The captain said, "I am sorry, Elder Bell. I know you do not approve. We must make concessions, however, to hospitality."

"Will there be cigars?" I asked.

"Regretfully, no," he answered. "I have never picked up the practice myself and do not have a supply."

Elder Bell spoke something too low to hear.

Smiling, I asked him to repeat it.

"I said, if we are to have spirits, we may as well have tobacco. It is fitting that they attend one another. Of the greatest sots I have known, none did not begin with the tobacco habit."

"You believe it is a strict progression?"

"It begets a thirst that will not be alleviated except by liquor. It is the working of the poison. They are Satan's twin ministers, ordained to the ruin of all health and morals. Of itself, tobacco leads to impotency and unnatural lust, to palsy, and, in due course, to lunacy and death."

"Both impotency and unnatural lust. That must make for great frustration."

He began to reply, but I was robbed of the benefit of his observations by Mr. Jones, who offered us a choice of cream soups and bouillon. Fish appeared, too, and a diversity of wines.

"The Elder is perfectly right," the captain remarked. "It is why I was easily won over to his idea of destroying the tobacco we captured."

"Shouldn't people's health be their own concern?" Susannah asked.

"Not if it burdens society. In all things, it is the welfare of the whole that must be considered. Always remember that service to the State should be a man's highest aspiration. A woman's, too."

"But there will be another crop."

"Oh, I know that we cannot eradicate the vice. The best we can do, I think, is discourage it. I am contemplating a sort of excise on its production."

"But not on its wicked twin?" I asked.

"That, too. On distillation. We can institute that measure immediately, because the activity goes on all year."

I looked conspicuously at his wineglass.

"We are not trying to do away with drinking," he said. "Just curbing the most irresponsible forms. Be glad that the Elder's position is merely advisory."

"This will not go down well."

"Acts of kindness are not always immediately perceived as such by their beneficiaries. They will comprehend in time and thank us. When their wills have been trained to accord with the common good, they will be truly free, at last."

"Yes," Elder Bell put in. "True freedom is had only in reconciliation with the Lord."

Captain Arnim smiled appreciatively. "And the State is the presence of God upon the earth."

"So, you are doing these things at the behest of the federal government?" I asked.

"No, but as its sole representative in the area—and the only effectual authority, as I have said—I can take that discretion upon myself."

The main courses included ribs and roasts of pork and beef, and a large roasted goose, besides untold and untellable vegetable dishes and breads. I wanted to stuff my pockets, but could not do it undetected with only the one arm. Susannah, for her part, had nowhere to hide anything. Mr.Guildford observed the proprieties for their own sake, as far as I was aware.

At a certain juncture, Susannah observed that there seemed to be more food available than the distributions to the people would suggest.

The captain was not disconcerted a whit. "If the provisions are to be distributed at all, there must be providers, and their needs must be seen to as much as anyone else's." He looked in my eyes. "You and I understand that."

I said, "I had a friend—in fact, you were at his funeral —who felt that the proper function of government is to prevent more government."

"That is fine," replied Captain Arnim, "for the privileged. Would your other friend, Anthony here, agree?"

"Only because of the government in Washington," said Elder Bell, "is there a chance of ending slavery. Only when our cause is victorious will Anthony share fully in the equality and liberty that others now enjoy, to the extent that the limitations of his race allow him."

The captain toasted Mr. Guildford with, "He will find genuine equality at last, in obedience to the State."

The dinner ended with cakes, and fruits, and cheeses. Then, the table was cleared so that a tray with port and glasses could be set down for us.

Captain Arnim toasted again. "To President Lincoln and the beginning of a new era. An era in which America will acquire that imperial glory of which Hamilton spoke so often, but in the pursuit of which we have been so lax. May the Stars and Stripes soon wave in every quarter of the globe, bringing freedom to all."

He caught himself. "Except France, of course."

I raised my glass to the last.

He sat and said, "I was at Lincoln's inauguration. I was distant from him, but he is tall and I could make him out clearly. I said to myself, 'There is the world spirit, there is history, in a stovepipe hat.' Where Napoleon failed, he will succeed. My apologies, but your emperor did fail."

"I would have disagreed not many weeks ago. We have an Empire, and it derives its grandeur from Napoleon's personal splendor. I used to believe he was the most extraordinary individual who had appeared in the world for many centuries, however pernicious the institutions he established. Now, I am not sure that even the grandeur is more than spectacle, and tinsel, and noise. I have trouble seeing the difference between uniforms and livery."

His features went very still and cold, and I knew I had struck him, finally.

"He may have been merely a murderous dwarf," I added.

"That is for you to say. I only know that we Americans stand on the threshold of a new age, a culmination of all history. A time when all of life can be put in order and directed to the general good. With strong, unified authority we shall even be able to rationalize the economy, at long last, so that it serves humanity and not narrow, private gain."

"So, Louis XIV is your *real* hero."

Puzzlement flickered in his eyes for a second, but he carried on blithely, "We shall deliver mankind from its animal nature."

"Its fallen nature," amended the Elder. "No portion of human life will be beyond healing. Man's most sordid, sensual appetites will lose their old dominion." His eyes went to Susannah and away.

"Yes," said the captain. "Even those energies can be harnessed for the higher good."

Elder Bell touched his fingers tip to tip. "And not for venereal excess. They were not given Man for the casual gratification of trollops." He looked at Susannah, again.

"Captain," I said, "I am faced with a dilemma. It would seem bad form to whip a man's dog in front of him, but yours appears sorely in need of discipline."

"Perhaps, then, we must bring the occasion to a conclusion. Anthony, you may stay."

He saw us off, icily proper, and had us accompanied to the main gate.

"If he's planning to tax the next tobacco crop, he must be planning on a long stay," Susannah commented to me, as we walked off under a waning moon.

"My impression is that these people mean to be around for the rest of time."

Pulaski County, Kentucky, U. S. A., 28 October 1861

Mr. Graham liked German immigrants. The only families with which he had experience were those that had been assimilated thoroughly to his own tribe's principles and customs. He also liked the Chinese and the Jews—he claimed they arrived already possessing the right attitude toward things.

He despised nearly everyone else as people who came over only after all the conflict and work of settlement was done: "People whose fathers and grandfathers were picking turnips for their masters while we were fighting the Revolution, and who then decided there was money to be made here, after all the danger was over."

I am not as dubious as he about these other newcomers or as sanguine as he about the Germans. It is not the latter's immigrants so much that I mistrust, I suppose, as the intellectual influences they import.

I spent two very agreeable and edifying months in Berlin a few years ago. My acquaintances were chiefly university professors and their families, by whom I was warmly accepted and made to feel at home. There was great intelligence there, and always a sincere simplicity of manners and life.

I cannot speak as well for their public life. They were what two hundred years of absolute government and sixty years of centralization had made them. The long practice of bureaucratic dependence—as administrators or the administrated—has shaped their philosophy in ways that could have done lasting harm if not for the gift that has fallen to us from heaven.

The incredible pace of German emigration to this country—140,000 a year at the time I was there—aggravates the threat, but it would mean little were it not for the commission they bear from the academics.

I could not get Mr. Graham to see things this way. He

thought his own folk, in their pharisaical dotage, were the bigger danger. Perhaps he was right. The moralism of the two madmen at the dinner reeked more of Ulster than Berlin. But the two spirits match so well that I suspect a hybrid was inevitable. Had it flourished, in a world without the shield...

Early this afternoon, Mr. Elliot came to me in such a troubled state that he could barely take the breath to speak. "Is what Anthony says true?"

"Probably. What does he say?"

"That the captain's farther off plumb than Elder Bell and he's going to help him force all his crackbrained ideas on us."

"Well, they were talking of imposing taxes on tobacco and whiskey. You should not worry about it. I doubt this unit will keep its position here for many weeks, whatever Captain Arnim believes—war moves quickly. If not, our communications should be restored soon, and you may lodge a complaint."

"They're already doing it! Or, trying to. They sent a squad around to the Hodgson farm to collect on their stills. The Hodgsons got their work in on three of them, but the rest got away, and now the place is surrounded."

We had been standing on my porch, but now I sat on the step and put my face in my hands. I had been telling myself it would not come to this—that the captain was a fanatic but not insane. That his own prudence would win through and stay his hand.

"What should we do?" he asked.

I replied without raising my head. "What do you want to do? Raise the siege?"

"I think we have to. But, this is a big step. It feels like we'd be crossing a line, somehow. It was different with the rebels. This lot are the real government."

"It had to happen some time. If not here, then elsewhere in the country or elsewhere in the world. It had to happen first, somewhere. For you, this is the

Rubicon. I crossed mine when I killed my first man. Once you have killed one, you are an assassin. The deaths after add nothing to that. Nor do their particularities."

"I never understand half of what you say. Should I collect the boys or not?"

"Let us find Mr. Selby and lay the onus off on him."

As it happened, he found us before we had gone more than a hundred paces.

"Have you heard about the Hodgsons?" he asked.

"We were coming to you," I said. "It has been proposed that we rally again and march to the rescue."

"There's no point. The Hodgsons are all dead."

"Then, revenge will be the point," said Mr. Elliot.

"I wouldn't advise that. For now. They are too many and too well trained. They could make a wasteland of this district before you made a healthy start. It's more important to start distributing the devices to the people around."

"I cannot help with that," I said. "It will be difficult enough to accommodate them to this alien apparatus. They will not accept it on the recommendation of an alien."

While the other two went off to organize their agents, I debated whether to go to the Armstrongs—and renew the long and unprofitable campaign to convince Susannah to carry a stone—or go to the camp and waste my time on the captain instead. I chose the captain, whose makeup I did not positively know to be unbending.

The gates were closed when I arrived, however, and the guard doubled. By chance, Lieutenant Fiedler was inspecting the perimeter and, when I caught his attention, was willing to take me to the command tent.

Captain Arnim sat at the large replacement table, no longer adorned with its convivial trimmings. "What does he want?" he asked his officer.

"I don't know sir. He requested to see you."

To me, the captain said, "Be quick about it. I have a great deal on my hands, at the moment."

"I wished to attempt to dissuade you from actions that are not strictly a part of your military duties. You have seen how ill considered they were. You will not get compliance from these people."

"Were the revenues all, I would agree. But, it is compliance itself that is at issue now, and I will have it. They have fired upon my men."

"And paid the penalty."

"I do not mean the farm family. My soldiers have been shot—some killed—in the streets and in the very camp. I have set patrols. I am dismayed that you did not meet one."

"I am most sorry, but the trouble will cease at once if you rescind the excises. I have the confidence of many months' association with the natives."

"It shall not be done. They will learn, to their cost if necessary, the obligations of civil life. I would sooner exterminate them than see them continue unregenerate."

"Your superiors will not see things in the same light, I much expect."

"My superiors would be sad to hear of it, I imagine, but—as they say in Ohio—they have bigger fish to fry. They will not encumber themselves with minutiae."

He picked up a pen he had laid down when we approached. "I do not think it will come to that degree of violence, though. If the situation does not improve, I am considering constructing a separate camp where the population may be concentrated peaceably. That is for the future, however. They are likely less obstinate than you judge, and some limited demonstrations of our resolve should settle the matter."

He mimed with his hands for the Lieutenant Fiedler to escort me back to the gate.

"I have talked with many men in your company," I

told the lieutenant. "They are as courteous and kind a group as any one might hope to meet. Are they capable of the things he seems ready to ask of them?"

He looked at me coldly. "They will follow orders, as any citizen would."

I have been brought to an appreciation of a *jeu d'esprit* of Mr. Graham that not all men are political animals, but too many are political livestock.

Pulaski County, Kentucky, U. S. A., 30 October 1861

Even as I spoke with Captain Arnim, I have learned, members of his patrols were being surprised and slain. It was none of our Irregulars doing. There were no killings that night, strangely.

Attacks on homes and farms resumed yesterday morning. None were successful and the troops, again strangely, withdrew. In the afternoon, the region was flooded with small detachments of three or four men who seemingly mapped the location of every dwelling they could find. Mine is charted somewhere, as is the Armstrongs'. Something large is imminent.

I heard of many plans to waylay the units, but no reported successes

Susannah and I spent most of today on the peak we found three weeks ago, when I was still clean of anyone's blood. I expected the colors to have faded, but they have only grown more fiery. The green is gone, except on the conifers, and there are large patches of simple brown overwhelmed by the red around them. It is an ocean no longer, but an exultation of flame.

We had our first frost last night, but there was little left to damage, so it was just another marker on our way into winter. It cleansed the air, somehow, and there was little wind, and sounds came to us clear and sharp from all the valleys. Early on, we thought we heard gunshots, but these ceased and left us with the unidentifiable creaks and murmurs of the hills and basins.

The day was warm, despite the lateness of the year and the sun's eerie, angled light. We took apples and maize cakes and cider, not having much else. I brought along the book of sonnets, which we have come to prize. We did not say much, nonetheless, until the sun was noticeably lower still.

"Time has run on," she remarked.

"The hour or the season?"

"Both. It's colder and sadder."

"*Sunt lacrimae rerum.* There are tears in things."

"I don't know the reference."

"Virgil. The *Aeneid.*"

"You'll have to get me a copy," she said, distantly, and got up. She walked in a circle, surveying the rolling land. "Tomorrow is Halloween. I see why the dead come out this time of year."

"You've seen them?"

"I've felt them. The barrier between is thinnest now."

"And you'll celebrate that. With fires in the mountains."

"Used to be just one, when I was a girl. Before we had so many people. We'd put out all other fires and light them again from the big one. It was mostly all a party, though, like it is now. People will dress up and play games. Ella's already carving pumpkins. "

"We did not have so much fun. When I was growing up, it meant we had to spend three days in church or in cemeteries."

"We have fun to drive away the feeling everyone gets from the dead being so close."

"What do they want?"

"You can't tell if they want anything. Anything at all. Whether they'll want anything ever again. That's the scary part."

"But, your religious beliefs have something to say on the subject."

"Those are fine any other time of year."

Without warning, she held me and kissed me longer and more deeply than she had ever before. I felt her little belly hard beneath her dress. "Something of the living always survives," I said. She smiled.

Paris, 30 April 1865

It took more time to gather the strength to reread
these volumes than it did to write them. The crate in
which they were shipped sat in an unused closet until
this last December, when a servant inquired about them.
I let it sit a few weeks more, then unpacked them and left
them in a pile on the floor by my desk. I thought to ease
my entry into them in that way, since it would require so
little to take up the first notebook as I passed one day
and read.

It was not that easy. I had worked to satisfy myself
that I was safely through the lowest passages of sorrow,
but, day by day, I could not open the journals. I feared
them as one fears to lift a rock in a field—a serpent may
wait there. My condition looked like health, and that
sufficed. Why test the appearance and risk losing even
that?

I have read them, now, and I am not destroyed. I am
as whole as I shall ever be. My soul, like my arm, works
well enough, if I do not ask much from it.

It is spring. I do not know what sort of weather they
are having outside. It was sunny the last time I looked,
and the smell of new growth was in every breeze.
Everywhere is green, and the gardens and the boulevards
are full of colors. I see it all as through a smoked glass,
accurately but somehow dilute. It does not move me,
and I prefer to keep the drapes closed. Yet, I am not
unhappy. I would even say I am content, and that is
something few can truthfully claim.

I shall never make use of this journal. Too soon and
readily, it wandered off from its purpose. That purpose
is no longer mine, in any case. I have done one great
thing—or shared in it—and that is as much as I wish to
do. Both greatness and doing have lost their old appeal.
Still, the story needs its end. I shall give it and return
these volumes to their closet, there to wait for someone

who can distill something of value from them. An historian, perchance. I, myself, am outside of history.

Twilight came early those last evenings of October. I reached the Armstrongs' place under a dark sky. Only the thinnest shaving of moon remained to light my way. I was to join with the family and Mr. Selby to attend a bonfire before returning for whatever Ella had planned.

She was on the porch, setting candles into jack-o'-lanterns, pumpkins into which faces were carved.

I greeted her and said, "I have heard two accounts of these pumpkins. One is that they commemorate the dead. The other is that they scare them off. Which is true?"

"Both. We want them to feel remembered, and we want them to do it somewhere else."

She was dressed all in white, and a mask of red clay or some such lay face up next to where she knelt. It had no features save for eyeholes and a mouth, and, with its uneven surface, that made it all the more uncanny and disturbing.

"Is everyone to be in disguise?" I asked.

"No. Just me. Toodie was going to, but she's being cross. Bob was supposed to be here, but he's down in the town." She was having difficulty fixing one of the candles into the melted wax that was to hold it. "Oh, and you're supposed to meet him there, but Susannah wants to see you first."

Inside, the others were wrapped to go out. "Good," said Susannah. "Bob wants to see you in town, but you might make it back in time. We'll be at the Maxwells'."

She instructed me how to get there, and added, "Bob says to bring a gun. Do you have yours?"

I swept my coat aside to reveal the revolver in its holster. The Yankee soldiers' odd behavior had unsettled me.

"And you brought that stupid stone, I imagine."

"And the Bowie knife."

"Then, you are set. We will see you later."

She kissed me, and I left without a further word, losing that last opportunity.

The paths and lanes were only just visible, but I had trod them often enough to compensate. As I came among the buildings, I left the road and stole along among the trees and shadows to the side. I could see the light from the torches and fires of the camp, but the low, mingled noise was missing that marked the place when the clamors of the day had stilled. In the hills around, other fires were coming alight, one after another, like the sprinkling of stars when the day is fading.

Meeting no one, I crept closer to the camp. Passing near to the house opposite the post office, I was seized by my coattail.

"Edouard," whispered a voice I recognized as Mr. Selby's. "Come farther into the dark."

"What is happening?"

"I can't tell, exactly. Something was obviously up, so I brought a couple men with me to watch the camp. Just in the past half hour, those little units of two or three men have been leaving in all directions. They're armed. It can't be good. I only had the two men with me, and I've sent them off to warn people. I've waited here for you, but I'm going off, too. You go warn the family."

I hurried to the Maxwells' as swiftly as the dying moon allowed. When I came upon what I hoped was the final track leading to their land, I began to hear gunfire, clear and immediate to my front, and distant and echoing from elsewhere in the hills. I left the path and took off directly through the forest toward the nearer sound.

The wood started to shimmer with orange light as I made my way, and I knew I was moving toward the fire. Emerging, at length, into the open, I saw several people standing around a pair on the ground, one a woman I did not know and the other Mrs. Armstrong, who held her in her arms.

I went to them, and there was a flash and a crack. Mrs. Armstrong looked up and cried, alarmed, "Don't shoot him! That's Mr. de Grimouville!"

"What has happened?" I shouted.

"We were attacked from the trees," she told me. "They just started shooting. Some of us had...the protections, but they came on us cold."

"Did you drive them off?"

"They left, at any rate. Joe Maxwell thinks he winged one, but I don't know. He took some fellows out after them. But, Mrs. Maxwell has been hit in the leg."

"I'm all right," the woman said. She raised her hand as though to have it kissed. "Emily Maxwell. Very pleased to meet you."

I bowed and addressed myself to Mrs. Armstrong again. "Where are Susannah and the girls?"

"Toodie's here," she said, and pointed to where the girl stood with a feral expression on her face. "We've sent all the children back to their homes. Susannah's taking Ella back through the woods."

For a second, I felt relief. Then, suddenly, it was plain to me what it all meant. "Overtake your children before they reach your houses! It is a trap!"

The bonfires would have served as beacons for the soldiers, guiding them through the night directly to groups of unsuspecting revelers. But it was a twofold strategy. When they had accomplished all they could at the fires, they would go to the residences they had mapped and wait.

"Do your children have shields?" I asked the gathering, and did not get as many nods as I would have liked.

One man cleared his throat. "My family doesn't. A lot of us didn't believe in them. You shouldn't have sent Johnny Elliot to peddle them."

"Ella has one. Susannah doesn't," said Mrs. Armstrong.

"Stay here," I ordered. "I shall intercept them before they reach home."

I could not run in the woods, and, when I reached the road again, found that I had to use the beaten ways to find my direction to the house. Through the trees, I could see that the fires on the hillsides had multiplied, and I had little doubt what that signified.

While crossing the last bit of ground to the house, I stumbled over something and fell. It was the body of a Union soldier, an arrow sprouting incongruously from his chest. I got up and ran the rest of the way to discover the door open and emitting smoke I had not been able to discern against the trees.

There were flames inside, but they were only feeding on one side of the room, as yet. From the other side, I heard coughing and turned to see Susannah propped against the wall, the floor stained dark around her, glistening in the radiance of the fire. Her shreds of clothing were so wet they looked one substance with the blood beneath her.

I bent to lift her, but she gave a jagged sob and said, "Don't. It hurts too much."

"The house is burning."

"It doesn't matter."

I saw then how savagely her abdomen had been wounded. She was right. I let her be and sat by her side. I remember how a lock of her hair had fallen before her face, and how it trembled with each short, quick breath.

"This will be the end of me," I said.

She shook her head, gently, and smiled. "It will be all right in time. It will pass, and you will make yourself content. My love."

"My love," I repeated, and then the tress of hair was still.

Paris, 4 May 1865

I carried Susannah's body out but left the building afire, giving no thought to the paltry remnants of the Armstrongs' lives, some of which I might have saved. I gave as little thought to Ella, who, I learned afterward, was in the safety of the forest, returning to the Maxwells'.

My mind came to a single point, a single precipitated desire: a need to find Captain Arnim and kill him. Failing that—or in the course of that—I would kill every Union soldier I encountered. I opened my holster and started for the camp.

I was not long from the house when I saw three moving shapes on the road ahead. "Wait, please!" I shouted, and they stopped. With the shield raised, I went close enough to see their blue uniforms, then dropped the shield and drew and fired three shots. Only one struck its target, and, as the other men raised their weapons, I raised my defense again.

Their guns discharged, and the balls hit the barrier level with my heart. Knowing they had only muskets, I felt safe in walking toward them, directing my remaining rounds at the nearer of the two. He went down, and the last man dropped his gun and ran.

I reloaded while my first victim groaned at my feet. Then, I hushed him with a shot.

Examining him, I found a pistol in his belt, which he might have used on me had he not been in such pain. I resolved to be more careful. It was a musket, of course, but it was loaded, and I took it. His comrade had nothing useful on him.

I was almost to the town when I realized that, though I could enter the camp safely through the main gate, I could not do it unnoticed. If I was to catch the captain unawares and vulnerable, I would have to find another means of access.

The woods, I knew, came within twenty feet of the

camp midway down the southern side of the fencing. There might be guards or a patrol there, but most of the men would be out on their murderous errands, and I stood a good chance.

It was too difficult to maneuver through the trees with the shield up, so I went unprotected, as stealthily as I could. Because of this, I could hear Mr. Routledge when he came up beside me and said my name, and I did not shoot him.

He had his coating of firearms, and carried a long rifle. "What are you planning on?" he asked.

"I am going into the camp to kill Captain Arnim and as many others as I meet."

"Same as us, then. We've got about ten others going in around the circuit of the fence, some with shields and some not. Some others are going to attack the gate, and the shooting will be our signal to go in."

"I am going in now, before the captain is forewarned."

"Do you have snips?"

"What?"

"Do you have a way to get through the fence?"

"No," I admitted.

"Well, I do, and you'll have to wait here with me until I'm ready."

The general attack began that instant, though, so it made no difference. We ran across the open space, and Mr. Routledge cut through the wires. Inside were other obstacles, but they had been constructed more as defense works than obstructions, and cost us little time. Thankfully, no defenders appeared until we had climbed out of a trench and had an open path to the tents. I pulled out the pistol I had taken from the dead Yankee, having decided to empty it and discard it before using the better weapon.

Then, a tent flap opened, and a young boy, perhaps fourteen or fifteen, came out. He was facing away, at first, and did not perceive us. When he turned and saw two armed men without uniforms, his eyes were wide and dark as a deer's. "Please, mister," he said, and I shot him through the body.

"Jesus, Duke," said Mr. Routledge. "What did you do that for?"

"He was there," I said. I threw the musket aside and drew the revolver.

The report was inaudible against the background of gunfire, so it drew no attention. "I am going to the command tent," I told my companion. "You may do what you will."

"I might as well come help."

There was movement to the front of the camp, but we met no one until we came behind the captain's tent. Mr. Jones, the butler, was standing there, as if on a break from his labors to take the air.

"Mr. de Grimouville," he said, and I shot him.

He looked down at the red spot on his shirt. "I wish...I wish..." he said, then sat slowly down and fell over on his side. His face went slack.

Mr. Routledge, meanwhile, had gone to the front of the tent, and I followed. He was there with his rifle pointed at Lieutenant Robson, who was seated at the table.

"Where is the captain?" I asked.

"He says he's gone to the gate," Mr. Routledge said, taking his eyes from the lieutenant, who immediately lunged for something on the table a few feet to his left. I did not recognize, then, what it was, but I fired three times, and he fell sideways from his chair, dead.

The canvas was slapped by a ball, and Mr. Routledge shot back at the soldier who had fired at us. The Yankee knelt coolly and started to reload. I fired at him once, then pulled the trigger again and got only a click. My companion set the rifle down and tried to take the man down with another of his guns, but to no effect.

As I reloaded, Jack Douglas, one of Mr. Selby's troops,

came running by. "They are forming up near the front. We're on all sides of them. Come along with me."

We all saw the Northerner take aim in time to put up our shields. When he had fired, he left, walking in the direction Mr. Douglas had indicated.

We went after him—not to catch him, but to find our people—and he did not run, but kept a measured pace until he reached his own ranks. He did make a detour to skirt the Kentuckians who stood out in the open. They shot at him, but he continued on and joined one of the lines into which the Yankees had formed.

In the light of the torches, I could see that they were drawn up into four ranks, two with their backs to the other two. They began to volley, one line firing while the other reloaded. The one massed report I heard encouraged me to keep my shield raised to save my ears. I was unwise enough to drop it once to refresh my air, and let in a sulfurous haze that I could barely breathe.

The volleys affected our men not at all, but our less systematic barrages had no better result. The Union formations lost no one, nor their rhythm, even as we advanced on them. I understood what was happening long before the shooting stopped and Captain Arnim strode out between the combatants with a stone in his upraised hand.

I understood, but ran out anyway, and emptied the revolver at him, my shield down, heedless of the bullets that might have come my way. I knew, as well, that I was to be cheated of my revenge.

He smiled, condescendingly. I let the pistol fall, and took out my knife and threw it down, and motioned him toward a wall made from bags of sand, where he could shelter from our guns. There, he too dropped his shield and spoke: "You see you have nothing we do not. You can do nothing against us."

"But, we do have it," I said. "We are equally thwarted. And you are the one who loses most by that."

"I, lose? What do you mean?"

"Do you not see that you have doomed your own hopes by picking up that stone? Do you think it can be kept a secret? That it will not find its way into the hand of everyone who wants it? In a world without violence, your State is dead and your ideals are so much vapor."

"What happens now will only show the falsity of that old lie. The State is not violence. The State is the march of God through the world. History itself will be its vindicator."

I had known that he was mad. Talk was futile. I left him there and walked back to my friends.

Paris, 7 May 1865

The shield is not perfect. A man among none but enemies must let it down at times, and, in the end, they will have him. Elder Bell left Stirling when the troops did, and where he went, I do not know. All were hot to kill him for delivering the secret of the stones to the enemy. He did not do it—I do not think he knew about it until Captain Arnim did. He did not have one, anyway, to serve as the germ for others. I have told no one the truth, because I do not care.

"I should have finished him that day I had him under my stick," I said to Mr. Guildford the last time I saw him.

"You should have," he agreed. "But he did not give the shield to the captain."

"Who did, then?"

"I did."

I had no feelings in those last weeks I spent in America. Not sorrow, not hatred, not guilt, not anger. I pondered his statement as I would a report on textile exports.

"Why?" I asked, finally.

"Because I realized that I could not give a stone to a slave and expect the stones to reproduce like yeast. Slaves don't have the materials to make electric batteries. They don't have the privacy. I could smuggle wagonfuls of the things into the South, but it would be years before all the slaves were freed. We need a Federal defeat of the rebels. That is the only cure for slavery."

"And will the North free the slaves?"

"I think they cannot help it. Their cause is withering now. They need to give their words about freedom some substance if anyone is to fight much longer. The Union has the shield, now, and they will win, if they act before the Confederacy gets it."

"They will get it soon, and the Union has not shown itself expeditious. It will end in stalemate. You have not shortened slavery's reign."

"There is at least a chance I have."

I rolled that about in my mind, idly. "There is something false, here."

He stared into my eyes. "There's an even stronger chance that every hour the North has the shield before the South means more rebels dead. Even one death would be a victory for me. I will have vengeance."

"You have stolen mine from me."

He broke his gaze. "I'm sorry, Edouard. I can't say how sorry. If there had been another way...But you will have your revenge in time. When the governments fall. The State is your real enemy. Captain Arnim was only a tool of the State."

"I would like a vengeance more direct and personal. More active. One that will let me live."

After a moment, he said, "Do not take this wrong. I would not minimize your grief. There's a course open to you, however. An active one. Do what I'm going to do. Spread the shields. Drive a blade into your enemy's heart." He smiled, uncertainly, and added, "Devour him raw."

I did not find his language as rousing as he intended it, but it was an idea. I had nothing better to do with my lingering, vacant life.

Paris, 8 May 1865

As I predicted, the 11th Independent Infantry Company was not around for the next tobacco crop. Within a month of our battle, the focus of the war shifted west, and the 11th was sent to Somerset. I have read that Captain Arnim's military career throve after his discovery of the shield and his successful use of it against "Confederate irregulars" in Stirling. He was not a captain for long.

How high he might have climbed is difficult to say, but his rise faltered when the war that made it possible began to flag. If he still holds a command, it is a titular one at this point. The old Somerset Artillery—the drinking club—was ahead of its time. It was the original for all modern armies, with its cherished martial displays and its lack of employment.

The good Elder Bell left with the troops, but whether he stayed with the unit, I could not say. I have heard nothing of him.

Mr. Guildford misjudged how speedily and wide the shield would spread, once people got the concept. The rebels had it only a beat behind the Union, and neither side was slow to put it in the field. The war exists on paper, and in the minds of politicians and the dwindling soldiery, but the identities of the antagonists are no longer fixed. The secession is an accomplished and unalterable fact. So are the lesser secessions that have robbed the two nations of states, and the states of counties, and the counties of towns, and the towns of people. The Union is a memory and the Confederacy last season's craze.

It was not simply the impossibility of combat that brought the war to a standstill. Without conscription, it could never have been feasible. It would have needed great slave armies and unimaginable deaths. And, of course, forced funding.

Slavery in its overt, unconcealed form is dead. Contrary to Mr. Guildford, again, a single stone could evidently have leavened the whole lump. Effective emancipation took less than a year. Mr. Guildford himself may have had some hand in this—he disappeared into the South before I left. He is another from whom I have not heard.

I was there at the beginning. After that night, the people of Salt Lick Creek took little persuading to accept the stones. They were safe during the weeks before the soldiers left. Though the food supply stayed with the soldiers, there was no hindrance to commerce with the outside—we no longer had a secret to hide and could walk openly down the road, impertinent and invulnerable. The stones began to flow into the world.

Toodie and Mr. Selby have married. Her mother and sister have gone with them to Kansas, where Mr. Selby does something for railroads. Mr. Moffat, however, has proposed that the mother join him in the new Arizona Territory, which still belongs to the United States.

Ella has decided that she wants to work as an assistant in a scientific laboratory. She has written letters to institutions in the East, but has received no encouragement. Perhaps in some connection with that, she has developed an interest in women's suffrage, which has proponents in Kansas. What the significance of voting really is, in a world without violence, is not clear to me, but there are other dimensions to freedom.

Pulaski County is still part of the Independent Commonwealth of Kentucky. This, despite the best efforts of Mr. Elliot. He has inherited leadership of Selby's Irregulars, which became the kernel of a political association trying to stop improvements to the road between Somerset and London. The argument, as I understand it, was that nothing good had ever come down that road. The effort only drew attention to the possibility of improvement, and enough private donations were raised to carry out the project.

The association then began to campaign for independence from the Independent Commonwealth. They have failed in this, too, to date. Mr. Elliot's new vocation has changed the man himself, however—at least outwardly. He sent me a photograph in which he is dressed like a banker of twenty years past, with trimmed hair and beard.

Whether all the new little principalities will regain an appreciation for the advantages of federation or confederation is impossible to say. It is too soon, and they are too filled with a youthful delight in autonomy. The dangers of such arrangements are foremost in their minds. It will take them time to assure themselves, deep down in their marrow, that those dangers are no more. Then, I think, something new will be built.

Americans may simply be turning back into Americans. In France, affairs have developed somewhat differently since I brought the first stone. Secession is no one's first thought, but the Second Empire is a hollow shell and will soon collapse. What will replace it, who can tell?

The stones are spreading beyond France, of course. It is not my concern. I have had vengeance, of a sort. It leaves me cold. It is abstract revenge on an abstract construct. I have no further interest in abstractions—in any politics that does not offer me a human face.

Even that overstates my interest. There is only one human face I wish to see, and I shall not see it again. In all the empty time since Susannah's death, there has been nothing to hold me to this earth, and through all the empty years to come, there will be nothing. Detachment is easy now, and acceptance of whatever the world brings upon itself.

As the old Roman says: "It is pleasant, when, on the great sea, winds stir up the waters, to stand on shore and watch the distress of another. Not because it is a pleasure to see anyone suffer, but because it is pleasant to know you are free of such evils." Here I shall stand, until death calls me away.